T0022496

"This book has something for ever, _____, ___
mystery, a sweet romance that blooms unexpectedly, and a
surprisingly suspenseful climax to the story. Historical fans
will love it!"

Susan Anne Mason, author of the
Redemption's Light series

"*The Swindler's Daughter* is a compelling story with characters
I enjoyed getting to know as they faced challenges in times
of uncertainty in their lives. If you like stories of romance,
mystery, and action set in realistic historical times and places,
you won't want to miss this book."

Ann H. Gabhart, bestselling author of
When the Meadow Blooms

Praise for *The Secrets of Emberwild*

"Christians will appreciate the conclusion's upbeat message. . . .
This charming story has lots to like."

Publishers Weekly

"This is a great pick for readers who like historical fiction and
cozy mysteries with a strong female lead."

Library Journal

the
SWINDLER'S
DAUGHTER

Books by Stephenia H. McGee

The Secrets of Emberwild
The Swindler's Daughter

the

SWINDLER'S DAUGHTER

STEPHENIA H. McGEE

Revell

a division of Baker Publishing Group
Grand Rapids, Michigan

Published by Revell
a division of Baker Publishing Group
Grand Rapids, Michigan
www.revellbooks.com

Printed in the United States of America

Library of Congress Cataloging-in-Publication Data
Names: McGee, Stephenia H., 1983– author.
Title: The swindler's daughter / Stephenia H. McGee.
Description: Grand Rapids, Michigan : Revell, a division of Baker Publishing Group, [2023]
Identifiers: LCCN 2022040154 | ISBN 9780800740245 (paperback) | ISBN 9780800744632 (casebound) | ISBN 9781493441365 (ebook)
Subjects: LCGFT: Novels.
Classification: LCC PS3613.C4576 S95 2023 | DDC 813/.6—dc23/eng/20220831
LC record available at https://lccn.loc.gov/2022040154

Published in association with the Hartline Literary Agency, LLC.

Baker Publishing Group publications use paper produced from sustainable forestry practices and post-consumer waste whenever possible.

23 24 25 26 27 28 29   7 6 5 4 3 2 1

Dedicated to everyone who has ever
struggled to understand their path,
for God has great plans for you.

And to my book-loving friend Patty,
whose faith and good humor inspire me.

I will instruct you and teach you in the way you should go;
I will counsel you with my loving eye on you.

Psalm 32:8

CHAPTER ONE

ATLANTA, GEORGIA
MAY 2, 1912

Her entire life was a sham.

Somewhere deep inside, Lillian Doyle had always suspected there was more to the story she'd been fed since childhood. Yet in that moment, as Mother lifted her chin in defiance, Lillian longed to be wrong.

The solicitor's stuffy office smelled of stale tobacco and pomade, neither of which helped Lillian's roiling stomach. She and Mother sat in matching leather chairs across from Mr. Riley, who regarded her from behind round-rimmed spectacles.

"As you can see here . . ." He jabbed a bony finger at the paper on the gleaming desk between them.

Mother maintained her poise. "Yes, of course." Her honeyed tone dripped from lips used to forming deceptions. "And she is to inherit everything, you say?"

"As he had no wife or legitimate children, yes."

The words landed with a crushing weight, shattering the last bits of the veneer Mother had maintained for so long.

No wife.

No legitimate children.

Just Lillian.

Mother's glance warned her not to breathe a word. She couldn't speak if she'd wanted to. What did one say to finding out a dead man had died?

If that were not scandal enough, however, it would seem Mr. Floyd Jackson had bequeathed the sum of his earthly possessions to the sole care of his estranged daughter. Whom he'd never met.

A strange whooshing noise filled her ears. He'd been alive all this time.

"Did you hear me, Miss Doyle?"

Lillian's attention snapped back to the solicitor's pinched face. "Sorry, sir."

He tapped his finger on the desk again. "You have claim to Mr. Jackson's portion of the business as well as his house and furnishings. The solicitor in Dawson County will assist you further."

Mother sniffed as she rose from the small chair. "Thank you, Mr. Riley." She ushered Lillian from her seat and gestured to the door.

"Do you understand what I've told you, Miss Doyle?" Concern pulled Mr. Riley's bushy brows together.

"She understands." Mother grabbed Lillian's elbow and tugged her from the office. "Thank you for your time."

The paperwork. Had Mother taken that? Lillian turned to ask, but Mother closed the door firmly behind them and stalked past the reception desk. Lillian lingered in the hall. Should she knock, or . . . ?

The door opened, and Mr. Riley nearly ran into her as he stepped out. "Oh." He straightened his glasses. "You'll need this." He glanced behind her, clearly looking for her mother. He lowered his voice, though Mother had already headed for the front door. "Are you all right, Miss Doyle?"

"Um, yes, sir. It's a bit of a shock, is all." Lillian accepted the paper that announced her father's death from an apoplectic attack.

In prison.

A knowing look entered the man's blue eyes, followed swiftly by pity. "If you have any questions, please feel free to stop by again."

He scurried back into his office and shut the door before she could reply. Lillian stood there a moment longer before tucking the page inside her skirt pocket and hurrying to catch Mother. She stepped outside onto a street teeming with people, horses, and the occasional automobile with a purring engine. Situating her hat on her upswept hair, she practiced the conversation she'd have with Mother.

"Why didn't you tell me my father was still alive?" she would ask.

Mother would tilt her chin in her defiant way. "You didn't need to know. As far as you were concerned, the man was dead."

She would set her shoulders and keep Mother's gaze. "That's hardly true. It seems I have much to be concerned with, as he has left me a sum of money. Me, his illegitimate daughter."

Faced with the unveiling of the truth, Mother would apologize and explain that she had been protecting Lillian all this time.

Then Lillian would say . . .

She blinked, unable to think where the conversation would go next. So much depended on how Mother responded. What else had she lied about?

"How did he know where to find us?" The question darted from her lips before she could stop it.

"Not on the street." Mother had the uncanny ability to bark words under her breath while still maintaining a pleasant smile to passersby.

Not on the street. As though any of these strangers would know what they were talking about. Lillian pressed her lips together and let the matter drop. For now. But the moment they stepped inside the privacy of their town house, Mother would have to answer her questions.

Her father had been alive all these years. Meaning Mother was *not* the bereaved widow as she'd claimed. Nor had she been Floyd Jackson's wife.

Were you ever planning to tell me I was born out of wedlock?

Lillian watched her mother retreat down the busy walk. If she wasn't a widow, had they survived all this time because she was a kept mistress?

If not for her father's will, would Mother have kept the truth of Lillian's birth a secret forever? Probably.

If Mother had been able to go to Mr. Riley's office and collect the inheritance without her, would she have? Apparently. Lillian's presence had been required or Mother wouldn't have taken her to the solicitor's office with nary a word as to what the call was for.

Lillian stepped to the side to let a lady with a baby carriage pass on the sidewalk. Too many questions. Her head swam with how she'd ask Mother each one. How she would insist on an answer.

Then there were the technical issues to consider. They would need to travel to a rural town and find the solicitor there. Had Mr. Riley given her the solicitor's name? She couldn't remember. Then there would be paperwork, followed by some legal procedures. Then she would need to sell the assets, leaving her with a tidy sum.

Then what?

For the next four blocks, Lillian's mind created and discarded several possibilities. Would the money truly be hers alone? If so, what would that mean for her future? For Mother?

The cool May breeze lifted the edge of her wide-brimmed hat, causing her to take notice of the surroundings she'd not paid much heed to. Where was her mother? Lillian turned, finding her now trailing behind. Lillian must have been more lost in her thoughts than she'd realized.

When she paused, Mother breezed past her, the heels of her fashionable shoes clicking as she mounted the steps to their modest town house. Lillian didn't waste a moment. As soon as the door closed behind them, she launched into the conversation she'd practiced.

"Why didn't you tell me my father was still alive?"

Mother lifted her chin in exactly the way Lillian had anticipated. "To save us from scandal, of course."

Lillian gaped. That wasn't what she'd expected.

"Good riddance to the man."

Good riddance? How terrible a relationship had the two of them shared? "But he knew where to find us."

Mother unpinned her hat and tossed it on the rack by the door. "Sally!" She tugged the gloves from her fingers. "Of course he did. This is where he sent the money."

The young serving girl they couldn't truly afford scurried

down the steps and stumbled to a stop in the entryway. "Yes, ma'am?"

"Tea in the parlor. I am expecting Mrs. Montgomery any moment."

Mrs. Montgomery? Now? Today was hardly the day to deal with that pretentious woman.

"I'm not up to answering a bucketful of questions," Mother said as soon as Sally rushed off to prepare tea and refreshments. She pulled back her shoulders, stretching the too-tight fabric against a figure that had rounded considerably in the past year. "Mr. Jackson did not accept responsibility as a father, though his guilt saw to it that we were cared for." She gave a derisive sniff. "Until whatever schemes he was involved in failed, and then my monthly allowance disappeared. Now it seems he died in prison, leaving you whatever property remains. A good thing too, as we are on the verge of becoming destitute."

Lillian blinked, all her practiced poise flying away.

Mother seemed to take her silence as acceptance and bustled into the parlor. "Sally!" She poked her head back through the doorway. "Didn't I tell you to have the parlor spotless?"

Lillian followed her mother into the room, finding nothing out of place or lacking shine. The end tables gleamed, and the curtains had been opened to allow sunlight to splay over the furniture upholstery and create stripes across the rug.

"But, Mother, why didn't you ever tell me that . . ." The words "I was born out of wedlock" lodged in her throat at Mother's pointed glance.

"We'll discuss the specifics of collecting what's ours later." She fluffed a pillow that didn't need fluffing and replaced it on the settee.

A knock sounded in the entry. When the hem of Mother's gauzy gown disappeared through the parlor door, Lillian's breath left her in a rush.

That hadn't gone at all like she'd imagined. Though she shouldn't have expected anything different. Mother had always been tightly guarded, even with her own daughter. Lillian shouldn't have anticipated a little thing like her father's death to spark any heartfelt moments of connection.

Cheery voices twittered in the hall as though this morning's events hadn't entirely altered Lillian's world. How dare Mother pretend at a time like this?

But then, was not pretending the whole of life?

"Smile, Lillian. You could at least appear glad to be here."

"Tell the grocer his payment was sent last Tuesday."

"Wear the gown for the station of life you want, and that is what people will see."

Lies, all of them. And those only from this week.

Lillian pinched the bridge of her nose to ward off a headache. She was in no mood for Mrs. Montgomery, and given the change in circumstances, she didn't see why she had to entertain the woman at all.

Mother would expect her to feign a smile and pretend to be the lady worthy of a gentleman out of her reach. What would Mrs. Montgomery think if she knew the truth? Mother would likely no longer be invited to any gatherings. Neither would Lillian, for that matter.

Reginald Montgomery would most definitely be out of her social circle. The man was pleasant enough as far as austere gentlemen went, and Lillian had decided he'd likely be a safe, if somewhat stifling, choice for a husband. But he would most assuredly remove his interest in her if Mrs. Montgomery discovered Lillian wasn't the perfect flower Mother tried to make her.

So much the better. She was an heiress now, after all. She didn't have to keep up any pretenses if she didn't want to. In fact, she would tell Mrs. Montgomery that she was no longer interested in further discussions about—

"Why, Miss Doyle, are you quite all right?" Mrs. Montgomery's airy voice snapped Lillian out of her thoughts. The woman's slim frame graced the doorway, concern etched on her delicate features.

Before Lillian could formulate any type of proper response, Mother patted Mrs. Montgomery's arm and leaned close, whispering something about "indisposed" and falling victim to "women's troubles."

Another lie. And today the very notion of playing along with another of her falsehoods made searing heat climb up Lillian's neck.

Mother pinned her with a warning glare. "Perhaps my dear daughter should lie down for a bit, hmm?" Her honeyed tone warred with the hard glint in her eyes.

Lillian stared at her.

"Oh my, yes." Mrs. Montgomery patted her perfectly coifed hair. Her assessing eyes slid over Lillian as though she wondered why Lillian didn't possess the fortitude to maintain herself even while experiencing a woman's discomforts. Such a girl wouldn't be worthy of her Reginald, certainly.

The woman had no idea.

The temptation to let the sordid truth take wing made her heart hammer. Instead, pitiful words she'd not meant to speak squeaked through her tight throat. "I do hope you will forgive me."

Mrs. Montgomery slowly tugged kid gloves from her fingertips. "Of course, my dear. You are such a delicate thing. Mrs. Doyle and I can handle these matters."

The name stabbed at Lillian. Mother had never been *Mrs.* anything.

"Certainly." Mother took Lillian's arm when she'd still not managed to move from the center of the room. "Mothers are supposed to help with such important decisions for the children."

She spoke as though Lillian and Reginald were both mere toddlers who needed every decision made for them. At the moment, however, Lillian had an escape, and she wouldn't let wounded pride steal it from her. They could plan whatever they liked.

Mother may intend for Lillian to marry Reginald Montgomery, but she would soon discover that Lillian would no longer concede.

CHAPTER TWO

ll a woman needed was fortitude and good manners.

The sharp train whistle pierced the air, announcing Lillian's arrival in rural Georgia. As the station slowly came into view, Lillian repeated the fortifying phrase to herself several times, hoping the notion would stick. Conversations bounced around the confined space, adding to the chaos swarming through her.

A list. That would help. She mentally ticked off the order of the things she would need to accomplish.

Depart the train. Locate the solicitor. Complete the paperwork. Return home with her own small fortune and refuse to marry Reginald. Use her inheritance to resurrect a dream she'd buried a long time ago, perhaps. The idea tingled through her with the treasured memory of a place she'd loved as a girl. All she had to do was claim her father's fortune and new opportunities would spread before her.

Lillian pulled in a deep breath of stale air as the train screeched to a halt.

Simple. Except for one problem.

Mother had never sent her anywhere on her own before. The fact that she had done so now filled Lillian with both annoyance and an odd sense of freedom.

Mother had refused to accompany her on this trip, with the flimsy excuse that she was needed at home. She had declined to help her daughter through this difficult time because she didn't want to face anyone finding out she was the mother of an illegitimate child. Not even strangers in a small country town.

Lillian grabbed her valise and stepped out into the train aisle, trying to get her fluttering nerves to settle. She'd never even ridden a train alone before. Yet she'd managed perfectly well thus far.

The thought brought a measure of that buried fortitude to the surface, and Lillian lifted her gaze from her traveling boots. Her grip tightened on the wooden handle of her valise as she scooted her way down the aisle.

If she were able to handle settling an estate, what other things might she be able to accomplish?

The woman in front of her tilted her head back, and the oversized feather on her hat brushed Lillian's face, tickling her nose. Lillian snorted and scrambled away, desperately trying to contain a sneeze.

She stepped directly into someone behind her. A woman yelped.

"Oh!" Lillian shifted her weight off the woman's foot. She looked over her shoulder at a lady whose glare did nothing to help her stark features. "I'm terribly sorry."

The older woman sniffed and gestured toward the front of the train car, indicating Lillian should move forward. Lillian darted ahead in the cramped aisle. Her valise banged against one of the seats and bounced back to smack against her knees. Heat bloomed on her face.

Refusing to let herself get lost in her thoughts again, Lillian managed to depart the train without further incident and stepped down onto a dusty platform. She scanned the collection of travelers calling to porters and watched a lady and her gentleman struggle to properly contain their enthusiasm at having been reunited. She'd never once felt the elation painted all over the woman's face in Reginald's presence. Not that it mattered. She no longer had to consider marrying the man. She turned away as the gentleman took the woman's hands in his and smiled down at her with obvious affection.

What would it feel like to see a handsome gentleman gaze at *her* like that? Lillian shooed the thought away. What was wrong with her today? She needed to focus on the task at hand, not get lost daydreaming about silly fantasies.

She tugged the small watch on a delicate silver chain from her pocket to check the time. If only she'd remembered more information from Mr. Riley. Like the other solicitor's name. She'd been so flustered that day in Mr. Riley's office that most of his instructions had escaped her. And Mother had sent her off before she'd had the opportunity to call on the man again.

Perhaps it wouldn't matter. There could only be one solicitor in a town as small as Dawsonville. Squaring her shoulders, Lillian returned the watch to her pocket and wove through the crowd until she'd exited the platform. People loaded trunks in and out of carriages and rear compartments in automobiles, greeting one another with smiles. Finally, she spotted conveyances for hire and asked three drivers for fares before securing transportation with the one most reasonably priced.

Safely ensconced in an aged carriage, Lillian watched as a

well-dressed family climbed into a shiny black automobile. Perhaps with her father's funds, she might indulge in a trip back to the train station in such a vehicle, if only to see what one of the rumbling contraptions felt like.

For now, the cracked leather of the seat beneath her and an open-air carriage suited her just fine for what the aged driver said would be a fifteen-mile ride. The trip from the station in the bustling gold boomtown of Dahlonega to Dawsonville passed quickly as Lillian paid more attention to her growing to-do list than the hilly countryside.

Her driver, a man with a farmer's cap and a ready smile, reined his two bay horses to a stop and turned to look at her. "This here's the courthouse, miss. Center of town."

Lillian swiped a strand of hair from her eyes as she surveyed the brick building. Solicitors would be near here, wouldn't they? "Do you know where the solicitor's office is?"

"No. Sorry, miss."

She thanked the man and handed over payment after he helped her down from the carriage. The wheels churned up dust as it rolled away. The May sunshine warmed the shoulders of her blue day dress, and she pressed her tan kid gloves over the folds of the fabric in an effort to smooth out travel wrinkles. My, but she did look a mess. Perhaps she should locate a hotel and freshen up before making her way to the solicitor's office.

Lillian crossed the street, mindful of muck that would stain her boots, and headed toward a large bank to ask for the necessary directions.

The bank bustled with farmers, ladies with children at their skirts, and businessmen in tidy suits. Lillian waited her turn in line and then stepped up to the high counter. "Good afternoon.

I was wondering if you might be able to point me in the direction of the local solicitor's office."

The man's eyebrows rose as he studied her. Lillian resisted the urge to shift under his gaze.

He adjusted his collar. "Are you looking for Mr. Carson or Mr. Newton?"

Her chest tightened. How foolish to not know who she was sent to see. Before she could answer, the man offered her a kind smile.

"Both can be found just down the street, past the mercantile. You'll have no trouble locating the signs."

Lillian nodded her thanks. "And do you have a hotel you might recommend?"

A glint of curiosity twitched over his features. "Yes, of course." He pointed to the left, the opposite direction from the law offices. "The Moore Hotel is in the square by the print shop and general store."

She thanked him again and wound her way through the patrons. One step accomplished.

Lillian pushed open the bank door, fumbling to pull her watch from her pocket again. She might have enough time to change clothes and still go to see—

A weight shoved into her back, pushing her forward. The pocket watch flew from her fingers as she pitched out into the street.

He finally had his chance. Elation swelled in Jonah Peterson's chest as he hurried out of the bank. With this new opportunity, he would finally be able to—

Oof. He caught himself just as he stepped into a woman lingering right outside the bank door.

"Sorry, ma'am." Jonah pulled back, but the lady was already stumbling forward.

Her feet tangled in the folds of her skirt, and she lost her balance. She tumbled into the mud.

For a heartbeat, he could only stare. Then his manners kicked in and he rushed forward to extend a hand to her.

"Heavens!" The woman looked up at him, brown eyes large. When she didn't take his hand, he reached down and grasped her elbow, gently tugging her upright. "Are you all right?"

The woman gathered her feet beneath her and pulled her arm from his grasp with a yank that had her stumbling again. Flashing eyes took him in with a glance, and she turned up a pert little nose. "You really must watch where you are going."

Where he was going? She'd been standing right outside the door, practically asking for someone to run into her. But he wasn't about to let a haughty woman ruin his mood. Not today.

He bowed, the gesture only slightly mocking. "My apologies."

She stared at him as though he had sprouted a pair of mule's ears. Then she brushed at her skirts and gave him an offended glare when her gloves encountered a large stain of mud.

He hadn't meant to sully her dress. She was rather fetching in a light blue that wrapped her womanly figure and complemented her dark hair.

They stared at one another. He wasn't sure what more he could say. Maybe she wanted him to offer to do something about the stain on her dress.

She straightened an already stiff posture, turned away from him, and started to stalk off, her hands in tight fists.

"Miss!" he shouted after her, but she ignored him. He scooped her dropped bag from the ground and hurried down the street.

She quickened her stride. What was wrong with this woman?

Jonah stretched his longer legs and gained her side. He lifted the burgundy bag into her line of vision. "You dropped this."

Surprise then annoyance filled her face.

He was tempted to drop the bag in the dirt. Here he'd been trying to help. What cause did she have to look so offended?

"Thank you." The woman's cheeks burned red. She grasped the handle of the bag, the tips of her gloved fingers grazing his hand.

He couldn't help a smile as the flustered woman took her bag, drew her shoulders back to what seemed an entirely unnatural stiffness, and resumed her stalk down the street.

Women. He chuckled to himself and adjusted his hat. Nothing quite like the delicate flower types who thought all the world should bow at their feet.

Jonah shrugged off the encounter and tapped the paper safely hidden in his pocket. Now that the bank had approved the loan, he'd soon have Ma and his two sisters safely settled into a place of their own. He could probably even start classes come fall. There was plenty to do, but hope cast a glimmer over the day and kept his mood buoyant as he fetched his gray mare from the stables and mounted her to ride home.

Two miles east of town, he rode through the rolling hillside country, breathing pleasant spring air and reveling in the anticipation of sharing his news with Ma. But first he had to present the papers to his employer. Prove the bank had loaned him the funds to make the purchase. Lewis had already given his word that he would sell Jonah the house.

Jonah rode past the wooden gate and into the expanse of the Watson farm. Acres of rolling land filled with swaying stalks of corn and barley spread on either side of the white farmhouse. Jonah reined up at the barn, surprised to find Lewis waiting for him.

Jonah dropped down from the saddle, his dusty boots hitting with a thud. He fished the paper out of his pocket and handed it to Lewis with a grin before turning to tie Mist to the hitching post.

When he turned back, Lewis hadn't looked at the papers. Nor did his face hold a smile. Unease wormed into Jonah's stomach.

"The bank approved the loan." He nodded at the papers in Lewis's hand. He willed the man to look at them and hoped for a smile to replace the sadness etched along the lines of his tanned face.

His employer tapped the paper against his palm, eyes holding apology. The unease in Jonah's stomach soured into dread.

After another heartbeat, Lewis handed the papers back. "We waited to be sure, but . . ." He shook his head. "There's been a change of circumstance." When Jonah didn't respond, Lewis rubbed the back of his neck. "I hate to go back on my word, Jonah. I truly do. But this is out of my control."

The declaration punched Jonah square in the gut. He still couldn't bring himself to utter a sound.

"It would appear my wife's uncle did not leave the property to us as we had assumed." A frown pulled down the edges of Lewis's neatly trimmed mustache. "It came as quite a shock to all of us when we discovered Floyd had left the whole of his assets to his . . . daughter."

"Daughter?" Confusion tripped through him. He'd thought Floyd Jackson had been a bachelor. Apparently, so had the man's family. "So, the house . . . ?"

"The house goes to her as well. All of it. We didn't get a thing." Lewis clapped him on the shoulder. "I'm truly sorry."

All Jonah could do was nod. In one day, his hopes had taken flight and just as quickly been dashed to bits.

What was he going to tell Ma now?

CHAPTER THREE

is mercies are new every morning. Lillian repeated the thought as she went through her dressing routine. The comb snagged in her hair. She worked out the knot and forced her jerky movements to slow. Once the strands slid freely through the comb, Lillian studied her tired reflection. She would certainly need plenty of mercies today. Yesterday had been a disaster.

Not only had an incredibly rude and dusty cowboy—*cowboy,* in the Georgia foothills, of all places—carelessly knocked her into the mud and ruined her good traveling dress, but she'd had to spend far more of her limited money on this hotel than she'd anticipated. The proprietress had offered for her to share a room with another woman for a lesser fee, but Lillian could hardly agree. Take a room with a stranger? How could anyone sleep a wink under such circumstances?

Lillian pulled long sections of the smoothed locks to the top of her head and twisted the length into a soft spiral. She lowered the knot so that the roots of the hair fell into a soft puff, then secured the twist with several pins. A few short, natural curls sprang free around her temples. Not exactly the fashionable pompadour Mother would require.

She gathered the papers Mr. Riley had given her and scanned the contents once more. No mention of which solicitor she was supposed to see. Perhaps that meant any man with an education in the law would suffice. More likely, she would suffer embarrassment for not remembering the name of the man Mr. Riley had told her to find. She tucked the paper away, secured her wide-brimmed hat properly over her hair, and tugged on her gloves.

If only her inner chaos could be as easily smoothed as her outer disarray. Lillian sent a prayer heavenward for an extra dose of those mercies and strode out the door.

The small town of Dawsonville bustled with activity as the countryfolk hurried about their daily tasks. Lillian made her way down the street, politely nodding to the curious glances of people as she passed. Near the courthouse stood a sheriff's office and a small jail. She swallowed the thickness in her throat as she passed the place where her father had died.

By the time she found the first solicitor's office—the sign naming him one Mr. Carson, esquire—the attention of the townspeople had started to gnaw at her. Did she appear odd? Or were there not many visitors to this town?

Lillian pushed open the door, and a bell announced her presence. The front room of the solicitor's office appeared dust free, with matching furniture in masculine shades of deep red and brown. Too nervous to sit, Lillian waited by the door and mentally rehearsed stating her reason for being here.

A moment later, a thin man with a pointed nose and a touch

too much pomade in his sandy locks strode from a door in the rear of the room. "Good morning."

"Good morning, sir. I am Miss Lillian Doyle, and I'm looking to settle the estate of my late father as was left to me in this will." She fumbled in her pocket. Oh, why hadn't she had these papers ready before the man came out?

The paper snagged on the chain of her pocket watch, and by the time she snatched it free, the document looked as though it had been dropped on the street and run over. Ignoring the heat rising in her face, Lillian held the paper out to the solicitor with as much dignity as she could manage.

To his credit, the man's face remained passive as he took the document and unfolded the crinkled paper. Lillian kept her stance still and her features serene even as she fought the urge to fidget.

Blue eyes lifted from the page and studied her. "Miss Doyle, you say?" Crinkles formed along his forehead. She'd chosen the wrong gentleman.

Nothing for it now. "It appears my father was a Mr. Floyd Jackson."

The man studied her for another few heartbeats and then returned his attention to the page. At least he hadn't shaken his head and sent her out the door. After what felt like another five minutes, Lillian began to fidget.

Was there a problem with Mr. Riley's papers? Or did Mr. Carson not believe her to be Floyd Jackson's daughter?

"I'll need an address." Mr. Carson turned his back to her before she could answer. "This way please, Miss Doyle."

Lillian followed him through the doorway at the rear of the reception area and into a hallway with blue-papered walls, then trailed him into an office that looked strikingly similar to the one she'd visited in Atlanta. Both Mr. Riley and Mr. Carson favored large desks and a bookshelf filled with impressively thick volumes.

Mr. Carson stood behind his desk and opened a drawer. He thumbed through a stack of papers. "Your address, Miss Doyle?"

"Oh." Lillian eyed a leather chair opposite the man's desk but remained standing. "Mother and I live on Mitchell Street in Atlanta. Number one hundred twelve." She worked past the dryness trying to clog her throat and lifted her chin another notch. "Mother is Mrs. Doyle."

Mr. Carson didn't even twitch at this bit of information, much to Lillian's relief. She should have said Mother was Florence Doyle and avoided the deceptive title altogether.

Mr. Carson gave a nod, apparently oblivious to the heat creeping up Lillian's neck. "And your birthday?"

"Twelfth of December 1888."

He gave another nod without looking at her. Seeming to have found whatever he sought, Mr. Carson sat in a chair that protested his weight. He waved a bony hand at the one in front of his desk. "Take a seat."

Relief loosened the tight muscles in her neck. The invitation appeared to signify his acceptance of her claim. Lillian perched on the end of the chair and folded her hands in her lap as Mr. Carson pulled several pages from his drawer and laid them across the desk.

"Who sent you here?"

"Mr. Riley."

Mr. Carson leaned back in his seat and regarded her. "As you already know, Mr. Jackson left the entirety of his property to you." He pushed a paper across the desk. "And as you learned from my letter to Mr. Riley, the estate includes Mr. Jackson's home here in town as well as a portion of his business, shared with Mr. Jeffery Tanner."

A bubble of satisfaction intercepted her nervousness. She'd guessed the correct solicitor after all.

"I'm sure there will be details to work out when Mr. Tanner returns to town." Mr. Carson tapped the page. "Sign here, please."

How long would Mr. Tanner be unavailable? She didn't plan on staying in Dawsonville long. However, this didn't seem to be the moment to ask. First, the burning question she had to know the answer to.

"Why was Mr. Jackson in jail?"

The solicitor barely glanced up. "Intoxication."

He didn't elaborate, and she couldn't bring herself to ask more. At least it hadn't been for something nefarious. Like murder. What would she have done then?

Lillian accepted the pen Mr. Carson handed over and marked her name across the bottom of the paper. He slid the page to the edge of his desk and fetched an object from another drawer.

"Here is the key to Mr. Jackson's property, located at the east end of Main Street. Number fifteen." He pushed the key across the desk.

Lillian could only stare at the slender black metal. A key to a house. A house that belonged to her. One filled with mementos of a man whose lineage she shared. The implications blanketed her with a sudden weight. Was she prepared to go through a stranger's private things? What would she discover about the man who had never bothered to visit yet had left all of his earthly possessions to her?

Mr. Carson cleared his throat. "Feel free to inspect the property while I file the necessary documents."

With that declaration, he rose and gestured toward the door. That was it? All she had to do was sign a paper and accept the key?

Lillian rose and clutched the key. Her mind scrambled with a dozen half-formed questions about her next steps and how long finalizing the estate would take, but none of them made their way past her lips.

"Are you residing in town?" Mr. Carson asked.

"Yes, sir. I have a room at the Moore Hotel."

"I'll send word as soon as I have the details in order." Mr. Carson led her down the hall and held the front door open for her expectantly.

She mumbled her thanks and hurried outside.

Well. That hadn't been so terrible after all. Lillian headed east down the street. After she passed several businesses, the structures at the edges of the town turned into well-maintained, modest homes.

A couple of houses down, she found a large number eight posted at the gate of the house to her right. The next house, a two-story brick structure with wide shutters open to accept the spring sunshine and a tidy porch hosting two rocking chairs, didn't have a number that she could see. The next few houses looked similar, one with a fenced yard and several with a host of flowering bushes.

A stray thought pounced, catching Lillian by surprise. Her *own* house. What would it be like to have a tidy little home all to herself? A space to manage as she saw fit? To arrange the way she desired?

She pushed the idea away. Charming as these houses might

be, she couldn't live here. No, that would be foolish. She knew no one in Dawsonville. She had no skills to live on her own. Yet the desire still tugged at her. The allure of independence—without Mother's overbearing influence or a man like Reginald dictating her every moment—awakened something inside her.

Something best left ignored. At least until she sold her father's property and figured out what to do with the sum left to her.

The next house in line differed sorely from the others. In need of a fresh coat of paint, the sad little house almost seemed to slouch in defeat. Two shutters drooped, the front step was sagging, and the yard desperately needed tending. A middle-aged woman stood in the yard with her hand to her brow, features set in concentration.

No number on that one. Lillian quickened her steps and looked to the next house. A neat white number sixteen was painted on the fence.

She slowed. She must have missed her father's house. She looked across the street and understanding dawned. Of course. The one over there didn't have a number either, but the houses must be numbered across from one another, even on this side and odd on the other. She lifted her skirt and crossed the road.

Oh my.

Lillian bounced up on her toes. This must be it. This belonged to her? She couldn't help the smile that wanted to bunch her cheeks. It was *perfect.*

Painted a pristine white, the house gleamed in the morning sunshine. Flowering bushes lined the short walk from the street to a dainty front porch. Her father must have been a tidy man. One who took care with his appearances.

Lillian slowly wandered up the sidewalk and admired the

porch railing and sitting benches at the front of the house. Wouldn't this be a lovely place to linger with a cup of tea? Oh, and she could put a vase on that table there, bringing the blooms up closer.

An excitement Lillian struggled to control bubbled through her. She would have to sell the house, but that didn't mean she couldn't enjoy it for a few days first. And besides, it would be much nicer—and cheaper—to stay here rather than the hotel. She could even buy a few supplies at the grocer and make her own meals.

Lillian mounted the porch steps and lifted the key. Her father had kept a nice home, despite his imprisonment. She had to admit she was rather surprised. What further clues would she find within?

She hadn't needed to worry over how long it would take for Mr. Carson to handle the affairs. She would need several days, perhaps even weeks, to sift through all of her father's belongings.

Lillian rolled the key in her gloved palm and drew a deep breath.

The key jammed in the lock, refusing to turn. She frowned and jiggled the handle. Perhaps it had become stuck with disuse. She tried again, but the key still wouldn't turn. Pushing too hard would cause it to break off in the mechanism.

Lillian stifled her disappointment. She'd simply have to find Mr. Carson and see if he had another—

Movement flashed in the window.

The front door tugged open, snatching the key from Lillian's hand. "Oh!"

A short woman in a green day dress stared at her with wide brown eyes.

Lillian stared back. What was this woman doing here? She worked her mouth, finally getting words to shake free. "Who . . . who are you?"

The woman lifted her brows. "Who are *you*?"

"I'm Lillian Doyle. This is . . ." *Oh no.* How had she been so stupid? She closed her eyes and drew a breath before meeting the woman's gaze again. "This isn't house number fifteen, is it?"

The woman darted a glance behind her. "This is twenty-six." She offered a kindly smile. "The houses are numbered up the right side until you get to twenty, then back down this side to number forty, which is closest to town again."

Lillian pinched her lips together, hoping the woman wouldn't utter the words she didn't want to hear.

"Fifteen is that house there, across the street." The dark-haired woman gestured behind Lillian. "Belonged to Mr. Jackson."

So much for hoping.

The woman plucked the key from the lock and handed it over. Somehow Lillian managed to mumble an apology before pocketing the key and numbly walking down the front steps. She should have known better. This home had been too good to be true. Too pretty to hope for.

Reluctantly, she lifted her gaze to the dilapidated house across the way, where the middle-aged woman in a worn work dress and ungloved hands stared at her.

CHAPTER FOUR

W hat do you mean, this is *your* house?"
Lillian stared at the tall woman standing with
her hands on her hips and a look of motherly
authority on her face. Almost as though she thought to chide
Lillian into giving up what was rightfully hers.

The woman lifted her dark brows, practically a dare.

Lillian smoothed her features back into a pleasant de-
meanor. "There has been a mistake, I'm sure. I'm Miss Lillian Doyle. My father, Mr. Floyd Jackson, left this house and
property to me." When the woman's expression didn't change,
she added, "His daughter."

"Well, now. That *is* a bit of a predicament, isn't it?" Oddly,
the woman's voice held a note of humor buried beneath a thick
layer of disappointment.

Who was she? A relative? Where Lillian had thin lips and
a somewhat pointed nose, this woman had a full mouth and
more of a button nose. Her hair, while also brown, was much
lighter than Lillian's. But since Lillian hadn't met her father's
side of the family, how could she know if there were resem-
blances?

"Who would have thought this would be the first problem I encountered?" The woman tilted her head back as though addressing the sky. "Couldn't make anything easy on me?"

Odd woman. Lillian laced her fingers together. Clearly this person had plans for the house. Plans Lillian's presence had interrupted. Though if she wanted to buy the dilapidated structure . . .

Lillian brightened. "I'll be selling it, so if you were hoping to buy . . ." The words trailed to a halt as the woman shook her head.

"This house is already promised to my son. It's ours."

"How can that be? I've just come from the solicitor's office." She held up the small object still clutched tightly in her hand. "He gave me the key."

They looked at one another long enough for Lillian to grow uncomfortable. Perhaps if they started with proper pleasantries. She snapped into the practiced charm Mother had instilled in her. "It is a pleasure to make your acquaintance. I'm Miss Lillian Doyle."

The matronly woman smiled as though Lillian had said something foolish. Perhaps she had in stating her name again, but as the lady had yet to reciprocate, she hardly had a choice.

"Melanie Peterson."

"A pleasure to make your acquaintance, Mrs. Peterson." Why did the woman look so infuriatingly amused? This was hardly a situation that warranted the spark of humor in her large blue eyes. Another feature Lillian didn't share.

"Where're you from, honey?" The warm tone, which felt entirely at odds with the predicament, caught Lillian by surprise.

"I'm, uh, from Atlanta."

"Atlanta. Hmm." She tugged on the sleeve of a clean but well-worn work dress. "That explains it then, I suppose."

Lillian narrowed her eyes. "Explains what?" If she was going to point out her family's shame, she may as well get it over with.

Mrs. Peterson gestured to the length of Lillian. "You."

Heat scorched up Lillian's neck, and she scrambled for something to say to such an unusual insult.

"I never had much cause to go into the big cities, so I haven't seen many fine ladies." Mrs. Peterson shrugged as she inspected Lillian's attire. "There's a few around here that play like they're more than what the good Lord made them, but you've got an elegance to you that can't be hidden. Not even under all your nervousness and attempts at stoicism."

Any retort Lillian could have summoned left her lips with an empty breath. She couldn't decide if she should thank the woman or be annoyed.

This conversation needed to get back on the proper path. "I've come from Atlanta because the solicitor informed me that my father had passed and left his estate to me." Regardless of what this woman thought about Lillian, the fact remained that she was Floyd Jackson's daughter. Therefore the property belonged to her. That was the only information that mattered.

Mrs. Peterson turned to look up at the house, and her soft voice drifted back over her shoulder. "We're at an impasse then, I reckon, because Mr. Newton said Floyd's sister—and we figured his niece as well, seeing as they are his only family— inherited his estate."

Mr. Newton. The other solicitor in town. Should she have gone to him instead? But Mr. Carson had sent the letter to Mr. Riley. Why wouldn't any of them have told her if the family had contested the will?

Her family.

Lillian's stomach fluttered with the realization. She had an aunt. And a cousin. What would they think of all this mess?

Mrs. Peterson turned back to her. "And Mr. Watson, the niece's husband, already promised this property to my son."

Lillian shook her head. This couldn't be happening. For all the kindness radiating from the woman before her, she also seemed to possess a determined streak. Lillian wouldn't be getting anywhere with her. She'd have to find this niece. Her cousin. Nervousness and excitement warred within her. She had an extended family.

One who would likely not be pleased to meet her.

Lillian cleared her throat and matched Mrs. Peterson's matter-of-fact tone. "I'm afraid you are the one mistaken." She spread her hands. "You see, two different solicitors already say this property belongs to me."

Mrs. Peterson offered a sympathetic smile. "I'm really sorry, honey. I hate that you came all this way for nothing."

There had to be a mistake. Jonah resisted the urge to pace across the parlor rug and satisfied himself instead with twisting his fingers behind his back. The news that Floyd Jackson had a secret daughter had thrown the Watson family into an understandable fit of confusion. He didn't envy their situation. Finding out a scandalous truth could cause any family dismay.

Jonah chided himself for likely the tenth time for being selfish, but the implications the discovery had on his own future wrapped him in cold dread. He'd counted on having that property. Had spent years of his life working and scraping together the funds to make sure his mother and sisters would be cared for.

He made a trip around the Watsons' parlor, his gaze sliding over the familiar setting without really landing on anything. How much longer would Lewis tarry in town?

Jonah couldn't afford anything better than what the Watsons had offered him. The family had been kind to him, giving him a job as a farmhand when he was but a boy of sixteen and suddenly his family's sole provider. They treated him nearly like one of their own.

And after the cabin burned . . . where else would Ma and the girls have gone? They'd already moved into Floyd's house. Jonah didn't have space for them in his small room attached to the barn, and he certainly could never allow for them to stay in the Watson house, even though the option was offered. His acceptance of charity could only go so far.

What would this mystery woman do? Evict a family already living in the house? When Floyd had died a mere three days after the cabin burned, the available house had seemed like a godsend. What would they do now?

Jonah stopped pacing and squeezed his eyes shut.

Maybe the daughter would want to sell the house. She couldn't be anyone local. But would she give him as good a deal as Lewis? Probably not.

"Did you hear me, Jonah?"

He snapped his attention to the face of his employer's lovely wife, a woman he'd cared for like a sister during the eight years he'd been working here. He shook his head and offered a sheepish shrug.

"I said not to worry. It will work out. I'm sure of it." Alma's sweet voice held a note of conviction, and Jonah didn't have the heart to point out how she should know that things rarely worked out for the good. Instead, he merely nodded and mumbled some kind of vague acceptance of her words.

Before Alma could start working on a way to convince him, Lewis strode into the room with sure steps but unreadable features. Jonah straightened. Finally.

"I've just come from Mr. Carson. Seems Floyd's daughter arrived in town to claim the inheritance. He's still working on the legalities, but it looks as though the lady in question is the daughter Floyd confessed to having."

"When did he confess to having a daughter?" Mrs. Edith Hampshire rose from where she'd been quietly tucked in the corner, knitting. Jonah had completely forgotten the sprite of a woman had been there at all. "My brother never confessed to me he had a daughter. How do we know this gal isn't running a confidence scheme?"

Jonah wanted to hug the tiny woman. Bless her for saying what it wouldn't be proper for him to voice. She glided across the blue rug and past the formal polished tables.

"Is it really so difficult to believe that Floyd had a child he never told us about?" Alma remained calmly perched on the settee near the window. The sunlight caused golden highlights to sparkle in her auburn hair.

"No." Edith snorted, then her features turned contemplative. "How old is this girl? And where is her mother? Is she an orphan?" The questions tumbled out of her at a rapid pace, though she snagged a bit on the last one.

Guilt punched Jonah again. What if this girl was an orphan? Alone and scared in the world, and then one day she thought God sent a miracle—a chance for her to have a home and a life outside of an orphanage.

Lewis shook his head. "The girl has a living mother, from what I understand. She came from Atlanta."

Atlanta? Floyd had a family only a few hours away and the Watsons never had the first hint?

Alma rose and clasped her hands together. "Think of it, Mother. You have a niece and I a cousin." She smiled brightly. "I would like to meet her."

The discussion fell into conjectures on how old the mystery woman would be and what she might be like, but Jonah could hardly listen. Regardless of the woman's age or temperament, she'd come to take what should have been his. Speculations on her personality didn't change anything.

Energy coursed through him, making it impossible to continue standing around in the parlor acting like one of the family. He had work to do. Work that wouldn't be ending anytime soon, thanks to Floyd Jackson and his deceptions.

Jonah tipped his head to Lewis and slipped through the doorway. When any further news came, someone would let him know. Until then, he should keep his hands and his mind busy.

He retrieved his hat from the rack at the door and stepped out onto the wide porch. The day blazed with bright sunshine, and the blue sky held wisps of pristine white clouds. A good day to move the cattle to the south pasture.

Max and Millie would enjoy the exercise. Lewis's pair of blue heelers tended to get into mischief if they were left idle for too long, and Jonah had already spent most of the last two days out of the saddle.

He stepped down from the porch and turned toward the large barn, which cast a shorter shadow across the lawn than he'd anticipated. How much of the morning had he spent inside the Watsons' parlor? By the time he got Mist saddled and gathered the dogs, he'd be running into time for the noon meal. He could probably get the cattle moved in one afternoon, but that might be asking for trouble. Maybe he'd check the fence lines instead.

Movement caught his attention, and he paused. A visitor?

Dust roiled up from the road with the approach of a cart or wagon. Jonah waited until the shape of a small cart became visible in the haze. He tipped his hat back. Was that a woman?

The massive feminine hat strained against the wind, threatening to dislodge itself from the woman's head. She held on to the reins so stiffly that the poor mare pulling her cart kept flicking her ears backward. The creature alternated between picking up a good trot and prancing back into a walk.

Clearly this lady didn't know how to drive. Jonah turned and let out a shrill whistle to alert Lewis and Alma that they had a visitor.

A *woman* visitor. The implication jarred through him.

Floyd's daughter. Had to be.

A moment later, the front door opened and several footsteps sounded across the porch.

"Think that's her?" Lewis rubbed a hand down his straw-colored mustache as he gained Jonah's side. "Didn't expect her to come out to the house. I reckon Mr. Carson gave her our address." He chuckled. "Doesn't look like she knows how to handle a cart."

Jonah watched the cart tug to one side of the road and back to the other. "I'd say that woman has never driven a horse before in her life." Not a good sign. What would a city girl who couldn't even handle a simple cart want with a small Dawsonville town house?

Probably to sell it at unreasonable Atlanta prices.

The woman pulled the horse through the gates and struggled to get the upset animal to come to a halt. The mare pawed the ground.

Jonah could sympathize. He should unhitch the bay and take her to a stall, but his focus remained riveted on the woman on the cart bench. Her giant hat was tilted low, covering her face. Despite the aged cart she drove, she wore a green dress of a finer quality than Ma or his sisters had ever had.

An irrational annoyance surged through him. This woman clearly didn't need what would mean freedom for his entire family. She fidgeted with the reins, evidently unsure where she should properly tie them.

As though coming out of a stupor, the Watson women scurried down the front porch just as Lewis strode forward and called out a friendly greeting. Jonah's boots remained planted in the grass as Lewis helped the woman down from her perch and the others crowded around her. They exchanged greetings, and Alma—from what Jonah could tell from the back of her head—seemed to bounce with enthusiasm for the newcomer.

Edith, true to form, remained more composed, the slow bob of her head as controlled as if she greeted a neighbor and not her brother's secret daughter. Alma turned back toward the house, her arms gesturing broadly as she said something about inviting the woman in for the midday meal.

"Oh yes, and this is Jonah. He takes care of all these cows for us. And the horses, of course." Alma beamed and stepped to the side, giving Jonah his first real look at the woman who had come to take everything from him.

She tilted her chin up, and his fingers clenched. Oh no.

44

The woman's pink lips formed a little O as her eyes widened. "You!"

Alma drew back, her gaze darting between the pretty viper and him. "You two have met?"

As suddenly as the surprise had overtaken the woman's features, it disappeared into a mask of cold indifference. "We . . . ran into one another in town."

The woman who had come to steal his chance at a new life was none other than the prissy little lady who had stood directly outside the door to the bank and then admonished him when he'd accidently run into her.

Jonah couldn't formulate anything polite to say. Alma's voice soon filled the awkward silence with frivolous pleasantries and unsubtle hints for Jonah to extend a greeting. Of course this would be the woman who had come to usurp his dreams.

When would he ever stop being surprised at his rotten luck?

CHAPTER FIVE

L illian hadn't really known what to expect, yet she was certain it hadn't been . . . this. Her new cousin filled the air with so many words that Lillian couldn't snag half of them and make any sense of what the woman said. The older lady, Edith, regarded Lillian with a somewhat reserved curiosity. The gentleman, Alma's husband, remained quietly thoughtful.

All of this she could have weathered without any cracks in her composure were it not for the tall man staring holes into her. She could *feel* his eyes on her back. She barely resisted the urge to shiver. What had caused this man so much contempt for her? Surely her being upset that he'd ruined her dress didn't warrant the glint of alarm she'd caught in his eyes when they recognized one another.

At least he stayed behind as Alma shooed her toward the house.

They stepped onto the wide front porch of a tidy farmhouse, the planked surface home to several rocking chairs. White paint covered the wooden exterior, and the windows sparkled in the sunshine. Curious about the family that called this cozy place home, Lillian put all thoughts of the churlish cowboy from her mind. He could think what he wanted. It made no difference to her.

Alma smiled brightly as she swept open the front door. "Come in, come in."

Every gesture her cousin made and every ready smile that spread over her cheery face warmed a small part of Lillian's heart. In truth, she'd expected hostility. Rejection. At the very least, suspicion. Alma Watson didn't show any of those things.

Lillian stepped into the front entry and let her eyes devour every detail of her new family's home. The wooden floors and papered walls weren't all that different from the house she shared with Mother, yet somehow the Watson home seemed to open its arms and invite a person in. The rugs on the floor were worn, the furniture scuffed but polished. Each feature spoke of a family that cared for their home yet wasn't afraid to truly live in it.

Lillian followed Alma and Edith into the parlor. Another room well-worn yet inviting. These people didn't reserve this space only to impress guests. The gentle slope to the seat cushions spoke of a family that gathered together to enjoy one another's company on a regular basis.

A sudden sense of longing opened up within her, so wrenchingly deep that she had to draw a steadying breath. She needed to get her thoughts together.

"See now, Alma. You've gone and gotten the girl flustered." Edith eyed Lillian as she scooted past her and dropped into a chair in the corner near the hearth. "Too many questions at once, dear. Give the child a moment."

Oh. She hadn't heard a single one of Alma's questions. She offered an apologetic smile as her cousin waved her to a chair.

"Do forgive me." Alma's voice held no contriteness, only amusement. Her brown eyes, several shades lighter than Lillian's own, sparkled with humor. "Mother is correct, of course. As always."

The older woman snorted.

Lillian had to contain a bark of laughter that wanted to leap from her throat. These people were rather interesting. The two women appeared to hold a type of relationship that Lillian could not quite grasp. Despite the words fired between them, they both seemed amused with one another. How odd.

"Now, let's see . . ." Alma perched on an upholstered chair. "One question at a time."

Edith gathered a ball of yarn and knitting needles, and soon the clack picked up a steady rhythm of creation.

Lillian tried for a gracious smile. One could hardly ask such awkward questions of a family member they'd just met, so in order to save this kind woman embarrassment, Lillian spoke first. "My mother and I live in Atlanta. Until a letter arrived from a solicitor requesting my presence, I had thought my father dead for many years. This entire situation—as I am sure you can agree—came as a shock. I do apologize."

Edith's knitting needles stopped. "What do you have to apologize for? You weren't the one who kept yourself a secret."

The woman's matter-of-fact declaration tugged a little of the tension from Lillian's shoulder muscles.

"That fool brother of mine. What a mess." The needles started again. "Not you, of course. You're rather lovely. And you have my mother's nose."

She had . . . ? Lillian stared at the woman who returned to her project as though she had not somehow altered Lillian's world. Edith's mother would be Lillian's grandmother. A lady she assumed no longer lived. A pang at the missed opportunity fluttered through her heart. She'd always wondered what it would be like to have a grandmother.

Edith glanced up and caught Lillian staring. Her cheeks heated.

"I'd thought for a moment you might be trying to deceive us, but you look so much like my mother that if I didn't know better I'd mistake you for my own daughter." With that pronouncement, she returned to her knitting.

Lillian swallowed a lump in her throat. There were so many questions. Things she wanted to know about her father. Yet sitting in the same room with his family—*her* family—she couldn't form the first one to ask.

Apparently sensing her thoughts, Edith pointed a knitting needle. "Don't worry. Floyd wasn't a bad man. A foolish and overly ambitious one who more often than not got himself into trouble, but he had a good heart." She tilted her head. "I'm guessing he sent money to Atlanta?"

Lillian nodded slowly. "It would seem so."

"Ah, well, that explains it."

Explained what? Before she could figure out a way to ask, Alma spoke again. "How old are you, if you don't mind my asking?"

"Twenty-three."

"Delightful." Alma nodded as though Lillian had answered something correctly. "Only four years younger than myself." She reached over to squeeze Lillian's hand with long fingers. "We are going to be such great friends."

The unexpected words wrapped her in a comforting embrace and pushed away some of her nervousness, but all Lillian could do was offer a small smile. Why were these people so welcoming? Mother certainly wouldn't have been if the situation had been the other way.

Footsteps sounded down the hall, and a moment later Alma's husband entered, carrying a tea tray.

"Oh, Lewis. You are such a dear." Alma rose and accepted the tray from her husband with a loving look. "I've completely forgotten my manners."

A man who made the tea tray and brought it to the parlor for the women? Lillian couldn't fathom Reginald ever doing such a thing.

Lewis grinned and took a seat near Edith. Dressed in a casual suit, he exuded a quiet confidence that Lillian had not seen in many men. As he caught her eye, his mustache twitched up into a smile. "Welcome to our home, Miss Doyle."

Lillian worked past the dryness in her throat. "Thank you."

"Are you staying at a hotel in town?" Edith asked.

"Oh, you should stay here." Alma plucked a teacup from the tray. "Shouldn't she, Lewis?"

Lewis's eyebrows lifted slightly before he cleared his throat. "Of course, my dear."

Alma was far too kind. Lillian accepted the teacup from her and offered a gracious smile—the one a lady used when extending a polite refusal to an offer not made in earnest. "I couldn't possibly impose. But thank you for the kindness of your offer."

Alma opened her mouth as though to protest, then held out the sugar jar instead. "One lump or two?"

"Neither. Thank you."

Alma served the others as the conversation settled into how delighted they were for Lillian to join them for their midday dinner and how they would like to meet her mother someday.

The very idea filled Lillian with dread, though she couldn't put her finger on why.

"I hope you'll forgive the directness, Miss Doyle." Lewis set his cup on the small table near his wingback chair. "But there is a matter of some importance that I'm afraid we must discuss."

"Yes." Lillian settled her own barely touched teacup on her saucer. She'd rehearsed this part. "According to my solicitor in Atlanta and Mr. Carson here in town, Mr. Jackson's property was left to me."

"That is what we were told as well."

Relief tingled through her. At least she didn't need to fight them over the will. "There is an issue I've run into, however."

Lewis nodded as though already expecting trouble waited.

"Strangely, there was a woman at Mr. Jackson's house who claimed that the property already belonged to her."

Lewis winced and shared a look with Alma. "There were some special circumstances, and we had no way of knowing that Floyd's property wouldn't be passed to us."

Special circumstances? Lillian rubbed her finger over the painted edge of the teacup. She could hardly blame them for expecting the inheritance to fall to Edith, or perhaps Lewis and Alma, but surely they should have waited for the will before selling off the man's property. Why the rush?

"We will get all that straightened out. Don't worry." Alma's cheery voice filled the silence that had started to stretch. "Jonah is a good man. I'm sure we can come to a solution that suits everyone."

Jonah?

"I'm sure we will." Lewis pushed up from his chair. "I'll fetch him, and we can discuss the options over Mother Edith's pork roast."

Jonah? The name repeated in Lillian's mind, rolling around and looking for purchase.

Oh no.

A sense of dread curled in her stomach and usurped any delightful stirrings caused by the delicious aromas drifting down the hall.

It couldn't be.

Mrs. Peterson's words echoed through her head. *"Mr. Watson already promised this property to my son."*

The dirty cowboy who had pushed her into the mud. The angry man who had stared holes into her when she'd arrived.

Lillian withheld a groan. From what little interaction she'd had with this Jonah, one thing was painfully clear.

He wouldn't be the sort to give up anything easily.

CHAPTER SIX

─────◈─────

To think he'd nearly declined attending such a strenuously awkward meal. Jonah gripped the fork in his hand so tightly the silver should have bent. Why hadn't he stood his ground and refused to subject himself to this? The answer was simple. Because he'd never really been able to tell Alma no.

Scents of roasted meat and perfectly seasoned vegetables hung in the air, and the family passed the platters around with their usual joyfulness. Jonah cast another sidelong glance at the prim woman next to him, who seemed to have done her very best to add to the awkwardness of the meal.

She could have at least attempted to be polite. Not only did she decline to look at him, but she hadn't once uttered a single "thank you." Not when he'd pulled out her chair or passed her the potatoes, green beans, or corn.

"Don't you think so, Jonah?"

The sound of his name snapped his attention back to Edith, who sat across from him. The sassy tip of her lips indicated she knew he hadn't been listening.

After another heartbeat, she tossed him a lifeline. "About coming to a solution that suits everyone, I mean."

There wouldn't be a solution, though he could hardly say so. The only logical outcomes he could foresee wouldn't work in his favor. Unless . . . "If Miss Doyle honors the price we agreed upon, then I am sure everything will work out for the good."

Silence settled on the room as the din of filling plates paused.

"Details for another time." Lewis placed his fork on his napkin. "Shall I ask a blessing on our meal?"

While Lewis prayed for the family, gave thanks for their many blessings, and even thanked the Lord for the unexpected new family member, Jonah attempted to keep his fists from tightening under the table.

And failed.

Why do you continue to take from me?

The thought came unbidden, and Ma would be ashamed of him. But it seemed that every time a plan came together, something upended him. God thwarted him at every turn.

Jonah held in a sigh and focused on his food.

"I'd like to know about your mother." Edith stabbed a chunk of roast and waved it over her plate. "I'm rather curious, if you don't mind."

"My mother pretends she is a widow when she is not. We live in Atlanta in a house I always thought left to us by my father, a man I thought dead for many years."

Miss Doyle delivered her words with as much electricity as a dead wire, her face never twitching out of her perfectly composed mask. But underneath, Jonah sensed something more. Did she think that if she delivered the truth with cold logic, people would accept her words and move on, thus saving her from embarrassment?

Edith, apparently, sensed no such thing.

"Ha. How like Floyd." She jabbed the bite of roast into her mouth, chewed thoughtfully, then set her fork down. When she spoke again, sadness laced her tone. "I dearly loved my little brother, God rest him. But the man always did have a knack for getting himself into a mess. He never learned that covering up his mistakes only led to more trouble. But at least he tried to care for you in some way."

Miss Doyle, to her credit, actually seemed to relax under the matter-of-fact statement. "Again, I'm quite sorry for the predicament I've caused. Until last week, I would have never fathomed such a turn of events."

"You've no reason to be sorry." Alma shot a look to her husband that said she wanted something. "Sometimes life is simply different than we expect, and we must embrace what has been given to us. How long do you plan to stay before returning to Atlanta?"

Miss Doyle shifted slightly. She spoke softly. "I'm not certain. I had hoped to go through the house prior to selling it."

"Splendid." Alma laced her fingers together over her plate. "Would you care for company and perhaps help with this endeavor?"

"I, um . . ." The poised shell surrounding Miss Doyle cracked ever so slightly.

"Jonah, his mother and sisters, and I would be—" At Edith's grunt, Alma popped a quick smile. "And Mother too, of course, would be happy to help you sort through the contents of the house, something we had been planning to get around to prior to your arrival. Besides, it will give us an opportunity to know you better." Her amber eyes sparkled. "Won't that be delightful?"

How could anyone resist anything Alma wanted when she presented her wishes in such a fashion? Probably why Lewis gave the woman everything in his power to provide.

"I . . . well, yes." Miss Doyle's shoulders stiffened. "I would like that."

Jonah nearly smiled at Alma's victory until he realized he'd also been pulled into the proposition. "I have work to do. I'm sure you ladies can handle your digging on your own."

Everyone looked at him, even Miss Doyle. Had he said something callous? He didn't think so. Why would they need him to dig through Floyd's personal belongings? And he *did* have work to do. Work the Watson family paid him for.

"If you will assist, I'll consider it a personal favor." Lewis held Jonah's gaze, but whatever the man wanted to communicate was lost on Jonah.

"Yes, sir."

Alma clapped her hands together. "Wonderful. It's settled."

Jonah felt anything but.

No amount of rehearsing worked with these people. Lillian felt constantly off-kilter in their presence and somehow at the same time enjoyed being among them. Lewis, Alma, and Edith were the liveliest people she'd ever encountered. They were entirely unencumbered by the strict mannerisms that had been schooled into Lillian for as long as she could remember. They spoke with a freeness both strange and inviting, asking her questions with an openness that would have had Mother fanning her face in shock. Good thing Mother hadn't come.

Lillian dared a glance at the sour man at her side while the family animatedly discussed the best place to store her father's belongings. What thoughts churned beneath that thick mop of dark hair and behind those strikingly deep-blue eyes? He clearly didn't want to have anything to do with her, yet he'd agreed to help with the house. Out of his own interests, she was sure. Whatever those might be.

He caught her staring. She looked away, but not before noticing the glint in his eye. Did he truly dislike her so much? It was hardly her fault her father had died and left his belongings to her.

"Do you have any hobbies, Lillian dear?" The endearment rolled easily off Edith's tongue and sent Lillian's senses into a spiral.

"I enjoy baking." Mother insisted baking was for poor women, but Lillian had always found joy in creating beautiful works of art that could delight both the eyes and the palate.

Alma grinned. "What an astounding coincidence." She tipped her head toward her mother. "Or perhaps providence?"

Lewis's eyebrows drew together as the two women held a conversation of looks. Next to her, the prickly cowboy had gone entirely rigid.

"I'm sure lots of women like baking." His words came out strained.

"Including your own dear mother." Edith started wiggling her fork around again, a habit she had whenever she spoke.

Jonah's mother. The stubborn woman Lillian had met outside her father's dilapidated house. Why did Jonah seem so upset that they shared an interest?

He turned to her, face somber. "Ma had hoped to start her own bakery in that house."

"Oh." Lillian twisted her fingers together under the table.

"Well, I do plan to sell. Once I sort through everything, of course." Her face heated. Why was he looking at her like that? "If she wants to buy it."

That flinty face of his remained unchanged. "We'll see."

What did that mean? She opened her mouth to call him out on his rudeness, but no words would escape.

"If you both enjoy baking, perhaps you could do something together." Alma smiled brightly.

"I'm not staying—"

"No, that's not a good—"

She and Jonah spoke at the same time and cut off their protests instantly. Just because she enjoyed the idea of her edible art didn't mean that she would spend her time here concocting confections for hire. Never mind that the thought of helping with a bakery sent a traitorous spike of excitement through her core.

Lillian cleared an annoying thickness from her throat. "We are agreed, I believe. I wouldn't presume to put upon your mother with my frivolous hobbies. My apologies."

Jonah watched her, his face unreadable.

An odd battle of wills played out between their locked gazes. Lillian didn't dare look away first, lest she appear weak. Her palms began to sweat.

The jovial feeling in the room dissipated, leaving unnerving silence in its wake.

CHAPTER SEVEN

This woman couldn't possibly be serious.

Lillian resisted the urge to pinch the bridge of her nose in frustration. This morning was already turning into a disaster. "Mrs. Peterson, I—"

"You can call me Melanie, dear. No sense standing on pretense."

Pretense? There was hardly any pretense in politely addressing a stranger. Especially a stranger insistent upon living in a home that didn't belong to her.

Lillian drew a breath. There had to be boundaries. "I don't believe I'm being unreasonable."

They locked gazes on the front porch of her father's town house, neither of them willing to budge on the matter.

Mrs. Peterson made a sound Lillian could only describe as part snort of derision and part chuckle. She waved a hand at the front door. "You think it's reasonable to snoop through someone else's home?"

"It's *my* home." As soon as the words left her lips, Lillian regretted them. "I mean, this was my father's home, which he left to me."

"And it is currently *my* home. Mine and the girls.'"

The woman was impossible. "Mrs. Peterson, while I don't mind—"

"Melanie." Her firm tone left no room for argument, but Lillian ignored her insistence.

"I don't mind if you and your daughters stay until you can find alternative accommodations, but in the meantime, I do need to settle my father's estate."

The older woman opened her mouth, no doubt to fire off some kind of retort, but boot steps silenced her. She whipped her head around fast enough to partially dislodge the massive pile of tawny hair on her head.

"Oh good." Mrs. Peterson—Melanie—let out a sigh. "You're here."

Jonah. Wonderful. Lillian tried to hide her annoyance at the arrival of Melanie's reinforcements, but judging by the grimace on the man's face, she'd failed.

He dipped his hat politely. "Ladies."

"Please try to get this lovely girl to see reason." Melanie waved a hand at Lillian. How did she manage to tangle insults and compliments together so seamlessly?

Lillian crossed her arms. "Going through my father's belongings and sorting out the estate he left to me isn't an unreasonable request."

Jonah's gaze darted between the two of them lightning quick. "The solicitor said the house is hers, Ma."

The disappointment in his voice sent a scurry of guilt through Lillian's veins. But why should she feel guilty? It wasn't her fault these people had moved into a house that didn't belong to them.

"I don't mind if they stay until they can find somewhere else, but I do need to continue with my affairs."

She stopped short of voicing her suspicions. Why would they care if she went through her father's things? Unless, of course, they were hiding—or stealing—something. She didn't want to make any accusations, but Melanie's reluctance seemed . . . well, suspicious.

Jonah rubbed the back of his neck. "I'm sorry, Ma. There's nothing I can do. The Watsons want to help her sort through Floyd's things and get the house ready to sell."

For a moment, no one spoke. Melanie turned her eyes up toward the porch roof and made some kind of tsking noise. "I know what I was told. So whatever is supposed to happen here, I reckon it just isn't going to look like I thought."

What was she talking about? Who had told her what was supposed to happen?

Jonah shifted his feet, his brows pinching together. His mother huffed at the roof again and then wiped her hands down the sides of her dress.

"Ma, I know what I told you, but things have changed."

"Not you, Son." She patted his shoulder, then drew herself up and offered a wide smile. "No matter. It will work out. You'll see."

What would work out? Did this mean Melanie would step aside?

Melanie nodded decisively. "We'll need to get all this stuff cleared out for the repairs anyway." She clapped and Lillian jumped. "Let's get to it, girl. Betsy and Rose will be home before you know it."

"Repairs? What repairs?" Lillian said. The house could use some work, but they would need to decide on the details and how everything would be paid for. If the Petersons planned on purchasing the house, they would need to come to terms on the price and how the repairs factored into it.

Melanie bustled past them, leaving Lillian confused and Jonah mumbling something under his breath. Her clear voice carried through the open doorway. "The bakery will go on the bottom floor, with a big kitchen and a small place where folks can sit and have their coffee and sweets. It's going to be so lovely and . . ." Her voice trailed off as she disappeared deeper inside the house.

Lillian looked at Jonah, hoping he might offer some insight.

He simply shrugged and spread his palms. "She wants to live upstairs and put the bakery below. She said if the doctor and the dentist can do it, so can she."

Lillian had heard of doctors having rooms to see patients in their homes, but she would have thought a bakery needed to be somewhere in town, nearer the courthouse and the pleasant little square. This house was technically on the main street, but none of the other houses also doubled as businesses as far as she could tell. What would the neighbors think of Melanie's plans?

"And one day we'll have electricity too, which will make all the difference." Melanie appeared in the doorway again. Had she continued the conversation all on her own?

"Electricity?" Lillian hadn't seen any electric lights since she'd left Atlanta. And even there, only the wealthiest families and the larger hotels and businesses featured them. "You have an electric company out here?"

"No. We don't." Jonah shot his mother a warning look and then stalked through the house.

Melanie bustled after him, saying something about how he only needed to have a little faith.

These people were strange. Lillian hesitated only a moment before stepping inside after them. Strange or not, she'd have to deal with them for a little longer. Good thing Mother had stayed in Atlanta. Lillian couldn't fathom Mother and Melanie in the same room together. Then again, maybe her mother would be the only person with a strong enough personality to counteract Melanie's stubbornness.

A tingle trickled up her arms as she paused just inside the door. Her father's home. Mother always said a lot could be learned about a person from their house. Their tastes, breeding, and manners could all be ascertained by a glimpse of their personal space.

If that was true, Lillian didn't quite know what to think of the man who'd lived here.

Her eyes traveled from the hardwood floors that were long past due for a good scrubbing and polish to the dark green paper on the walls. Wood molding and trim matched the curved railing of the staircase and the heavy doors leading away from both sides of the foyer. The inside of the house seemed to be in better condition than the outside, thankfully, though still in need of a heavy cleaning. She hadn't thought her father had been in jail long, but this place looked as though it had been abandoned for quite some time. Odd, considering there were people living here.

"Where'd she go?" Melanie poked her head through a doorway to Lillian's right. "Oh. You're still standing there." Her eyebrows arched. "What's wrong?"

Lillian straightened. "Nothing."

Melanie's expression said she didn't buy Lillian's lie, but at least she didn't call her out. "Then come on." She gestured into the room behind her. "All of this will need to be opened up, of course. We'll want room for the tables over here since the kitchen and the display will go on the other side of the house."

Jonah said something about support walls and making sure Melanie wouldn't bring the house down on their heads.

Lillian stepped into a parlor overflowing with dusty furniture, stacks of books piled on the floor, and all manner of odd boxes and crates shoved haphazardly around the room. *Oh my.*

Were these her father's things or Melanie's? The woman certainly didn't seem concerned with housekeeping. Lillian pressed her finger under her nose to keep from sneezing as Jonah stirred up dust moving one of the crates out of the walking path to the next room.

She followed the two through another doorway into what might have once been a study, with the most charming set of bay windows. With a bit of work, this could be a lovely place for reading. She could picture herself sitting in the sunny window with a Jane Austen novel and a cup of tea.

Lillian mentally shook herself. What was she thinking?

The two rooms on the opposite side of the house offered more of the same, an overcrowded space stuffed with furniture that didn't belong and more crates and boxes. Had this been another parlor or a dining room? She could hardly tell as she wove her way through the debris.

"Thankfully, the kitchen is attached to the house, so we won't need to worry with that." Melanie waved her hand toward a small room with a large fireplace and a tiny wood-stove, located to the back of what Lillian finally decided must have been the dining room. "We'll need a large modern oven, of course. And plenty of tables for preparing pies. Oh yes, and two iceboxes." She bobbed her head, speaking to no one in particular. "I heard that a man has invented an electric icebox. Can't you just see me with an electric icebox?"

There were electric iceboxes? Why did a person need an electric light in an icebox? And heavens, no one needed two. Lillian kept her thoughts to herself as they looped back around to the front entryway of the house.

"I saw an advertisement in the paper last month." Melanie smiled up at Jonah, who appeared strangely uncomfortable. "Porcelain-lined iceboxes. They aren't supposed to scratch or hold germs. We can get one with polished oak for thirty-five dollars."

Lillian could have sworn Jonah paled. She needed to get this conversation under control.

"Are these belongings yours or Mr. Jackson's?"

Melanie and Jonah both turned to her, looking like they had forgotten she'd followed them all through the house. "Jonah put everything down here when we moved in." Melanie gestured around them.

So these were her father's things. Apparently the Petersons had taken all his possessions and piled them up in the lower rooms. As if they had the right to do so. Lillian turned toward the staircase.

"Why are you going up there?" Melanie scrambled forward to halt Lillian's trespass.

"To see the rest of the house."

Melanie exchanged a look with Jonah that Lillian couldn't decipher. "None of Floyd's things are up there except that big bed."

So she said. Lillian ignored her and mounted the first step. She'd ascended half the staircase before she heard Melanie's footsteps behind her. At the top, Lillian paused. Where the lower floor smelled of dust and disuse, the upper hallway gleamed with polished molding and held the fresh scent of soap. She threw a glance back over her shoulder just to be sure she was still in the same house.

Soft carpet muffled her feet. No pictures lined the hallway, and not a single stick of furniture broke up the space between doors. Melanie mumbled something behind her but didn't stop Lillian from opening the first door she came to.

The polished door swung open on silent hinges, revealing a large but sparse space. Lillian stood frozen with her hand on the doorknob. A simple, lumpy mattress sat on the floor, topped with a well-worn quilt. A pitcher and washbasin huddled underneath a clean window framed by faded curtains. A small, battered trunk sat on the opposite wall.

"This is my room." Melanie's voice sounded small and rather unlike the woman Lillian had first met.

Lillian closed the door, unsure how to respond. The next room revealed much the same, though with two mattresses on the floor and two milk crates stuffed with folded clothing. Melanie's daughters must occupy this one.

"They are staying a few days with a friend of mine," Melanie said. "Until things are settled."

Meaning Lillian and the mess she'd brought with her. Again Lillian closed the door to the room without comment.

There were two more rooms on the floor. The first was empty yet spotlessly clean, and the second, the largest by far, was bare except for a massive canopy bed atop a brightly colored rug. Curious, Lillian stepped into the room and crossed to the bed. The wood gleamed with fresh polish, and the mattress had been kept clean.

"This was Floyd's room." Melanie spoke behind her, still in that quiet voice. "Bed was too heavy to move."

"Why did you move everything downstairs? And why . . . ?"

She wanted to ask why the top floor was so clean while the bottom floor was, well, what it was, but she couldn't think of a way to ask without sounding rude.

"Why does the lower floor look so terrible?" Melanie shrugged. "I had to start somewhere, and Rose tends to get sickly when there is too much dust. Better for her to just pass through it than to sleep with it."

But where did they eat or sit in the evenings? No. That was none of her business.

Lillian gave a small nod. At least the second floor of the house didn't seem like it would need much attention. "Why didn't you want me up here?"

Melanie lifted her palms. "Nothing up here but Floyd's bed."

Had she been embarrassed by the sparse belongings? "I did want to see the entire house, nonetheless." Lillian stepped out of her father's bedroom and closed the door behind her.

They made their way back downstairs and found Jonah standing at the front door with Alma and Lewis Watson. Alma's face brightened with a grin as soon as she saw Lillian, and a strange warmth spread through Lillian's middle. Her cousin radiated joy, and to have someone so openly glad to see her was a feeling Lillian had rarely experienced.

"What do you think?" Alma shared a glance with her husband, her eyes gleaming with expectation. "It will make a lovely bakery. Don't you agree?"

Lillian's pulse skipped.

Oh no. She thought— Was that why—? Lillian's thoughts tumbled together. She'd been such a ninny. She'd thought Alma wanted to help her go through her father's things. Spend time together. Maybe even develop a type of kinship.

Why hadn't she realized that Alma and Edith would team up with Melanie? Had her mother taught her nothing? These were the same tactics the women in the sewing circle used.

Why in the heavens had she let herself think that for once she wasn't facing trouble alone?

CHAPTER EIGHT

———❦———

What a mess. Jonah scanned the entryway to Floyd's house, the space stuffed to bursting with discarded objects, flustered people, and the tension pulsing between them. The Watsons shared looks with Ma, who then turned to him for answers. How would he understand Floyd's daughter better than any of the rest of them? One moment he'd thought she was about to embrace membership into the Watson family, and the next she seemed one breath away from dismissing them entirely.

He turned his attention to the statuesque Miss Doyle. She perched on the bottom of the staircase, her face as smooth and unaffected as marble. He'd known her to be rather stiff and a bit pretentious, but up until this moment he hadn't considered her outright rude.

Miss Doyle lifted her chin another unnecessary notch. "Again, I'm sorry if my decision causes any distress, but I really must be clear on my intentions."

Was that a slight waver to her voice? Jonah studied her but saw no other indication that she wasn't as cold as a block of ice in one of those fancy iceboxes Ma wanted.

Alma's smile faltered. "You said you were also interested

in baking." She turned out a gloved palm. "So I just thought . . . well, I didn't mean to cause . . ." She let the words trail off with a slight shake of her head.

"I do enjoy baking as a pastime, Mrs. Watson."

Miss Doyle managed to speak with the most unusual mix of gentleness and haughty reprimand.

"But I am not prepared to convert my late father's home into such a business. Nor do I have any intention of staying in a strange town. I have a life to return to in Atlanta."

There it was again. The tremor in her voice. Jonah didn't mistake it this time. Maybe the woman wasn't quite as flinty as she appeared.

Alma must have noticed as well. She cast her husband—who seemed to be trying to blend into the wallpaper—a loaded look before turning back to Miss Doyle. "Oh, my dear cousin. I'm so sorry. I wasn't trying to be pushy."

A little of Miss Doyle's armor loosened as surprise flickered over her face. She shifted, further undoing the stiffness of her bearing. "It is a lovely idea, truly. And if Mrs. Peterson wishes to purchase the property, I'm sure she will have great success."

Ma muttered something that thankfully the rest of the room couldn't hear. He hoped. He loved his mother. Her conviction when it came to something she believed the Lord had told her was commendable. But others often mistook her faith for obstinacy. Probably best if he reminded the group of the focus for today.

He stepped forward, garnering everyone's attention. "Why don't we start with Floyd's things in here?" He gestured toward the front room directly behind him. "That's something everyone can agree on."

Miss Doyle's shoulders drooped, his pronouncement somehow deflating the determination holding them in place. "Yes. That would be fine. Thank you." She shot him a grateful look that should not have caused a strange heat in his chest. His lips tipped upward of their own accord, which earned him a tentative smile in return.

She was a rather pretty woman when she let a smile soften her face. Dismissing the impulsive thought, Jonah strode into the parlor. This room alone would take them the remainder of the day.

A feminine sigh followed him. "I have no idea what to do with all of this stuff." Miss Doyle appeared at his side, her soft voice urging him to offer advice that probably wasn't welcome.

"Anything you want, I suppose. Seeing as it belongs to you." He swept an assessing gaze over the clutter. "We could organize an estate sale if you'd like. Or I can make arrangements for a shipping car to take anything you'd like to keep back to Atlanta."

Why had he just offered that? He had more than enough work already.

Her face turned up to him, and hope flickered in her gaze. "That's very kind of you, Mr. Peterson. I am grateful for the help." She blinked long lashes, and the coffee-colored depths of her large eyes drew him in.

He caught himself leaning toward her and pulled back. Before he could stop himself, he said, "I'm sorry about Ma."

Curiosity stole over her features. "How so?"

"She can be rather . . . determined."

Miss Doyle's cheeks bunched with a sudden grin. "Something that hasn't slipped my notice." The expression was gone as quickly as it had appeared. She pinched the bridge of her nose and squeezed her eyes shut. When she opened them again, the sincerity in her gaze rattled him. "I never intended to cause your family trouble. This entire situation is simply more trying than I anticipated."

Tears shimmered in the corners of her eyes, and his chest constricted. He rubbed the back of his neck. "I can imagine this must be difficult."

"It *is* rather shocking to discover one's life is not what one thought it to be." Her small laugh carried a twinge of pain.

Guilt pricked at him. Had he been too quick to judge her? He could only imagine how he might react if their situations were reversed.

Miss Doyle turned those luminous eyes on him again. "Thank you for understanding."

He clasped his hands behind his back. How did he respond to that?

After a moment of silence, Miss Doyle sighed. "Well, anyway. Like I said, I'm sure your mother will have success with her endeavor."

Glad the conversation was back to the matter at hand before he said anything foolish, Jonah focused on the crates jammed in the space. He took another step deeper into the room and kept his gaze from lingering on the woman at his side. The viper he could handle. This other version of her, however . . .

He had no idea what to do with the decidedly unfathomable urge to pledge his aid like some kind of medieval knight. Perhaps it was merely the urge to protect a vulnerable woman. A sort of brotherly protectiveness like he had for his sisters.

Miss Doyle watched him, an odd expression he couldn't name stirring in her eyes.

"Ma will be glad to get everything out." He cleared his throat and pointed to the closest box. "She's been asking me to help her move these crates, but I've been busy."

"Right." Miss Doyle straightened, and all the sunshine disappeared from her gaze. "A good solution for all of us."

The haughtiness had entered her tone again. Had he said something wrong?

Alma and Edith chose that moment to enter the room, Edith tsking over the state of affairs. "My gracious, Melanie. You could stash an entire family of mules in here and not find hide nor hair."

"Now, see here. This place was a mess before I . . ."

Jonah tuned the two women out as they started bickering like hens. After another few moments and a substantial increase in volume, Miss Doyle's clear voice rose above the chatter.

"I do thank you for coming, but you don't need to put yourselves out." She gestured toward the door in an almost comically big motion. "Really. I can tackle this space on my own, I'm sure."

Jonah nearly chuckled. A perfectly polite way to say she didn't want any of them here. Given the crowded space and the quick-fire verbal jabs between the older women, he could hardly blame her.

"Nonsense." Alma planted a fist at the curve of her hip. "We have all come to *help*, and that's what we will do." She shot a glare at Edith. "Isn't that right, Mother?"

"What?" Edith scrunched her nose and turned away from Ma. "Oh. Yes. We are here to help." She shook her head at Ma and then scurried to Alma's side.

Jonah darted a look at Lewis, the two of them likely sharing the same thought.

Trapped in a room full of opinionated women. Exactly how a man wanted to spend his day.

Heavens. Lillian resisted the urge to stick her fingers in her ears like a child. What had she stepped into? Edith and Melanie continued to argue over the state of the house, though it didn't seem as if either of the women meant any actual scolding with their quick-witted banter. If anything, they looked as though they were having quite a lovely time sparring with one another.

Mother would be aghast.

In addition to the two older women's rapid-fire tongues, Alma kept up a steady stream of cheerful words that had started to run together in an incoherent flood of lively syllables. The men discussed the best way to organize the crates and in what order they should be searched.

All Lillian wanted was space to learn about the man who'd abandoned her.

She stood in the center of the room, fighting against a persistent feeling of suffocation. Her fingers twitched with the effort. She needed a quiet moment to think. She mumbled her excuses to Alma and darted for the door. Her cousin would think her terribly rude, but she simply couldn't help herself.

Just a moment of fresh air. Then she could reorient herself to handle the chaos. She slipped through the front door and closed it behind her, muffling the sounds within.

She exhaled. Much better. The warm sunshine beckoned, and she ambled down the sagging porch steps to stand in the center of the yard. She tilted her face heavenward, the touch of the sun reminding her of the comfort of the Lord's presence.

I could use a little help, if you're willing.

She needed a plan, some mental fortitude, a bit of peace, and wisdom on how to handle both the Watsons and the

Petersons, but God surely knew all of that and had applied those needs and perhaps others to the simple word "help."

"Sorry if they overwhelmed you."

The masculine voice startled her, and Lillian spun around.

Jonah stood on the porch, watching her with an unreadable expression. "Ma is a good woman. She just has her own way of thinking."

Lillian smirked. "My mother is the same. Actually, your mother is quite different from mine. But I know what you mean about a mother who has her own way of thinking."

He leaned against the post, his steady gaze unnerving. What was it about this somewhat uncouth man that did strange things to her composure? He'd been gentle with her in the parlor, almost as though he and the churlish cowboy she'd first met were two different men. He'd gazed at her with concern and compassion, something she didn't remember any man doing before.

"If you don't mind my asking, why didn't she come with you?"

A legitimate question, and one that should not elicit a throb of shame. "She thought I could handle matters." The lie stabbed hot and quick through her center. Lillian sighed. "Actually, I suspect she didn't want to entangle herself in any kind of scandal."

"So she left you to navigate all of this"—he gestured behind him—"on your own?" His tone didn't hold judgment, merely curiosity.

Lillian twisted her fingers together. "Mother is quite conscious about appearances and how they affect one's standing."

Jonah studied her for several heartbeats, thoughts churning behind his eyes. "I see."

Pride stiffened her spine. What did that mean? That he understood why no one would want to associate themselves with the illegitimate daughter of a man who'd died in jail? Her face burned. Her birth was hardly her fault. In fact, if there were any shame to be had, then Mother should be the one here bearing it, not—

"So then, what do *you* want to do?"

She opened her mouth, but no answer formed. What *did* she want to do? The reality of her desires hit her with force. She wanted to live a peaceful life that was honest and simple. She didn't want to keep up airs or pretend to be someone she wasn't.

"I mean, I assume your mother had a plan for you coming here and what you would accomplish."

"I suppose." Mother had simply told her to get what belonged to them and come home. She'd left out any kind of helpful details.

"But what about you? What do you want to do with what your father left you?" Jonah stepped off the porch and came closer. "He did leave everything to you, after all. Not you and your mother."

The words locked Lillian's stomach into a painful knot. She'd known that already, but hearing him say it out loud somehow brought a distinction she had not let herself consider.

Could it be that this choice, this opportunity, had been given to her alone for a reason? Her father had left her a blessing. One that was up to her to decide what to do with.

A strange lightness filled her. She flashed a smile that Jonah immediately returned.

"You know what, Mr. Peterson?" She strode toward him. "You are exactly right."

He beamed at her, and her heart did the strangest sort of little pirouette.

CHAPTER NINE

She was ready. After hours of discussion yesterday with Melanie, Alma, and Edith on how best to tackle the mess of her father's house, Lillian had retired to her room at the hotel, where she'd spent some time in prayer. And while God hadn't laid out a plan as she'd requested, she'd started this pristine spring day with a serene sense of purpose. The blessing had been given to her. Now she had to decide what to do with it.

The day outside of her hotel brimmed with sunshine, and she enjoyed the warmth of it cascading over her shoulders during her short stroll to the Farmers & Citizens Bank. She entered the moment the man inside unlocked the door and turned the OPEN sign.

"I'd like to meet with Mr. Grimly." She tugged her kid gloves from her fingers and tucked them inside her rose-print handbag before meeting the gaze of the banker.

"I can assist you if you are looking to start an account." He tugged on his lapels in a manner that reminded Lillian of a cardinal when it puffed its feathers.

"Thank you, but I'm not opening an account." At least, not at this moment. She may need to do so once she sold off her father's property. That way she could request a bank transfer of her funds and not have to worry about traveling alone back to Atlanta with such a sum. "My solicitor listed Mr. Grimly as the banker on my father's estate."

The bell above the door chimed as another customer entered behind them. The banker cast the customer a quick glance, then gestured toward the rear of the building. "Right this way, please."

Lillian followed him through an archway and into a hall lined with doors. He knocked briefly on the first door, and when a voice barked out a response, he poked his head inside. "A lady is here to see you, sir. Says it's in regards to her father's estate."

"Ah yes. That would likely be Miss Doyle." The rich baritone rumbled past the thin man taking up the doorway. "Send her in."

The banker stepped back and gestured Lillian inside, then quickly disappeared the way he had come. She entered into a well-appointed space one might expect of a man of finance, complete with the deep masculine hues of leather and dark wood.

Mr. Grimly rose, buttoning his black coat over an ample stomach. "Miss Doyle. A pleasure to meet you."

"I'm pleased to make your acquaintance, sir." Lillian perched on the padded chair Mr. Grimly indicated and tucked her ankles beneath her. The room held the faint smell of tobacco smoke and a spicy type of aftershave.

Mr. Grimly settled back into his chair, releasing the button on his jacket. "I take it Mr. Carson sent you?"

"He said that you would be the best person to speak to in regards to Mr. Floyd Jackson's business." She still wasn't entirely sure what type of business her father had owned. Something to do with transporting goods from factories and distributing those wares to various locations. The solicitor hadn't given many details beyond that.

"Indeed." Mr. Grimly studied her a moment as he leaned back in his chair. "I am sorry for your loss."

The words landed on her with a sudden weight. She'd been given a heap of unexpected information, been peppered with dozens of questions, and been expected to muddle her way through the aftermath of her estranged father's death, but no one else had thought to offer her condolences.

Heat burned behind her eyes, and she blinked back sudden moisture. "Thank you."

"Your family has been in our prayers." Mr. Grimly's rich tone had an oddly soothing quality. "I imagine this situation has been difficult for you all." The sincerity in his voice seemed like more than simple platitudes, and Lillian inclined her head in thanks.

Her family. The people she'd left to sort through the next room of the house. A twinge of worry poked through her sense of calm. That probably hadn't been a great idea. What if they discarded things without her consent? No, they could have done that—probably had—long before now.

Lillian straightened and met Mr. Grimly's patient gaze. "Yes, sir. It has been an adjustment for everyone."

"If I may ask, have you met with Mr. Peterson?"

"Yes, sir. I believe the Petersons still plan on purchasing Mr. Jackson's residence." As soon as they came up with an agreed-upon price.

Mr. Grimly nodded, though Lillian sensed a hesitation in the gesture. He leaned forward and placed his hands on his desk. "The other matter is Jackson and Tanner Distribution. Mr. Jackson's company."

Jackson and Tanner? It took a moment for her brain to catch up. She'd forgotten that Mr. Carson had mentioned her father's business partner, who was currently out of town.

"The matter of the debts would be best settled with all parties present, but I can tell you that the amount Mr. Peterson planned to use to purchase the residence won't be able to pay the company's debts in full. According to the terms in Mr. Tanner's loan, both owners of the company share the burden."

Lillian stared at him. Had he said *debts*? A sinking feeling started in her throat and lodged in her stomach as the rest of his words took hold. Would she have to sell everything just to cover her father's loans, leaving her with nothing in the end?

"However," Mr. Grimly continued, "Mr. Tanner is currently on a trip that he assures me will right the state of affairs." The smooth words carried both a tinge of comfort and hope.

"Yes, sir. Thank you for the information."

They sat quietly for another moment.

"Is there something else you would like to discuss?" he asked. "Any questions I can answer?"

Her pulse thrummed in her ears. "Do you know what type of business this is, and what share my—Mr. Jackson—held?"

"Jackson and Tanner Distribution transports wares from factories and delivers them across the southeast. Mr. Jackson held the primary portion of the company, a sixty-forty split with Mr. Tanner."

So she would carry sixty percent of the debt as well. "Do you know when Mr. Tanner will return?"

"I'm afraid not." He laced his fingers together on the polished top of his desk. "But when I see him, I will be sure to inform him that we must set up a meeting for the three of us."

Lillian rose. "Thank you, sir. I am currently residing at the Moore Hotel but may also be found at Mr. Jackson's personal residence."

He offered a polite response and a wish for a good day that

Lillian barely registered. She numbly exited the office and wandered outside, thoughts churning. Her father had left her a sagging house in need of repairs—claimed by a family with big plans but not enough funds, as far as she could tell—and a business that offered more debts than assets.

The peace she'd felt this morning drifted away, swiftly replaced by a bubbling anxiety. What would Mother say? What about the plans that had been simmering in her own heart? Without any assets, she was right back to where she'd started before she'd first learned of her father's actual death.

Except the process had changed something within her. She could no longer see herself in her mother's world. No longer consider marriage her duty to raise their station. Coming here, facing this challenge on her own, had awakened a spark of independence she didn't think she could smother.

Miss Doyle wasn't going to like this. Jonah lined another crate along the wall for her to sort through and then stretched his back. "Ma, she's made her opinion pretty clear."

"Oh, fiddle. That's only because she doesn't know the plan yet."

He skirted his mother as she waved a dust rag in the air and grabbed another box. "I'm quite sure she does. You told her no less than eight times yesterday while we worked in the parlor."

"Well, yes." Ma followed him back across the room, where he lined the box up neatly next to the others he'd mentally labeled "personal effects." "But that was just *my* plan."

He paused. He probably shouldn't ask. "And the difference is?"

Ma beamed, clearly pleased he'd taken the bait. "Now she needs to hear the Lord's plan."

Oh boy. "Ma. You can't go around telling people what they are supposed to do and call it God's will. They have to figure that kind of thing out on their own."

Ma crossed her arms and huffed. "And how do you figure people learn about God's plans?" She held up a finger, and Jonah mentally groaned. "One, they receive a vision or an angel comes to them. Two, they get a quiet sense in their soul as the Holy Spirit leads, usually while immersed in his Word." She wiggled three fingers. "And three, someone else tells them."

Of course they did. He loved his mother and her faith, but how could she really know anything about God's plans for someone else?

"Prophets were always telling people what the Lord said, you know."

Jonah picked up another crate and dropped it next to the previous one. "Are you saying you're a prophet now?"

She planted her hands on her hips. "In a manner of speaking." She grumbled something he didn't catch.

Jonah focused his full attention on her. "What did you say?"

Ma arched her eyebrows. "I said, I should have known better than to let your father name you after a man who ran from God's will. What was he thinking? Speaking that over you." She gestured to the full length of him. "And see here, you've done just that most of your life."

Jonah gaped at her. Then he clamped his teeth together tight enough that the muscle in his jaw convulsed. Such statements did not require a response.

"Oh, now, Son. Don't get upset. Jonah eventually yielded." She patted his arm. "You will too."

He shook his head. "Regardless of my name or what you think it means, the fact remains that Miss Doyle has already said she has no interest in your baking business." He waited until she returned his steady gaze and her face softened enough for him to know she was actually listening. "And even if she did, I don't think proposing to go into business with a woman you don't know and who clearly doesn't share your sense of work ethic is a wise choice."

A sympathetic smile turned up the corners of Ma's mouth. "Oh, my sweet boy. You'll understand one day."

Irritation spiked, and he struggled to keep it from his voice. "Understand what?"

"That just because something makes little sense to us"—she shrugged—"or sometimes no sense at all, I suppose, doesn't mean that it's not exactly what we are called to do. In fact, I think we get promptings to do the things we least understand so we can learn to lean on God's understanding."

Jonah sighed. Lord help Miss Doyle. When Melanie Peterson decided God had a plan for someone's life, there was no stopping her making it a personal mission to see it carried out.

"I don't think it will work." Jonah held up a hand, and she paused whatever retort she'd been about to refute him with. "Why don't we find you another place? This isn't the only building available in town. I think the old Millner place is for sale. I was already approved at the bank." He took his mother's hands. "We can accomplish your dream another way."

She opened her mouth to respond when an enthusiastic banging from the foyer interrupted them.

Jonah gave his mother's hands a gentle squeeze and headed for the foyer. Time to see what new problems pounded on their door.

CHAPTER TEN

———— ✦ ————

*N*ow what? Lillian picked up her drudging pace as she neared her father's house. A man of average height and build with a balding head of sandy hair stood on the front porch, holding what Lillian could only describe as an animated conversation with Jonah. She hurried up the walkway, the click of her shoes drawing the men's attention.

"Here's the lady now." Jonah gestured in her direction. "You can speak with her yourself."

The other man grumbled something. As he turned, his thin lips transformed from a snarl to a welcoming smile. He extended his hand as he lightly bounded down the steps. "Miss Doyle! A great pleasure to meet you." The long fingers extended so close to her person that she had little choice but to offer her own gloved hand in greeting. He wrapped her fingers in a tight grip. "My, look at you. You do have your father's eyes."

Did she? Lillian could only stare at him.

"Where are my manners?" He dropped her hand. "Allow me to introduce myself. Mr. Jeffery Tanner. Your late father's business partner."

Mr. Tanner! A rush of hope filled her. Had he returned with something that would help with the status of the loan?

She offered a genuine smile. "Pleased to meet you. Mr. Grimly said you would be returning with a solution for the debt?" The words darted from her lips before she could catch them. Hardly what Mother would deem an appropriate introduction.

Questions flickered through Mr. Tanner's eyes, but his smile remained in place. "I've come to you straightaway, having just returned this morning. You've already taken over Floyd's accounts?"

Lillian pressed a hand to her hat as a sudden gust of wind threatened to pluck it from her head. "Not yet. Mr. Grimly just informed me of the state of affairs this morning and mentioned you were seeing to matters with a loan against the company."

Mr. Tanner scoffed as though such matters were inconsequential. "Not to worry, my dear. It's a trivial thing. No need for you to fret."

An odd sensation tingled though her. His words should have brought relief, yet she couldn't shake the strangest feeling of suspicion. Mr. Grimly hadn't seemed to find the matter trivial. But perhaps whatever Mr. Tanner had needed the loan for had been secured, and the money would soon be returned.

The man watched her expectantly. Mother always said she kept too many of her words inside her head and too often forgot to let the right ones out. "Won't you come inside? I'm afraid everything is a bit of a mess at the moment, but—"

"I don't think that's a good idea." Jonah's clipped words cut her short. She'd forgotten he still stood on the porch.

She shot him a questioning look, but whatever he might have been trying to convey with his gaze was lost on her.

"Yes, thank you." Mr. Tanner tugged on the hem of his jacket in a satisfied way. "I had asked to come inside to wait upon your return, but your"—he cocked an eyebrow at Jonah—"your fellow here refused me entrance." He chuckled, but it sounded forced. "I've frequented this house on many occasions. The home of my dearest friend, now lost to me."

How did she respond to that?

"Good morning, sir!" Melanie's voice drifted over the silence that had settled in the wake of Mr. Tanner's pronouncement. When had she come outside?

Melanie straightened her apron. "I'm sure you'll forgive us. We're in the middle of cleaning and organizing Mr. Jackson's personal effects for Miss Doyle, and I'm afraid there isn't a stick of furniture available for us to sit a spell on." She beamed brightly. Too brightly.

Confliction flashed over Mr. Tanner's face, but he gave a polite half bow. "Most understandable, ma'am." He turned back to Lillian. "As that is the case, I'll have to ask you to forgive my rudeness in discussing business on the front lawn. However, I do have a matter of some importance to take up with you. I've been running Jackson and Tanner Distribution for some time now, and I know that my partner would have wanted me to continue doing so. And of course a lovely lady such as yourself won't want to have to deal with the difficulties and labor of such an enterprise."

Lillian bristled. How did he know what she did and did not want to do? She didn't really see herself aspiring to get involved with a shipping business, but only she had the right to that decision.

"A lady has other matters to worry about, I'm sure." He gave her a warm smile she didn't return and spread his palms. "Floyd was my oldest friend, and he wanted to make sure that his only child was provided for after his death. Therefore, I've come with a proposition for you."

"What sort of proposition?" Melanie leaned off the porch rail, face intent.

Did the woman have no sense of propriety?

Jonah must have been thinking the same. He took his mother's elbow. "Why don't we finish moving those boxes while they talk?"

Melanie looked like she was about to refuse, then finally strode inside, her son a half step behind her. Thankfully, they didn't close the door. Lillian couldn't put her finger on why, but she didn't want to be out here with this man entirely alone.

"I would like you to sign over the portion of the company Floyd left you," Mr. Tanner said.

Sign it over? She hadn't gotten any paperwork giving her control of the company yet, and at this point she had far too few details to make an informed decision.

"Mr. Tanner, I can understand your desire to have full control of the business. However, I don't think—"

"I would purchase it from you, of course, as well as repay the loan I procured. I'm a fair man."

That was well and good, but she'd still need more information. She opened her mouth to tell him as much, but his next words stopped her.

"One thousand dollars." His smile stretched. "Quite a lot for a young woman."

The modest amount was far less than the two thousand dollars Jonah had offered for the house. Not that she knew much about such things, but surely the controlling portion of a successful business garnered more.

Mr. Tanner watched her expectantly. Lillian twisted her

fingers in front of her, mentally creating and discarding several responses. Simple honesty would be best.

"Thank you for your offer, Mr. Tanner. I will take it under consideration, and we'll speak on it further after I've had time to come to an informed decision."

A glint of something that passed over his face was quickly swallowed by a friendly smile. "Of course, Miss Doyle." He fished a calling card from his jacket pocket. "I'm available at your convenience."

He bid her a good day, and she returned the pleasantries. She'd hardly reached the top porch step when Melanie poked her head out. Had the woman been listening the entire time?

"Are you all right?"

"Yes." Why wouldn't she be?

Melanie narrowed her eyes. "Something about that fellow doesn't sit right." She made a dismissive gesture at Mr. Tanner's retreating back before her eyes focused intently on Lillian. "Before you get started on the next boxes, I want to talk to you about something."

Again? Lillian pinched the bridge of her nose. "Mrs. Peterson, I've already told you that you can do whatever you wish with the house if you purchase it, but until then we're not going to start on any repairs." She couldn't afford to start spending money she hadn't yet acquired.

"I want to ask you to be my partner." Melanie beamed. "We'll do the bakery together."

What? Melanie wanted her to . . .

Oh. Of course. The momentary spark of delight fizzled quickly under a harsh reality. Lillian owned the house. Of course Melanie would want to partner with her so that she could use the property without purchasing it.

"And before you get to thinking I'm taking advantage of you by trying not to buy the house, that's not it." Melanie wagged her finger as though Lillian was a wayward student who'd thought to sass her governess.

An errant tip of her lips must have given her away.

"I've prayed a heap over it, and that's what the Lord said you needed to do."

The pronouncement froze Lillian's breath. The woman couldn't be serious. She herself had prayed heartily and hadn't heard a single whisper from God. Why would he give her answer to Melanie? The woman had simply mistaken her own desires for divine direction.

That hadn't lasted long. Jonah grunted as he placed the final box in the neat row along the wall. Ma never could keep something to herself. From the spooked look on Miss Doyle's face as she'd followed Ma back inside a few hours ago, Ma had already fired off her thoughts despite his warnings.

A surge of sympathy had put him at Lillian's side, and he'd offered bracing support to her elbow before he could think better of it. She turned her face up to him, and for the briefest instant, vulnerability, worry, and something else he couldn't identify galloped over her features. Then cold indifference met him once more. Politely, she stepped out from under his touch and marched into the parlor, where she spent the next five hours alone with Floyd's boxes. She'd even refused to join them for sandwiches at noon. She had to be starving by now.

"This is much better." Lillian's voice startled him from his thoughts. She stepped up beside him, surveying the work he'd done in the adjoining study. "Thank you for your efforts, Mr. Peterson."

"My pleasure." The half-truth of the statement pricked him. He didn't mind helping a lady in need. But given the circumstances, he continually felt torn when it came to the woman who'd upended all of his plans. He rubbed the sweat off the back of his neck. "And please, call me Jonah."

A tinge of pink colored her cheeks. "Thank you. And you may call me Lillian."

He fumbled for something else to say as she scurried to the first box and knelt in front of it, but he couldn't think of anything beyond how fetching she looked when her cheeks colored.

The sound of girlish giggles saved him from any verbal fumbling. He smiled. "My sisters have arrived."

A moment later, Rose and Betsy burst through the door. Spotting him, Betsy launched herself forward, customary pigtails flying up behind her. She bounded into him and he wrapped her in a hug.

"Hello, Brother. Did you miss me?"

He returned her squeeze and tapped the end of her nose. "Well, now. Let's see. Did I miss the prettiest little blond gal with mischievous eyes and a winning smile? I sure did."

She beamed at him.

He winked. "So if you see her, be sure to tell her for me, will you?"

Betsy squealed and swatted at him playfully. "You're such a rogue!"

He gestured behind him, pulling her attention away from an attempt to climb up him. "We have a guest."

Sufficiently distracted, his jubilant little sister whirled to face the woman standing across the room, watching them.

"This is Miss Lillian Doyle. Lillian, these are my sisters. This is Betsy"—he patted his youngest sister's shoulder—"and over there is Rose." He gestured toward her. Rose, Betsy's opposite in nearly every way, stood quietly in the doorway, her chocolate eyes studying Lillian.

Lillian stepped forward and offered a polite smile. "Hello. A pleasure to make your acquaintance."

Betsy bounced on her toes, hair bobbing against the back of her yellow dress. "You sure are pretty." Her big eyes swooped back to Jonah. "Isn't she pretty?"

His throat tightened, and he awkwardly cleared the thickness. "Um, yes. She certainly is."

Lillian's cheeks flamed red, but her composure never wavered. "Why, thank you, Miss Peterson. You are quite lovely yourself. You have the most beautiful hair."

Before his little sister could attach herself and keep Lillian from her task, Jonah guided her toward the door. "I think Ma still has a few of those peach turnovers you like."

She gave Lillian a little wave as she grinned and bolted through the doorway, nearly knocking Rose over in the process. Rose turned to follow, but Jonah stopped her.

"Did you miss me as well?"

Rose shifted her attention to Lillian and then back to him and offered a slight smile. "I'm hardly a girl anymore."

At fourteen, she was very much still a girl. Though he didn't know what the statement had to do with his teasing.

"Betsy is far too exuberant for one who has nearly reached her first decade." Rose nodded decisively, her petite face far too serious. "Ma should tell her so." Her lips tipped downward. "Or you."

He had no intention of snuffing out Betsy's exuberance.

Rose could do with a bit more cheerfulness herself. She'd hardly smiled since the cabin had burned. She smoothed her hands down a worn skirt that no longer reached the top of her scuffed boots. He'd need to buy her some new dresses and another pair of shoes before the next school year began.

"Betsy is fine, Rose," he said. "There's nothing wrong with being joyful."

Lillian quietly returned to unpacking one of the boxes and gently opened the cover of a book before stacking it neatly on the floor with three others.

Rose cut a glance at Lillian and lowered her voice. "Will our *company* be staying for supper?" She put a strange emphasis on the word, coating it in an emotion he couldn't place.

Red splotches formed on Lillian's cheeks, but she kept her eyes glued to the book in front of her.

"If she'd like to," he said loudly enough for Lillian to hear. "She's certainly welcome."

Rose nodded solemnly and retreated. His chest constricted. What he wouldn't give to see his sister smile again. He watched her go, wishing he understood girls better. The age difference between them had always made him feel almost more like a father than a brother, especially given his responsibilities.

"Your sisters love you."

Lillian's soft voice tugged him from his thoughts. Such longing filled the words that he didn't know how to respond.

Lillian suddenly rose and brushed her hands together. "Thank you again for your assistance. The organization makes the job easier." She looked around, fiddling with her skirt. "I should probably return to Mr. Carson's office now that Mr. Tanner is back and check on matters with my father's company." She bobbed her chin. "Yes. I think that will be good.

Then I'll retire for the day and start fresh on this project tomorrow."

What had gotten her flustered? Rose and Betsy? Rose had been a bit rude, but the behavior wasn't solely directed at Lillian.

"Won't you stay?" he asked. "I do believe the Watsons will be here soon, and Ma has planned a large supper for everyone."

She hesitated, then shook her head. "It's best if I don't."

He moved closer, trying to decode her expression. "I'm sorry my sister made you feel unwelcome. She is . . ." He let the sentence drop, unsure how to describe Rose's temperament without somehow betraying her.

"It's fine, really." Lillian moved closer, heading toward the doorway.

"Alma will want you to stay. She enjoys your company." Why was he trying to convince her?

Her expression faltered. "I appreciate everyone's kindness in these circumstances, but there's no reason to pretend this is something other than what it is. I'll do my utmost to be fair in the situation we've found ourselves in. There's no need to try to sway me."

The words hovered, not quite finding purchase. "Are you implying that my mother and the Watsons are only nice to you because they . . . what? Are trying to manipulate you?"

Lillian's face blanched. "I hardly blame them, of course. No one expected me to be here. I hold no ill will against them that my presence is unwanted. I'm simply saying there is no reason to pretend otherwise."

He stared at her. "That's really what you think?"

She tilted her head, reminding him of one of the heelers when it encountered a new noise.

"Despite what you believe, Alma is thrilled to have a new family member, and my mother has already decided that God himself wants you to be a part of our lives. And once Ma thinks God has spoken, there's no dissuading her."

Lillian gaped at him.

Why had he let himself spout off? He clenched his jaw.

Lillian's momentary shock dissipated, and she straightened herself once more. "I can see how my providing the house for your mother's business would be beneficial for her, but I don't think that is the best—"

"What will you do with the money when you sell everything?" He'd been taught never to interrupt a lady speaking, but the question demanded attention.

She faltered. "I, well, I'm not sure yet."

"You never thought about what you would do with your inheritance?"

Lillian blinked rapidly.

He'd found a chink in her icy armor. He tapped at it again. "Not even before you knew the complications?"

"I . . ." She pulled in a long breath. "I once dreamed of a little coffee shop and bookstore, but that's hardly worth discussing." The words burst out of her, and she snapped her lips shut.

They stared at one another, a strange energy stirring between them. How could he be so attracted to an angry woman? She looked as though she wanted to shove him off a cliff, yet he had the oddest desire to pull her into his arms and see if he could direct her passion in a different direction.

Unable to help himself, Jonah let out a laugh. There was no explanation for the electricity buzzing between two people who had every reason to go their separate ways. It was almost as though a current moved beyond his control, positioning

STEPHENIA H. McGEE

strangers, making connections, and weaving a pattern that
knotted them all together.

Despite Lillian's shocked expression, his chest rumbled with
ironic mirth.

Maybe Ma was right about providential circumstances after
all.

95

CHAPTER ELEVEN

———— ❧ ————

What nerve. Lillian tried to get herself to form any sort of intelligent response to Jonah laughing at her, but she couldn't get anything to squeak past her lips. He found her dreams laughable.

Worse, maybe he'd discerned her wayward thoughts about how she somehow felt drawn to him as he kept pulling her secrets from her. Probably because she'd let her eyes indulge in the appealing lines of his strong jaw and linger too long on his lips like some kind of addled ninny. No wonder he was laughing at her. Apparently her brain no longer functioned.

"If you will excuse me." Lillian moved to skirt around Jonah.

"Wait." Another chuckle rumbled through his chest. A sound she might find pleasant if the man wasn't entirely uncouth. "Please. Let me explain."

She paused, despite every muscle demanding she keep walking toward the front door.

"My mother told you that she thinks the two of you are supposed to open a bakery, right?"

Lillian kept her gaze level. "So?"

He sobered. "You wanted to take the money from your father and, I assume"—he spread his hands—"use that money to purchase a building where you will open a coffee shop and bookstore?"

"It was one possibility I considered."

"And here you have a house and my mother wants to open a bakery. With you."

She stared at him. His mother wanting to use her father's house for her own business had nothing to do with Lillian's dream. One she should *not* have let slip free.

He took a step closer and looked down at her, eyes intense. "Maybe my mother is right. What are the chances that two women are connected to the same property with the same dream?"

A bakery was hardly—

The thought was cut short as a sudden vision of confections served along with coffee filled her mind. Memories of afternoons when she'd slipped into the little shop on her way home from school uncoiled inside her. The smell of coffee and books. Happy patrons sitting in comfortable chairs, newly purchased adventures spread open on their laps. There had been warmth and friendliness there that had filled a cold place inside her.

Lillian shook her head to clear the fantasy trying to form. "I live in Atlanta."

Even as she spoke, the notion persisted. She could stay. Start a new life here. Make this house like the one across the street she had immediately adored. But she had Mother to consider, and these people were strangers. It would never work.

Jonah watched as the thoughts flew through her mind like a dozen darting hummingbirds. After a moment, he stepped back, out of the way of her exit. "The invitation stands. Maybe it wouldn't hurt to get to know your family and their friends a little better?"

The question grabbed at the place deep within her that longed for connection. Before she could think better of it, she found herself nodding.

A smile pulled up one edge of Jonah's mouth. "I'll let Ma know you're staying to eat. I'll start on the next stack of clutter while you finish here." He slipped out of the room.

Lillian drew a long breath, thoughts swirling. She'd been praying for an answer. A plan to move forward. But could this really be it? Even though something within her heart tugged toward the idea, she had to be logical.

She shot another prayer heavenward and waited. She'd take the tiniest scrap of a divine nudge.

Nothing.

After another few moments, Lillian turned back to the disarray surrounding her. The only thing she could do was focus on the task at hand. With a sigh, she moved toward the boxes of books her father had left behind. She situated herself on the floor and ran a finger down the spines of the first stack she'd made. Had he loved the works of Dickens? Or were they a matter of decoration on a shelf? A gift, maybe? Though they were over a quarter of a century old, the spines didn't appear to have been more than cracked open.

Over the next couple of hours, Lillian lost herself going through crate after crate of books. Wouldn't this collection of Mark Twain novels be perfect on a set of shelves lining that bay window? Patrons could enjoy them with their coffee. Of course, if she planned on opening a shop, she'd also have to purchase new books to sell. She didn't mind sharing those left by her father, but she didn't want to sell them. Where did one buy books to sell in a bookstore?

Lillian filed the question away for later and stretched her aching back. How long had she been sitting on the floor? By the tilt of the light through the windows, the rest of the afternoon had slipped away. Had she missed the Watsons arriving for supper?

Even from her place on the opposite side of the house, Lillian could hear their voices rising and falling with a pleasant rhythm, the melody of laughter playing in swells. How wonderful would it be to have a house filled with people, warmth, and laughter? She moved past the crates to the bay window. It seemed bigger now without all the clutter.

The window would make such a lovely reading spot.

The polished floor would house several small tables. Aromatic coffee and delectable treats would top each one, and the people would come inside to find a few moments of escape from the troubles outside these doors. She could nearly smell the fragrant coffee in the air.

Lillian blinked, surprised to find moisture sliding down her cheeks. She quickly wiped the tears away. What was she thinking? Lovely as it would be, the idea was entirely impractical. Mother had always said foolish dreams led to broken hearts.

If only there wasn't a large sum owed to the bank. If only she didn't live in Atlanta . . .

She pushed the thoughts away. There was no point in thinking about things being different.

She counted seven boxes of books. She'd keep them all. The eclectic collection of poetry, fiction, and history volumes had given her at least a little insight into her father's personality, but so far she hadn't come across any personal effects that did more than hint at the true nature of the man. At least she knew he favored books. For today, that would be enough.

Lillian passed through the parlor, across the foyer, and into the dining room. A delicious aroma stirred her appetite. Was that cherry pie? She took slow steps toward the kitchen at the rear of the house, listening to the sounds of the two families interacting.

They spoke of everyday matters, their tones light. No forced pleasantries. No veiled attempts at outdoing each other in one form or another.

Simple. Real.

She closed her eyes, imagining for a moment what it would have been like to be part of a large family. A home filled with many voices and abundant laughter.

"There you are!" Alma stepped out of the kitchen into the dining room. "I was just about to come find you. We wanted to give you some privacy as you went through your father's belongings." She grabbed Lillian's hand and tugged. "But I'm practically starving. Aren't you? Mother made her famous pork roast and gravy—you liked that at my house, remember?—and Melanie baked a cherry pie for dessert."

Lillian allowed herself to be coaxed into a kitchen brimming with family. They'd packed the space with seven people already. No one seemed to notice that there was hardly any room for her or to care that Betsy perched on the prep table, flour clinging to the apron wrapped around her middle.

The girl grinned and waved at her. Lillian returned the gesture, the child's bright smile contagious.

Melanie lifted a spoon in the air like a band director's baton. "All right. We're all here." She turned to her son. "The blessing?"

They intended to ask grace before anyone sat at a table? Come to think of it, where did all these people plan to eat? The dining room was certainly in no condition to serve guests.

Jonah's rich baritone lifted, and the room quieted as the others bowed their heads. They prayed together as genuinely as they did everything else. Transfixed, Lillian couldn't help but let her gaze wander over those gathered as Jonah asked a simple blessing over the meal they would share. She managed to duck her head just as a chorus of "amen" rang out.

The room erupted into a flurry of activity. Melanie scooped hunks of pork onto white porcelain plates and smothered them with gravy. She then passed the plate to Edith, who added scoops of green beans and corn. Edith handed the plates off to Lewis to finish with a roll, and he in turn gave a plate to each person.

What an interesting and efficient procession. As soon as the family members gathered their meals, they disappeared through the rear door.

Why were they going outside?

Alma took her elbow and guided her toward Lewis and the plate he offered. She accepted with a soft thanks and, not knowing what else to do, stepped through the rear door.

The backyard looked nothing at all like the front. Why had she never come out here? A tall wooden fence wrapped a large patch of lush grass in a cozy embrace. Two towering oaks spread their limbs over the space like an umbrella, and underneath stood two wooden tables. Each table had been set with silverware and glasses of iced water.

Along the fence, a host of colorful flowers bloomed. A perfect little garden, tucked away. In the few short weeks she'd lived here, Melanie seemed to have put all her efforts into the family's portion of the house rather than the portions anyone else would see.

Rose and Betsy took a place at the table farthest from the house. Alma swept outside, plate in hand, and gestured toward the other table. "Shall we sit there?"

Lillian wanted to ask why they ate outside and why no one else seemed to find such a thing exceedingly odd, but she merely followed along behind her cousin and settled into a chair that wobbled beneath her.

"Isn't this lovely?" Alma's amber eyes sparkled. "I've always loved a picnic. My Lewis used to take me up to Amicalola Falls for picnics when we courted. You really must see it someday. It's the most mesmerizing waterfall. Not that I've seen any others, mind you, but I'm sure you will still find it spectacular."

Lillian had never seen a waterfall. Nor had she eaten out of doors, except for the time she'd been invited to the Montgomery house for croquet and tea had been served in the garden with cucumber sandwiches. That didn't seem quite the same.

Soon Lewis and Jonah joined them at the table while Edith and Melanie took the other two seats at the girls' table. Lillian chewed thoughtfully as she watched Jonah and the Watsons interact. Was he not under their employ? If she didn't know better, she would think them all family. They acted more honestly with one another than even she and her mother did.

The realization left a hollow place within her.

Deep into the languid meal, something loosened within her. The longer she sat among them, the more she let herself live in the moment.

"This gravy is heavenly." Lillian closed her eyes, enjoying the rich flavor on her tongue. "Did she use rosemary?" She opened her eyes to find the others looking at her.

Alma grinned. "Ha! She's figured out the secret."

"What's that now?" Edith's voice carried over from the other table. "Who has a secret?"

Lewis laughed. "You do, Mother Edith, and your niece has rooted it out."

How easily they looped her into the family. A longing for there to be sincerity and not opportunity behind the inclusion pinched her heart.

Lord, guide me.

A gentle wind stirred, caressing the back of her neck. She'd often imagined she could feel God in the wind.

"Well, now." Edith laughed as she pointed a fork in Alma's direction. "Looks like at least someone inherited my skills in the kitchen. Lord knows it wasn't you." Both women laughed before Edith turned back around in her seat.

"I don't know what we'll do when Mother Edith is no longer around to feed us." Lewis cast a mischievous grin at his wife. "My dear bride has many talents, but I fear kitchen skills are not among them."

The family continued to banter, and Lillian let their jovial mood wash over her as she ate. She finished the piles of vegetables, finding both just as tasty as the pork and gravy. Perhaps they should consider having Edith cook a simple dinner to serve to patrons as well.

The sudden thought surprised her, and she forcefully brushed it away.

"Jonah tells me you're thinking of opening a coffee or bookshop in Atlanta." Alma's voice broke into Lillian's thoughts and washed away the sense of comfort that had settled on her.

She shot Jonah a look loaded with her annoyance at his betrayal. "He asked if I had thought about anything I would want to do with the inheritance, and I mentioned something that had crossed my mind. That's all."

A smile played on Alma's lips. "And you also enjoy baking. What an interesting turn of coincidence."

Lillian straightened. "That doesn't mean I intend to turn my father's house over to Melanie for her bakery." The words shot out of her like a bolt of lightning, and she instantly regretted them.

Silence settled on the table a moment before Alma spoke again. "No one is saying you must. Though if I'm being honest, I find it quite interesting that you've been given exactly what your heart desired." Sadness crept over her face. "I tend to think a person should hold fast to such a blessing, even if it doesn't look exactly like they thought it should."

The statement hung between them, carrying more weight than just Alma's thoughts on a bakery.

Jonah tapped a finger on the table. "I happen to agree with Miss Doyle."

Her eyes snapped to him. What?

"I'll find another way to give Ma what she desires." His gaze, filled with meaning, lingered on her. "I'm certain Miss Doyle is quite capable of carrying out her own plans as well."

He thought her capable? Could he truly be giving her the space to make her own choices?

Jonah lifted a shoulder in a shrug that appeared tense. "Besides, we all know things usually don't work out the way we want them to."

The statement sliced through Lillian's growing sense of peace. The man seemed of two minds.

Alma lowered her eyes, hurt washing over her face. She picked up her fork and cut at her pork. Lewis and Jonah shared a look weighted with a meaning Lillian didn't understand.

"I know you had plans to leave, Jonah, but maybe that's not the path meant for you," Lewis said.

Leave? Where was he going? And what did that have to do with the house, the bakery, or Lillian returning to Atlanta?

The muscle in Jonah's jaw twitched. He pushed back from the table and scooped up his plate. "If you will excuse me."

Lillian watched him stalk away, confusion over the sudden turn of mood knotting her insides. Only one thing seemed clear. She wasn't the only one whose dreams remained out of reach.

CHAPTER TWELVE

———— ❦ ————

A telegram for you, miss." The proprietress's voice drew Lillian's attention and forced her to take notice of her surroundings. She'd been lost in thought since she'd left the strange supper at the Jackson/Peterson house and had hardly noticed entering the Moore Hotel.

Mrs. Moore, the widowed owner, hurried over with a folded paper in hand. Her gray hair was contained in a knot at her nape, and her face held the kinds of lines that attested to years of smiles.

Lillian accepted the outstretched page. "Thank you."

"Of course, of course." Mrs. Moore's smile lines crinkled, yet the effect didn't seem to age her. "Do you know if you will be staying with us longer?"

Lillian had completely forgotten she'd only paid for her room through tonight. Had the time passed so quickly? What little funds Mother had sent had dwindled, and she still hadn't gotten the money the solicitor said would come with her inheritance.

The proprietress waited patiently, poking at strands of silvered hair that hadn't actually escaped their pins.

"Would you mark me for another night, please?" Lillian

said. Despite what Mr. Tanner promised, right now as far as the bank was concerned, her father's estate still had to cover sixty percent of the company's loan. Hopefully Mr. Grimly wouldn't need to use all of the assets against the debts.

Mrs. Moore bobbed her head and wished Lillian a pleasant evening before she spryly hurried away to whatever tasks occupied her time.

Lillian clutched the telegram and trudged up the stairs. The message could be from only one person, and she was rather certain she already knew what it would contain.

She closed the door to her room and breathed out slowly for a moment. After placing the telegram on the polished but scratched surface of the dressing table, she took her time removing her gloves, hat, and hairpins. She unhooked her boots and slid the stockings from her feet, wiggling her toes. How she wished for a long soak in a hot bath. Mother said that some of the fancy hotels had indoor plumbing and hot water that could be pumped right into the rooms.

"Isn't that the kind of life you want for us, Lillian? Keep your tongue controlled and your smiles demure. Make Reginald determined to have you, and in turn we can have every luxury you ever dreamed of."

The memory filled her mind. She could still see the hope in Mother's eyes. The determination. Lillian had complied. She'd learned just the right way to tilt her smiles and lower her eyes. How to place her hand with the lightest touch on Reginald's arm while looking up at him through her lashes.

But had she ever really dreamed of luxuries? At least, as Mother thought of them? Lillian rubbed her foot, stimulating the aching muscles. To her, luxury was those moments where she could simply be herself. Those rare times when she didn't have to put on a veneer of perfection. When she could relax and laugh or curl her legs under her and find a quiet place to read.

She shook the thoughts aside and plucked the telegram from the table, then perched on the edge of the bed and unfolded the page.

```
Send funds immediately for wedding and
wardrobe
Taking too long
Return quickly
```

Lillian stared at the words. Wedding? And whose wardrobe? Heat flushed through her. Mother didn't ask how she was faring. No hint of worry over her longer-than-anticipated absence. Only an insistence she send money right away. Money Lillian didn't even have.

Mother would know that if she'd come along instead of sending Lillian to deal with this on her own. Lillian closed her eyes.

"Why can't you be poised, like Mrs. Jefferson's daughters?"

"Must you always embarrass us? Really, Lillian. You should think before you open your mouth."

Lillian settled at the dressing table, snatched the comb, and ran it through a particularly tight knot. She slowed as her scalp smarted from her effort. If only she could—

A knock sounded at the door. She froze. "Who is it?"

"Alma. May I come in?"

Lillian grabbed her long hair and pulled it over her shoulder. "I, um, have already started to retire for the evening."

"I don't mind."

Lillian stared at the door. Alma may not mind, but did *she*?

Then again, she could use someone to talk to. Bracing herself, she swung open the door. Alma stood alone in the hallway, her face gentle.

Hesitating for only a breath, Lillian gestured her cousin inside. She glided into the room with graceful steps and waited while Lillian closed the door behind her.

"You can take a seat at the dressing table if you'd like." Lillian nodded toward the seat she'd vacated. "Please do forgive my appearance." She gathered her hair again and twisted it into a coil at the back of her neck. Where were those pins?

Alma chuckled softly. "No need to pin your hair on account of me, Cousin." She removed her gloves and hat and set them on the dressing table next to Lillian's own. "Thank you for seeing me this late in the evening."

Lillian folded her hands in front of her. She was quite unaccustomed to receiving company in her bedchamber. How did one conduct herself properly under such unusual circumstances?

"I'm sorry for the way I behaved this evening." Alma's shoulders hunched as she leaned closer to Lillian, tone sincere. "I let my own thoughts carry me away without any consideration for how you must feel, and for that I am terribly ashamed." Her pretty eyes glittered with moisture. "Would you forgive me?"

Lillian's sandy throat resisted her swallow, and she nearly choked. "Of course I'll forgive you."

No one had ever come to her in such a manner. More than one lady had bordered on snide and once or twice crossed over into cruel, yet none had ever approached Lillian for forgiveness. The kindness warmed through her, releasing some of her tension.

Alma smiled softly. "I can only imagine what a shock all of

this must be to you, and I fear my family hasn't given your situation due consideration. We became excited when we learned that you and Melanie shared such similar interest, but I can see now how that must look to you." She laced her fingers together and gave a small shake of her head. "We're not trying to take anything that is rightfully yours, and I'm sorry we made you feel that way."

The admission slid over Lillian like a velvet blanket, warm and soothing. She sank down on the bed, all thoughts of maintaining a semblance of propriety forgotten. "This is all a bit . . . overwhelming."

Alma tilted her head in concession, even the simple movement graceful. "Certainly." She folded long fingers that looked suited for the piano in her lap. They sat in silence a moment before she spoke again. "I don't mean to overstep, but what *do* you want to do with what your father left you? Lewis says I shouldn't ask, but I truly wish to know." She gathered a quick breath, her next question coming out in a fusillade of words. "Do you think you and your mother would consider moving here?"

No. The word lodged in her throat.

The quietness of small-town life would not appeal to Mother in the least. But Lillian had to admit that the notion had tugged at her own heart from the moment she'd arrived— from the first time she saw herself with a book on the front porch of a tidy little house. "I don't think my mother would leave Atlanta, and I must care for her."

A look of understanding passed between them. The answer made perfect sense. Why, then, did she feel an ache of loss pushing against her ribs?

"I've always found that talking through an issue with a

friend helps me find clarity." Alma spoke so sweetly that the longing inside Lillian breached its confines.

"It's only that Mother—" Lillian clamped her lips together.

Mother's words fired through her. *Think before you speak, Lillian, lest you open your mouth and let loose something you can't recall.*

"Only what?" Alma leaned closer, as though nearness would be the spark Lillian needed to continue.

One variation after another flitted through Lillian's mind as she tried to decide exactly how to frame her words. "I wouldn't want her here." The truth brought a wave of guilt. She dropped her gaze.

"I take it you two share a difficult relationship." Alma's words held no judgment, only tender compassion.

Lillian gave a slow nod. Mother's affection always felt just out of reach. Something Lillian could almost touch if she was good enough, if she obeyed quickly enough, or if she accomplished something to make Mother proud. Those times were few.

Tears stung the back of her eyes, and she blinked them away. "Mother wants me to get my inheritance and return immediately so that I can wed a man of standing she's chosen for me."

Alma was quiet for a long moment. "Do you care for this gentleman?"

"I don't dislike Reginald. He is a decent man. But Mother sees the Montgomerys as a means to further our lifestyle. She worked tirelessly to secure the match between me and Reginald, and she'd be furious if I"—Lillian hesitated—"chose something else."

"I need you, Lillian. A good marriage is our only security."

Guilt churned in Lillian's stomach. Was it not a daughter's duty to see her own mother cared for? Without an affluent husband to provide for them, what would they do? Mother could hardly be expected to learn and take up a trade at her age. If Lillian didn't care for her, who would?

"Why do you suppose Floyd left everything to you rather than your mother?"

Lillian snapped her gaze to Alma. If he had left everything to Mother, she would be cared for and no longer Lillian's responsibility. Would she then still insist Lillian needed to marry well for standing and security? Something Mother herself had never done.

"I don't know." Lillian's thoughts churned. "Though I suppose . . ." She trailed off. No matter how she looked at it, the idea was vague and illogical at best. There were simply too many unknowns.

"Come, Cousin. You can share your thoughts with me." Alma smiled brightly, and Lillian found herself wanting to oblige.

"I'm not sure what . . ." She drew a breath and started again. "Well, I don't yet know the value of the company, and there are debts. And of course Mr. Tanner's offer is far less than what I expected, but—" The tumbling words snagged to a halt. She swallowed.

Alma waited, her expression merely curious.

"But perhaps . . . if there is enough . . . I could send whatever I sell the company for to my mother."

Ideas fired through her, each one slipping by too fast for her to fully grab and examine. If she somehow did manage to start a business of her own, would she be able to send her mother a monthly stipend as her father had? Would that plan allow her to care for Mother and at the same time discover her own life?

"Perhaps so," Alma agreed, sitting back in the dressing chair. "We never looked into Floyd's business dealings. We only took possession of the house because the Petersons' cabin burned down and they needed somewhere to stay."

"Oh." Lillian's heart squeezed. That explained Melanie's attitude when they'd met and the family's sparse belongings. "I didn't realize."

"They lost everything. We had an empty house and they needed a home, and at the time we assumed Floyd's property would be left to us."

A reasonable assumption. How many other secrets had her father kept? "How well did you know him?"

Alma pressed her lips together in thought. "Not well, I'm afraid. My uncle was always gone on one venture or another, and we hardly ever saw him. Sometimes not even during holidays. That made Mother sad, I think, though she rarely spoke of it. I know his death was hard for her. There is much regret there."

Silence settled as Lillian digested this new insight into her family. After a moment, she brought herself to ask the question that had been pressing on her heart. "Do you know what happened to him? There at the end?" She scarcely contained a wince.

A sympathetic look washed over Alma's features. "Sheriff Whittle said he'd been taken in for public drunkenness. When my mother went to visit him the next morning, he was . . . gone. Doctor Andley said his heart gave out sometime during the night."

The same simple truth she'd learned from Mr. Riley.

"I'm sorry I don't know more," Alma said.

"It was strange finding out he died while sitting in a solicitor's office, hearing the news from a stranger. I never even got to attend my father's funeral. That might have been something, at least." Lillian sighed. "I wonder why Mr. Riley didn't inform me immediately." She spat a bitter laugh. "He probably did. Mother simply didn't tell me until she absolutely had to, well after the services."

Alma's eyes glistened with sympathetic tears. "That must have been difficult for you. I am so sorry you've suffered such."

Lillian could only offer a weak smile in response.

They sat in companionable silence for a moment longer. Having someone to talk to lifted burdens Lillian had been carrying on her own.

"About what Jonah said at supper." She shifted her bare feet and tucked her hands underneath her. "A long time ago I used to love this little bookshop in Atlanta. Sometimes, if I knew Mother would be too busy to notice, I would stop in for a little while. Just to smell the fragrance of the coffee and walk past all the bookshelves."

The memory bloomed in her mind, as vibrant as though it had been just yesterday. The owner had died and the doors closed some six or seven years ago.

"There was always light and laughter there. People seemed happy." Lillian shrugged. "But I know nothing at all about owning a shop. I've never served customers. It's a silly childhood memory, is all."

Alma regarded her thoughtfully. "I believe that sometimes God places a spark of something within us as a hint to where he wants us to focus our time and attention. Do you think it's possible that he's leading you toward such a venture? And perhaps has even provided you the means to start?"

What did God care about bakeries and coffee shops?

Lillian shook her head, even as verses that reminded her of God's plans surfaced in her thoughts. "I can't work out how such a venture could be possible. There are too many unknowns."

"Ah, yes. That is rather true of all of life." Alma's tone held humor, but the words sliced right into Lillian's center.

There were *always* unknowns.

But working with Melanie? Living in Dawsonville? Those were enormous changes. Insurmountable obstacles. Not to mention Jonah. She hadn't even begun to untangle the knot of emotions she felt when it came to him, and she simply could *not* let a man and the odd way he muddled her senses hold sway over her logic.

"Whatever you decide, I want you to know that my family and I are glad to have you with us, no matter how long you stay." Alma looked around the hotel room. "Which brings me to the other reason for my visit. We'd like you to come stay at the house with us." Before Lillian could protest, Alma held up a hand. "You're family, and family shouldn't be in a hotel."

"Truly?" The longing pressed its way out of Lillian's throat. "You want me in your home?"

"Of course!" Alma rose and grabbed Lillian's hands. "I've always wanted a large family." She laughed. "I've tried tirelessly to bring Jonah and his mother and sisters into my fold, though they do tend to resist." She swung their clasped hands between them like a schoolgirl. "You, however, are blood. I will insist harder should you attempt the same."

The ache deepened within Lillian's chest until she knew such resistance would be pointless.

"Say you'll come?"

Unable to work words past the thickness in her throat, Lillian dipped her chin in a single nod.

Alma squeezed her fingers. "Wonderful. We'll get Jonah or Lewis to move your trunks tomorrow." She pulled Lillian into a hug. She smelled of lilacs. "Goodnight, Cousin."

Lillian returned the embrace and managed to speak her own goodbyes. After Alma closed the door behind her, Lillian picked up the telegram on the edge of the bed. She read the words over and over until determination hardened into resolve. Mother would get her reply first thing in the morning.

Lillian had no intention of returning to Atlanta anytime soon.

CHAPTER THIRTEEN

How had he managed to find himself in this situation? Jonah rubbed the fur between Max's ears, then chuckled as Millie pushed her cold nose under his hand, demanding her turn. He'd neglected the dogs while he'd been busy at the Jackson house. Despite Lewis's insistence that he could slack on his duties around the farm while they settled matters in town, the notion didn't sit right with him. Especially since today he'd received his usual weekly payment.

He'd planned to use that money to start on the repairs Ma wanted. But now? He groaned, earning a whine from Millie as she rubbed her furry head underneath his arm. God alone knew. Lillian Doyle was as fickle as an entire gaggle of women. One moment declaring she would return to Atlanta, and the next . . .

He shook his head. "I have no idea what that woman is thinking."

Max looked up at him with sympathetic eyes. Jonah rewarded him with another scratch.

Alma had found him early this morning before he'd saddled

Mist and informed him Lillian had decided to stay. Here, of all places.

Millie nuzzled him again, and Jonah gave her a fond pat. He tried to push away Alma's confusing declaration and rose from where he'd been crouching in the barn. He'd probably be expected to move Lillian's trunks this afternoon.

Lillian Doyle living at the Watson farm planted her all the deeper into their lives. Why was a woman who had made it perfectly clear she intended to sell off all her father's belongings and bustle back to the city suddenly settling in?

The woman was like a banty rooster caught in a tornado. Didn't know which way she wanted to go and stirring up trouble whichever way she went.

Not that he had any say on such matters.

He still needed to move the cattle to the rear pasture and check the herd for any signs of bloat after letting them graze on seed heads too long. He saddled Mist, and he and the dogs spent the day seeing to the tasks around the Watson farm. By the time he returned to the barn, the sun had dipped low into the western sky. He'd spent the entire day thinking through Miss Lillian Doyle's pronouncement, but he still couldn't wrap his mind around her sudden shift in thinking.

She wouldn't commit to running the bakery with Ma, though of course his mother considered the matter settled. Lillian also hadn't officially agreed to the price he'd offered for the house. If she hoped to get a better price from someone else, what would that mean for him and his mother and sisters? Would she expect them to pitch in with the work and then sell the property out from under them?

He slid the saddle from Mist's back and led her into her stall. Then again, helping with work in exchange for continuing to live in a house not theirs wasn't a bad trade. At least she'd never insisted Ma and the girls leave.

A strange situation.

He grabbed a curry comb and worked the tool over Mist's coat. Even if by some strange turn of events Ma and Lillian opened a bakery together, would such a venture succeed in Dawsonville?

He'd hoped for Ma to have a nice home and a pastime that might bring her extra income. She seemed to think the business would do more. What did Lillian expect? This wasn't Atlanta, where people had ample amounts of both time and money.

Regardless, he would see to it that Ma got her wish. He would also make sure his mother and sisters were cared for by any means necessary. Even if that meant he'd never leave this farm and the monotonous cattle work he dreaded.

The day's work completed, Jonah exited the barn, sweat cooling on his skin with the evening breeze.

Lewis strode across the yard and lifted his hand in greeting. "Jonah! I was just coming to call you inside. Edith is making ham and sweet potato hash for supper."

Another invitation to eat with the family. These offers were becoming too common, especially after Ma and the girls moved to town and he could no longer spend his evenings in his childhood home.

"Thank you, but I still have some work to do." He rubbed the scruff on his chin. Surely there was something that needed tending.

"I already know you didn't eat dinner, and Alma would have my hide if you didn't get supper either." Jovial tone or not, Lewis would see to it Alma had her way. "Get washed up, then come inside."

He strode away before Jonah could argue.

A half hour later, dressed in clean trousers and shirt, Jonah knocked on the front door. Lewis answered and gestured him inside. Women's laughter drifted down the hallway, bouncing off the papered walls.

They stepped into Lewis's study, the only room in the house where Jonah felt truly comfortable. The masculine furnishings didn't make a man worry he might damage the dainty fabric and spindly legs. Here a fellow could settle his full weight into a sturdy leather chair with ease.

They took the two wingback chairs near the hearth. "Any problems with the cattle?" Lewis asked as he reclined.

"No, sir. Didn't see any cases of bloat, thankfully. I also didn't see any signs of those coyotes, but we still need to keep a close eye."

"Agreed." Lewis stroked the edge of his mustache. "What do you make of this proposition your mother and my wife's cousin have come up with?"

"Proposition?"

"Your mother didn't tell you? She wrote an entire page of details and gave them to Lillian today. Appears she listed out all of her ideas for the bakery."

Ma had done that? He'd never seen her do anything similar. "So now Miss Doyle wants to enter into a partnership?"

"Don't know," Lewis said, his tone thoughtful. "But Alma seems to think she's more open to it now that Melanie has a feasible plan."

How much had he missed moving cattle today?

Jonah let out an exasperated sigh. "I don't know what to think of Miss Doyle. One day she's adamant that she will not consider a bakery, and the next she's decided to stay on and she's making future plans. For what purpose? She's nearly finished sorting through her father's belongings." He clenched the arms of the chair in frustration. "The woman makes no sense."

Lewis chuckled. He must understand women far better than Jonah. "Whatever Alma said to her, it must have been rousing." He steepled his fingers, lips tugging into a bemused smile. "From what Alma says, Lillian is considering Melanie's designs for altering the house."

Jonah hardly found such waffling amusing. Especially when it concerned his family's welfare.

His expression must have relayed his thoughts because Lewis turned his palms out. "All I know is that Alma asked to stop by the hotel last night. She insisted that Lillian stay as a guest in our home. I can only assume whatever else they discussed had quite a sway on the lady's opinions about Melanie, the house, and the plan for the bakery."

Something had been nagging Jonah about the entire situation. "I don't picture Miss Doyle as one who will dirty her hands in common labor. Why would she want any part in Ma's bakery?" He could hardly reconcile the stiff and haughty woman he'd first met on the street with a working woman spending her days seeing to customers.

"Perhaps you should take a look in the kitchen."

"Sir?"

Lewis chuckled. "Those women have flour everywhere. They've been baking ever since I brought Lillian home." He lifted his brows, a sort of knowing expression that Jonah couldn't quite decipher brushing over his features. "The kitchen seems to have unwound her quite a bit."

He could hardly imagine it, yet the idea intrigued him. Jonah had suspected her aloof manner was a protective shell, but he'd seen only hints of what the true woman was like underneath. Maybe tonight he'd have the chance. The notion sent currents of anticipation coursing through him, and he suddenly found himself glad he'd been invited to supper.

He chuckled to himself. Which of them was the fickle one now?

In the kitchen, Jonah found exactly what Lewis had described and yet not at all what he'd expected. Lillian's hair had escaped several pins, and tendrils bounced in little curls around her temples. She had flour smeared on her cheek and a fine dusting of it on her apron and hands. But it was her eyes that stopped Jonah cold.

Flour had unlocked her armor, and Lillian's entire countenance had shifted. Her posture was relaxed. Her eyes were beaming. A glowing smile had transformed her pleasant face into radiance.

A strong hand clapped him on the shoulder, jarring Jonah back to his senses. "See?" Lewis chuckled, his voice low.

Alma noticed them and gave her husband a sly smile, her gaze flitting to Jonah.

"Smells delicious, ladies." Jonah's words drew Lillian and Edith's notice, and they looked up from the lattice pattern they were creating on the top of a pie.

When Lillian's warm gaze found his, her smile said she was pleased to see him. What *had* she and Alma discussed?

Unable to think of anything better to say, he asked the obvious. "Making a pie?"

Her eyes twinkled. "Cherry. Do you like cherry?"

"My favorite."

"I thought your favorite was blackberry." Edith arched an eyebrow.

"A man can have more than one favorite."

Edith laughed. "Is that so?"

"It is when it comes to pie. I also favor cobbler. And turnovers."

They all laughed, the mood of the room drawing Jonah in.

"Anything I can help with?" he asked.

"Since when do you help in the kitchen?" Edith wiped her hands on a rag, an impish turn to her lips.

"Since our kitchen gained a pretty new addition," Alma quipped before Jonah could respond.

He ignored the heat clawing up from his center. Lillian ducked her head, but not before he caught her smile. He shoved his hands in his pockets.

Lillian bustled across the room, finished pie in hand, and opened the oven. She glided with graceful ease, not at all like the stony woman who usually moved as though she'd been born with an iron spine.

After closing the oven and wiping her hands, she stepped over to Jonah. "I could use some assistance setting the table, if you don't mind." Without waiting for his response, she swished past him, the sweet scents of fruit and lavender wafting with her.

Lord help him. This version of Lillian Doyle might well land him in a heap of trouble.

Even as the thought bloomed, Jonah cast it aside and followed right along behind her.

CHAPTER FOURTEEN

There was no going back now. Lillian forced her trepidation down. "I see no problem enlarging the kitchen."

Melanie practically bounced on her toes, eyes sparkling. "And a bookshop." She clasped her hands. "That will be the perfect addition to our plan. Simply perfect." She eyed the parlor and study in the Jackson house and nodded.

Yesterday, prior to her supper with the Watsons, she and Melanie had moved all of the remaining clutter from this room. Lillian had organized the boxes into what she planned to keep and what she would donate to the church for those in need. The space now stood empty, ready for a new future.

She was still uncertain about the extent of the debts against her father's company—which, as far as she knew, Mr. Tanner hadn't yet paid—and the amount of money that would become hers when the estate was settled. But she had agreed last night—on an emotional whim, of all things—to the remodeling Melanie wanted. She tried not to let herself worry overmuch about the level of commitment it implied. Looking at the excited woman now, however, she feared she'd jumped headfirst into a fast-moving current.

The back door closed and voices approached. A moment later, Jonah and Rose appeared in the parlor door.

Melanie twisted around. "Jonah! Go get that sledgehammer. We're widening this room for Lillian's bookshop."

Jonah didn't move. His eyes flitted to Lillian, questions in their blue depths.

She pushed her lips into a smile. "Remember? We discussed moving forward with your mother's design ideas at the Watsons' last night."

"I remember." His tone said he hadn't believed her, though perhaps he'd wanted to. The surprise—or maybe appreciation?—that filled his eyes now clenched her heart in a way she didn't understand.

"A bookshop?" Rose took a step further into the room. "You want to have a bookshop here in our house?"

"Well, yes, I thought it would work well with the bakery your mother wants and—"

"Jonah," Melanie barked with a wave of her hand. "Go get that sledgehammer. We can start right away."

Lillian shifted her gaze between the child she'd been trying to speak to and the man still eyeing her warily. She gave a small nod. It seemed all the answer he needed. He and Melanie exited the room, Jonah with steady steps and Melanie chattering as she hurried him along.

Rose still watched her expectantly. Lillian smoothed her hands down her skirt, not sure why the girl's penetrating gaze made her feel a tad nervous. She pointed to the nearest wall. "There could be shelves all along here, with an upholstered bench tucked there in the bay window where girls like you could sit and read." The words leaked out of her, stirring a yearning.

Suddenly she could envision every detail. A dining area would serve tea, coffee, and confections, and over here on this side, they'd have shelves stocked with books. Along with the enchanting bay window, customers could sit and read in a couple of other cozy nooks around the room.

The vision came with such a wave of longing that Lillian had to place her hand on the wall to steady herself. No longer could she look at this as Melanie's dream alone. Somehow her own dream had bloomed right along beside it.

"Truly?" Rose's voice held a longing that mirrored Lillian's.

She sucked in a breath in an effort to regain logical thinking. "People lingering over a book might want to do so with a confection in hand, don't you think?"

The first true smile Lillian had ever seen from the girl brightened Rose's face. "We could have matching curtains to go with the cushions. Oh! And they could coordinate with the napkins and linens for the bakery." She tapped a finger on her chin. "I wonder how many yards of fabric we would need." She grabbed Lillian's fingers and gave them a quick squeeze. "I'll do some measurements and calculations." She scurried from the room, only to poke her head back through the doorway a second later. "Thank you, Miss Lillian." With another grin, she disappeared once again.

That was unexpected.

Before Lillian could think too much on Rose's behavior, Jonah reappeared with a long-handled hammer clenched in one hand. Lillian tried not to gulp. The iron head must weigh at least ten pounds. He could certainly do plenty of damage with that thing.

Perhaps they should discuss the specifics of the remodeling a bit more. Formulate an exact design. Melanie had given her a well-thought-out plan for running the business, including the names of suppliers and a daily schedule. She'd even included a drawing of what changes she wanted to make with the house. But removing walls felt . . . permanent. A little more discussion certainly couldn't hurt.

Yes, that would be good. Lillian opened her mouth to say so when the massive hammer made contact with the wall.

Wood splintered and cracked. Within seconds, dust filled the air. Lillian stared, transfixed. Jonah swung again, and the sound of the hammer echoed through the house.

Soon the entire parlor of her father's house was filled with dust, clogging Lillian's nostrils and threatening to make her sneeze. Through the haze, Jonah hefted the sledgehammer, the muscles in his exposed forearms bunching and uncoiling with each swing. Dressed in dungarees with suspenders over a loose-fitting shirt that hung open at the neck, he looked very much the man for the job.

Lillian's stomach clenched with worry even as her heart danced an enthusiastic jig. How could a person feel both elated and terrified by the same decision?

Jonah's shoulder muscles tensed. He swung.

She covered her eyes as splinters of wood exploded inward with the weight of the hammer.

This was really happening.

The finality of the massive hole in the wall proclaimed in no uncertain terms that the Petersons had taken her seriously. And they hadn't spared a moment or an inch of wiggle room for Lillian to reconsider. Now all she could do was watch as Jonah made quick work of tearing through the wall. She should probably find something else to do, but watching Jonah swing that giant hammer had her entirely mesmerized.

Lillian had no idea how long she'd been standing there staring when Jonah finally stopped and stretched his lower back, examining the work he'd accomplished. Wiping her eyes after withholding a sneeze, she joined Jonah in surveying the wall.

The previous mahogany-trimmed doorway that had stood between the parlor and study now gaped open with jagged edges. With the doorframe and a good portion of the wallboards gone, Lillian could get a sense of how large this new space would truly be once Jonah finished widening the single doorway into a larger pass-through. It looked a mess now, but she could envision the room filled with sunlight and happy townspeople.

Well, that did it. She'd been praying for confirmation, hadn't she? The happiness Lillian had brought—both to Melanie and her girls and to the book-loving girl she'd once been herself—wasn't something she could undo.

Decision truly accepted, she let a relieved breath whoosh out of her.

Jonah must have mistaken the sound as one of displeasure. His shoulders stiffened. "Looks a lot different, doesn't it?"

"It's far bigger than I'd first thought."

He nodded, casting a sidelong glance in her direction.

She probably should make an effort to put the poor man at ease. Mother always said men could wind themselves into knots when they thought a woman stood on the verge of changing her mind and thus redirecting what they'd already started.

Lillian lifted her chin, infusing confidence into her tone to reassure him. "Your mother is right. This will suit her business well."

"Hers? Aren't you joining in this venture?" His tone said he hadn't yet decided if he was keen on the notion.

Lillian did her best to gauge the feelings behind his words, but he turned his attention to the jagged remains of the wall, expression unreadable. She smoothed her skirt. "Of course. And if that doesn't work out, then I'll sell the house to your mother for what you and Lewis agreed on. We can work out an affordable payment system to cover the construction and other necessities from a portion of the bakery's proceeds. Once it's profitable, of course." She lifted her shoulders when he still didn't relax. "Undertaking the construction will be beneficial either way. No reason to worry."

He stared at her. "You're going to sell us the house for the same price?" Disbelief hung on each word.

True, she probably would have been able to sell the house to another buyer for a higher sum, and waiting for the business to be profitable and trusting Melanie to pay back what Lillian spent would be a risk. But for some reason entirely unexplainable, Lillian felt drawn to Melanie.

"I see no reason your mother shouldn't continue as she put forth in her plan," Lillian finally said into the silence. "And I may still choose to keep the house." She tilted her head, thinking out loud. "If I do, then we can work out a rent instead." Not a bad idea. She still hadn't decided if she would actually stay in Dawsonville and take part in running the shop. But even if she returned to Atlanta and let the shop earn an income for her, that would still give her freedom. No need to marry to survive. And besides, as the owner, she would have a perfectly reasonable excuse to visit from time to time.

Jonah's face flickered with an emotion Lillian couldn't place. Then, without bothering to respond to any of her efforts at easing his concerns, he hefted the hammer and swung at the wall with more force than necessary.

That man! He could at least have the decency to—

Another hole opened up along the left side of the doorway, and something caught her eye.

"Wait!" Lillian leapt forward, holding up her hand.

Jonah grunted and paused mid-swing. He lowered the hammer to his side, his eyes quizzical.

Lillian stepped around him and shooed the dust away. "I saw something." She poked her fingers inside the opening and felt along the edges of the wall. "I think it dropped down deeper." There. Her fingers brushed against something. With a tug, she lifted a hefty rectangular bundle wrapped in protective oilcloth.

"What is that?" Jonah crowded closer as he peered over her shoulder.

He smelled like cedar and . . . sage? Lillian blinked and shifted away from him. The package was large, with the weight and feel of a book. How had it gotten inside the wall? She pulled the string securing the oilcloth and it fell away, revealing a thick, leather-bound tome.

Jonah once again looked over her shoulder, his breath tickling her neck. He remained silent as she opened the cover and scanned the contents. Lines of dates filled one column along the edge, dating back five years. The next two columns contained some kind of abbreviation system.

"What is that?" Jonah's repeated question scurried across her cheek.

"Looks like some type of ledger." She should move. Acute perception of his nearness—an odd sensation that had never happened with Reginald—tingled along the nape of her neck. "Do you know what it means?"

He grunted again and stepped away from her. "What was it doing in the wall?"

Lillian let a shrug speak for her.

Had her father hidden the book? Why? She thumbed through the pages, finding more of the same system, with lists of dates followed by a series of letters. She ran a hand down the lines.

3WHRM
18FFRM
2DMS, 5EWL

She had no idea what the notations meant. In the column next to the first series of numbers and letters was a second line with much the same.

GT, S
LL, A
M, A

The letters *A* and *S* appeared most commonly, though others occasionally appeared as well. More of the same followed down each column on every page.

"I guess this is how he did it." Jonah's statement tugged her attention from attempting to decipher a pattern. He'd opened a rectangular portion of the wall, the edges too smooth to have been caused by his hammer.

Lillian neared, studying what looked to be a little door. How hadn't they noticed it before? Where the top portion of the wall had been papered like in the parlor, the bottom half had been lined with wainscoting. Beneath the chair rail, strips of wood created little boxes spaced evenly down the wall. She'd seen this design in the parlor of Mother's friend Mrs. Presley, who'd favored colonial architecture.

The top half of the hidden door had been busted away, along with the wainscoting above it. But now that she looked, she could see that the decoration had clearly been a hidden compartment.

Lillian set the book on the ground and placed her fingers along the edges of another square on one of the intact walls. Jonah did the same on the wall opposite. Lillian worked her fingers around the edges of each strip of molding, but nothing pried free. She tried again with the next square and the one after it, working her way around the room until she met Jonah at the hearth.

"I didn't find another one." He frowned back at the gaping hole.

"I didn't either. I wonder why someone put that in there." She picked up the book again and flipped to the last page. Blank. She thumbed back until she found the final entry.

Dated February 26, 1912.

A coldness seeped through her. The entries had stopped not long before her father's death. What had he been hiding?

A knock sounded at the door. While Jonah went to open it, she took the book to the kitchen and tucked it inside a cupboard. No sense carrying around a hidden book in the presence of uninvited company.

Stiff male greetings sounded from the porch through the open front door. One a tad gruff. The other smooth and groomed.

Mr. Tanner.

Outside, she found the men eyeing one another like a pair of roosters.

"Mr. Tanner," she said. "Good day to you, sir."

He doffed his hat, revealing the shine of his balding head.

"Good afternoon, Miss Doyle." His gentlemanly manner mirrored that of men in Atlanta. "Might I come in?"

"I'm afraid not." She kept his gaze, her words sweet and delicate while not leaving room for argument. Just as Mother had taught. "Now that we've started construction, there are even fewer spaces for entertaining company than before."

"Construction?" Mr. Tanner nearly barked the word, then cleared his throat. "I didn't know you planned on redesigning the house."

"If you've come to inquire after your offer, I haven't yet come to a decision."

Jonah gave another one of his wordless sounds, this one with an edge of annoyance, were she to guess. At Mr. Tanner? Or her?

He excused himself and slipped back inside. Mr. Tanner's eyes snaked after him, his gaze probing the open foyer for a moment before darting back to Lillian.

"Yes, about that." He straightened. "I've come to tell you that I've worked out the matter with the bank." He waited a moment, but when she gave no response, he hooked his thumbs under his linen jacket and into his suspenders. His tone shifted to one used on a confused child. "As I have covered all of the company debts, my offer to purchase Floyd's portion of Jackson and Tanner Distribution leaves you with a considerable sum."

The implications swarmed like startled bees through her head. The offer gave her immediate access to a thousand dollars, plus whatever money her father had in his bank account. With that, she'd have enough to modestly support her mother for years, and—with careful stewardship of what the shop earned—likely for the rest of Mother's life. Which meant she could do as she liked with her own life.

Mr. Tanner apparently took her continued silence as dismissive. He cleared his throat again, gaze sharpening. "I've come with another offer." Another quick glance inside. "I wish to purchase the house."

Shock brought her eyebrows scrunching together.

Mr. Tanner stroked his chin. "Sentimental value, you know." He snapped his fingers as though just coming to a decision. "Whatever the others are paying, I'll pay double."

Lillian stared at him, unable to form words. Finally, she said, "I . . . I'll have to think about that, Mr. Tanner."

"Think about it?" He scoffed. "What is there to consider? My offers are more than fair. Quite generous, in fact."

Lillian's eyes narrowed at his condescension.

"On account of my good friendship with Floyd, you see."

His assurance did nothing to quell her suspicions. Why offer so much for the house? And why now? Did he know something about the ledger hidden inside? "I will consider your offer, sir, against my own desire to keep the residence."

He opened his mouth—likely to object—so Lillian hurried on.

"As for your previous offer concerning the shipping company, until I know for sure what Mr. Jackson's portion of the business is worth, I cannot judge its fairness." She spread her hands. "However, I'm certainly glad to hear the matter of the loan has been settled."

Mr. Tanner's eyes flickered. "Wise." After an awkward heartbeat, he chuckled. "You're Floyd's progeny after all, aren't you?"

How did she respond to that?

He sucked in a long breath. "Very well. I'll have Mr. Grimly draw up an official appraisal of the business." He nodded toward the house. "Though I assume since you have already deemed one price fair on the house that my offer is sufficient?"

"I'll still have to think on it. Melanie already has plans for the house."

"*Your* house." A sneer started at one corner of his mouth, then quickly disintegrated. "Or is it hers already?"

Lillian tried not to bristle at the insinuation. "As I said, I'll need time to consider all of my options."

His lips curved into a smile, but it didn't reach his eyes. He placed his black derby on his head and tugged on the brim. "I do have a business to run, Miss Doyle. I'd appreciate your answer by the end of the week."

She clasped her hands together to keep them from fidgeting. "You shall have it."

He bid her a good day and strode from the porch. Lillian leaned against the rail, her thoughts churning.

A strange hiding place in the parlor. A secret book filled with coded lines. And now her father's partner's sudden offer. An uneasiness uncoiled in her center.

What sort of trouble had she inherited?

CHAPTER FIFTEEN

————— ❧ —————

He should have known.

Jonah tried to slow his breathing. He shouldn't have been listening at the door. He'd told himself he would stay near in case Lillian needed him, but truth had a way of burning through whitewashed lies. He'd wanted to know what she and Mr. Tanner discussed because he didn't trust her not to go back on her word the moment it suited her.

Turned out he'd been right. Lillian Doyle had gotten Ma's hopes up, only to cast everything aside when Tanner offered more money. True, she'd said she'd consider the offer and hadn't accepted it outright, but if she'd meant to turn him down, she would have already.

He clenched the hammer and returned to the hole he'd made in the wall. If Tanner purchased this house now, then he'd do it with walls missing. Jonah hefted the meaty hammer and slammed it into the wall with a satisfying crunch.

Another swing. Another.

His body fell into a rhythm of swing, slam, swing, slam. The coiling and release of his muscles did little to help the anger building inside him.

If Tanner took the house, would he ever be able to get Ma and his sisters stable enough for him to attend university? The concept of electricity and directing those currents through the wires fascinated him. He'd read of the engineering program at Clemson University and their classes on electrical engineering. If he could only learn the skill, perhaps he could bring that knowledge home to Dawsonville. Improve the lives of his families and neighbors.

A big, foolish idea.

Swing, slam.

Who did he think he was? He was no scholar. He knew little beyond the basic education he'd received before his father died and he'd had to care for his mother and sisters.

Swing, slam.

But if he could get through the reading portions and focus on the hands-on training, maybe he could make something of himself, prove that he could be more than a struggling farmhand, and give his family a better life.

Maybe someday.

Swing, slam.

"Jonah!" The alarmed voice reached through his self-pity.

He paused mid-swing, chest heaving. Ma stood beside him, her eyes large and wild.

"What are you doing?"

He lowered his arm and surveyed his work. The entire wall was nearly gone. He stepped back and rubbed his shoulder. How long had he been swinging? "Widening this doorway. Like you wanted." *Though it probably won't matter now.*

"You were about to demolish the entire wall." She crossed her arms and gestured with her head. Pieces of the paneling had splintered and ripped away in a far larger section than they'd planned.

He grimaced. If he'd taken out too much of the structure, he could have brought the ceiling down.

"Everything all right, Son?" Ma eyed him, her motherly instincts reaching out to hook into him.

Your plans are about to go up in smoke. Right along with mine.

"Everything's fine."

She cocked an eyebrow. "This have anything to do with that pretty yet fickle little gal?"

Didn't everything these days? "Just trying to finish this wall before I have to get back to the farm."

Ma scoffed. "If I hadn't stopped you, you mighta torn down the whole house."

Jonah rolled his shoulders, loosening overly tight muscles. "Anything else you need me to do before I go?"

Her gaze slowly swept over the piles of debris all over the floor. Right. He'd best get this cleared out.

"That front porch step is a bit of a danger. Rose tripped on it yesterday and it sagged under me this morning. I'm afraid it's going to snap the next time someone uses it."

Jonah nodded. "I'll handle it."

She patted his shoulder. "I know. You handle everything." Warmth spread in her eyes. "Pretty soon, though, things are going to be different. You'll see."

A weight settled on him, but he couldn't bear to tell her the truth of Lillian's deception. Instead, he shouldered the burden alone.

Like always.

Mother would think her mad. Lillian didn't care. Her steps were featherlight as she moved to the final room of crates and boxes filled with her father's things. She'd made her decision. Truthfully, it hadn't taken long. Mr. Tanner had offered her more, but she'd already made her plans.

Besides, she liked it here. No harm in staying at least a little longer. Long enough to get to know her cousin and aunt. Long enough to help Melanie get her business started. Surely Mother would see the value in the investment. Eventually. And Mother would never know what offers Lillian had turned down. She'd only know what Lillian decided to tell her.

Lillian lifted the lid off the first crate and sorted through a stack of table linens. They'd keep these. The extra bed linens as well. She scooted the box to the side.

Though she'd been momentarily tempted to consider Mr. Tanner's higher price, she was already getting far more than she'd ever dreamed. Mother would understand. Perhaps.

Lillian reached for the next box. No, Mother wouldn't understand. But it didn't matter. This felt right.

She opened the next box, revealing a set of painted china. She ran her finger over the yellow flowers dancing along the edge. Where had her father gotten these? They had a feminine grace. Had there been another woman? She shook her head and put the plate back with its fellows. She'd ask Edith if they'd been passed through the family.

An odd satisfaction bubbled in her as she pushed the crate next to the one with the linens.

Three more crates held various items that must have come from the kitchen and dining area. All of which Lillian would keep in the house.

Finally, she came to the section of boxes she'd thus far

avoided. She settled on the floor and pulled a crate to her. These had come from the most personal portions of the house—her father's bedroom and study. Perhaps today she'd finally learn something about the man who had abandoned her and Mother.

The telegram she'd sent Mother replayed in her mind, sending tingles along her arms. It would most surely send Mother into fits.

```
Nothing to send yet
Lots to do
Will return when able
No wedding
```

Lillian could picture her reading the note, her face flaming red and her eyes flashing. Lillian had never been happier to be in the rural parts of Georgia, far from Mother's lashing tongue.

The sudden cessation of Jonah's rhythmic hammering made her pause. Had he finished the wall? She rose, ready to see what the open space looked like. The room would be massive now. How far would she be able to stretch the bookshelves? Could Jonah build them, or would she need to hire a carpenter?

So much to consider. She found herself relishing each choice to make, excitement for the venture welling.

Jonah had agreed to help with the construction labor to save the women expense, but he could only do so much. He still had employment with the Watson family.

Unless she could hire him.

As soon as she gained access to funds, she'd offer Jonah official employment. Lillian smiled to herself, having made another decision that felt right.

She wandered across the front hall and into the rooms on the other side of the house. Well, one room now. She put a hand to her throat. "It's lovely!"

Jonah snorted. "Dust and debris she finds lovely."

What had up and bitten him? Lillian lingered at the edge of the room, taking in the dirty man before her.

He gripped his large hammer in white knuckles, his exposed forearm corded with strain. His shirt was still unbuttoned at the collar, revealing more tension in his neck. A muscle in his jaw twitched, and his eyes landing on her held an intensity that had her easing back a step.

Melanie swatted Jonah's arm, but he didn't seem to notice. His poison-tipped gaze remained trained on Lillian. What had she done to offend him?

"Don't mind him." Melanie sighed but offered no further explanation.

"Yes, don't mind me at all." The words had a weight to them. Nearly ominous.

Lillian took another half step back, darting her gaze between the grizzly bear and his sighing mother. "Did I do something wrong?"

"Did you?" Jonah kept his voice even, though it was with obvious effort.

He had no idea of the risk she took trusting these strangers or yielding to the tug she felt in her heart toward Melanie and her grand ideas. And he treated her as though she was muck to scrape from his shoe?

A storm welled inside her. She set her shoulders. "If you have something to accuse me of, sir, best you be about it."

Jonah snaked a glance at Melanie and pinched his lips into a tight line.

This had something to do with Melanie?

Lillian studied her would-be business partner. Dressed in a sturdy day dress with her hair tucked into a neat coil, Melanie returned Lillian's gaze with sympathetic eyes. Whatever ire Jonah felt, Melanie didn't seem to share it.

What had transpired between the commencement of the construction this morning, when they'd all been pleased with one another, and this current turn of unexpected hostility?

Mr. Tanner.

Heat pooled in her center and inched up her neck.

Jonah must have been eavesdropping. On matters that were none of his concern. Lillian pulled in a deep breath, held it, and let it out again. She'd decided not to accept the man's offer. Not that Jonah could know that.

Pride tipped her chin upward. "Pray, do tell, Mr. Peterson. I'd appreciate it if you'd state the cause of your obvious disdain."

Jonah clasped his hands in front of him, making his shoulders roll forward and pronounce the muscles. How did men manage to puff themselves up like that when facing confrontation?

Well, if he could do it, so could she. She pulled her shoulders back a mite more, forcing her form to the peak of her height.

"It's best if you say it." His voice rumbled low. He shot a pointed glance at his mother.

Melanie frowned.

He hadn't told her.

Some of Lillian's phony bravado seeped out of her, replaced by a tug of guilt. She didn't want Melanie to know that she had so easily considered going back on her word. Or that she'd considered, even if only briefly, ousting the woman and her children in favor of more money.

She deflated. "I'm sorry, Melanie."

The woman's eyes darted between Lillian and Jonah. Jonah tensed as though waiting for Lillian to deliver the news that she had deceived them. So little he thought of her.

Who could blame him?

Lillian swallowed against a sandy feeling in her throat. "Mr. Tanner came here this morning and offered to pay me double for the house."

The pronouncement hung on the air a moment. Anger and betrayal flashed in Jonah's eyes, the tight set of his jaw proof of his assumptions.

She cleared her throat, trying to dislodge the persistent scratch. "Though I'll have you know I decided against it."

Jonah narrowed his eyes, studying her.

"Of course you did, child." Melanie waved her hand as though to brush away ridiculous concerns.

Lillian and Jonah unhooked their gazes to stare at Melanie.

"What?" Melanie scoffed at their scrutiny. "I already told you, Jonah. I don't know why you look so surprised."

Jonah's mouth tightened. He shook his head. "Ma. She told the man she'd consider it. Probably would have taken that offer if the guilt of admitting the truth to your face hadn't stopped her." His shoulders lifted and lowered with a long breath. "She most likely will still take the money when you're not looking."

I will not!

The words froze on Lillian's tongue. Nothing she could say would ever convince him otherwise. Any favor she'd found with him had been lost.

Why did that cause an ache in her chest? The man was a brute. Uncouth and unpolished. Why should she care what he thought of her?

"Nonsense." Melanie drew out the word as though Jonah had said a purple sun had risen in the west. "She was merely being polite by not dismissing the man out of hand." Not a hint of mockery peppered her voice. "She wouldn't have gone back on her word. I already told you there's a plan." A sharp nod. "And I believe in Lillian."

Melanie's words burrowed into Lillian's heart, tugging and shifting until they settled deep. Someone believed the best of her. Trusted her and thought her honorable and true. And that person believed God had a plan for the two of them. Together.

Emotion welled within her, burning its way into her throat and searing the backs of her eyes.

Maybe it was time she started truly believing too.

CHAPTER SIXTEEN

———— ✦ ————

Three days. Lillian ventured a quick glance at the reticent man beside her. For three days she had been riding from the Watson farm to her town house with Jonah, and he'd hardly spoken two handfuls of words to her the entire time.

She adjusted her gloves and tried to focus on the passing landscape of green trees. Perhaps she could find a colorful bird or a rambunctious squirrel playing catch with its fellows—anything to steer her mind away from the man sitting next to her.

No such luck. Nothing but the sound of the horse's clopping hooves to break the silence. Only gently swaying trees and a deserted dirt road to claim her attention. Her thoughts swung right back to contemplating Jonah.

Despite becoming insufferably tight-lipped, he hadn't been rude. He'd helped her from the wagon each morning, asked if she needed assistance with anything, and then offered polite goodbyes. But he hadn't really talked to her.

Why that bothered her, Lillian couldn't say.

The warm summer air brushed over them, stirring her

riding hat and teasing the ends of Jonah's hair where it escaped from his wide western hat. He'd pulled the brim low, shielding most of his face. She couldn't get a good look at him unless she leaned forward.

Which she would certainly never do.

"Got something to say?" Jonah's tone held an odd mix of amusement and . . . well, something that wasn't quite annoyance but could probably masquerade as such.

Her cheeks heated. "What?"

"You keep looking at me. Figured you had something to say."

How had he known? She'd thought herself covert.

She could brush this moment aside. Sniff haughtily and stare forward, reminding him that he shouldn't treat a lady in such a manner. That was what Mother would say to do.

"I want you to know," Lillian said instead, "that I had already decided not to accept Mr. Tanner's offer." Thankfully, the words came out smooth and even. "You'll likely never believe me, but that's out of my control."

Jonah tipped his hat back and regarded her thoughtfully for a moment, then turned his attention back to the road.

Lillian twisted in her seat to face him. "I admit to being momentarily tempted by the sum and what it would mean for my mother and my livelihood, but the notion was fleeting. I had already made a commitment."

Silence reigned for several moments, with only the clack of the horse's hooves on the hard-packed road and the crunch of the wagon wheels to fill the void.

Lillian shifted to face forward again. Very well. Let him believe what he would. She had no control over what others chose to think. In fact, she honestly didn't care a whit.

She nearly laughed. What a novel sensation. She'd spent

the majority of her life deeply concerned about the thoughts of others. But no matter what she did or how she acted, she'd failed in one set of eyes or another. Doing her best and letting others think whatever they would felt much better.

Pulling in a deep breath of earthy scents, Lillian tipped her head back and let the sun warm her face. She focused on the tickle of a breeze across her cheeks.

"You didn't change your mind in the face of my mother's disappointment?" Jonah's contemplative words broke the silence and Lillian's welling sense of contentment.

She tipped her hat back down to shade her face. "No."

"Very well, then. I believe you." The words held a ring of truth.

Lillian turned her body again to face him. "So we have come to a truce?"

"Truce?" He chuckled. "Are we at war, Miss Doyle?"

It certainly seemed so. A war of silence and veiled animosity, if nothing else. Lillian adjusted her gloves again and kept her manner pleasant. No sense letting the man know she found his statement irritating when they were trying to reconcile.

"I would like for us to live happily together." There. That hadn't been so hard.

Her fingers tightened on her skirt at his silence. She replayed her words in her mind, horror warming her cheeks.

Oh dear. That had sounded far more intimate than she'd intended. She hastily added, "For your mother's sake, of course."

A smile played at the corners of Jonah's lips, the grin reined in just enough not to give full exposure to his amusement at her bumbling. "Of course."

She set her jaw. He'd drawn that last word out a touch too long. His amusement might be worse than his stoicism. Before she could come up with something to redirect his focus, Jonah changed the subject.

"I agree about building the bookshelves along the side wall by the window seat," he said as though they had been talking about the construction the entire time. "A good place for customers to linger and decide they want another confection."

"I hope people will find it cozy. I'd still prefer something in the heart of town, but Melanie insists they will come."

His chuckle rumbled low and deep in his chest. "Ma is rather inflexible when she puts her mind to something."

They fell into an easy discussion about the height of the new bookshelves, contacting the local general store about how to order new cabinets and a stove for the kitchen, and other various details for the shop. Had Lillian known sooner that confessing the truth about her consideration of Mr. Tanner's offer would decimate the wall between them so completely, she would have spoken up earlier.

Perhaps.

But probably not. It had taken a good bit of courage to gather herself enough to do so. And she'd had to scrub a bit of her pride out of the way.

Well worth the effort.

She relaxed a bit more as they talked about the construction plans, which projects Jonah thought he could accomplish for them, and which ones they would need to hire someone else to complete.

"I'd like to hire you for your part of the construction, if that is agreeable," she said.

He cast a look at her from under his hat. "I'm already doing most of the construction."

"Yes, but you should be paid. As soon as I get the funds

from the bank and can hire other workers, it only seems fair you are compensated as well."

Jonah remained silent for several moments. "You purchase materials, and we will consider my labor a trade for the difference in price you would have received from Mr. Tanner."

Lillian opened her mouth to refute but had the feeling she'd be somehow disrespecting the offer. Another little loosening of her grip on her pride. She tipped her chin. "A generous trade. Thank you."

The satisfaction on his face said she'd chosen well.

She let her mind wander to all the grand possibilities for the future and smiled wistfully. "It's a shame we can't get electricity. Wouldn't that be lovely?"

He went rigid beside her.

Lillian cast him a look. "You don't want electricity?" She'd heard some people didn't care for the unnatural lights and currents of dangerous voltage.

"Not feasible." The clipped words hung on the air. Not unfriendly, simply . . . wary.

How odd.

After several moments of silence, he sighed. "I'm sorry. Truth is, I'd hoped to study electrical engineering someday. Maybe bring it back here." His shoulders hiked up a notch, and he shook his head. "Far-fetched, I know."

Lillian patted his arm. "It's an admirable dream. I find electricity quite fascinating. I imagine the men who work with those currents have an exciting vocation." A thought occurred to her. "Is that what Lewis meant when he said you'd wanted to leave?"

Jonah gave a tight nod. After another few moments of silence, Lillian decided that he wouldn't say more on the topic.

She understood. Discussing a dream one believed out of their reach could be painful.

"How are your sisters enjoying their studies?" she asked. A safe turn of topic might bring back the easy comfort they'd shared only moments before.

"Betsy is ready for the end of classes." Jonah nodded at a farmer on an approaching buckboard, nudging their horse to the far right of the road until the man passed. "Though she has a few more days yet. Ma will have her hands full with the girl underfoot all day." The affection in his tone belied any hint the girl would be considered an annoyance.

A memory flared of her own mother admonishing her for being too pesky and "underfoot" when she'd been a girl of around Betsy's age, seeking attention.

"And Rose?"

He was quiet for several moments as they neared the edge of town, the cart bumping along the more deeply rutted section of road. Lillian gripped the handrail to keep from tipping into Jonah.

"Rose is still struggling with losing the cabin."

"Did your family lose a lot in the fire?"

"Everything we owned, save what little I had in my room at the Watsons.'"

The reality of the situation settled on her. She had seen the sparseness of the upper rooms. Had noted the few changes of clothes Melanie and the girls owned. Yet she'd been so wrapped up in her own situation that she hadn't truly considered the magnitude of theirs.

"Is that why your mother is so intent on the bakery?"

Jonah cut a sidelong glance at her as they passed the walled square in the center of town and moved beyond the courthouse. "The bakery gives her a way to use her skills to provide for her and the girls."

Didn't Jonah provide for them?

"Ma claims that the fire gave her the courage to move forward with the dream she'd buried under the normal pressures of life."

Lillian's stomach twisted. She'd always believed that good could come from the bad, as God worked all things to the good of those who loved him. At least, she'd always claimed to believe it. In practicality, she found hardships anything but a blessing. Would she have had Melanie's faith after losing everything?

They pulled up next to the house, and Jonah reined the mare to a stop. Lillian gazed at the little town house. Here she'd been given a heap of blessings that had come from tragedy. Circumstances had intertwined her bounty with another's need, another's skill with her own interests.

A sense of knowing there could be something bigger at work settled on her. *Someone* bigger. Lillian blinked sudden sentiment away before mustering a smile for Jonah as he handed her down from the wagon. "Thank you."

He tipped his hat and moved to return to his seat.

"I mean, thank you for all of it. The work you've done here." Her voice softened. "Your support of these lofty goals."

Jonah paused, his gaze searching her face. "You're welcome." He continued to look at her a moment longer as if to mine some kind of truth from her expression. Then he tipped his wide hat again and leapt into the wagon. "I'll be back after I finish checking the fence lines."

She nodded her thanks and watched him drive away.

Inside, she found Melanie kneeling down, her head close to the floorboards. "Melanie? Are you all right?"

The woman snickered. "Yes, dear. Just measuring."

Measuring? Lillian looked around the massive room, every hint of dirt and debris cleared away. Had Melanie spent all night down here cleaning? Lillian should probably stay later in the evenings to help. "I'm sorry, I don't understand."

Melanie rose and dusted off her palms, though Lillian still didn't see any signs of dirt. "Helps if you get the right perspective."

The floor was the right perspective?

"Have you finished the last of those crates?" Melanie ambled over as though she hadn't just been doing something entirely odd. "I'll get Jonah to move them out when he gets back."

"I have two left." One contained all the items from her father's desk, and the other held his personal effects from his private bedroom, minus the clothing she'd already donated. She'd donate most of what she didn't intend to use to the local Baptist church to be distributed to those in need. The majority of the furniture had been cleaned and either moved upstairs or placed in the front room on the other side of the house, waiting to be used.

She'd put off going through those final boxes. Perhaps because once she finished, all remaining chances for discovery would be completed. Or maybe because she feared learning something she didn't wish to find.

"I was thinking we'd put the tables in the other room." Melanie gestured to the other side of the house. "Next to where we'll have the display counter. What do you think?"

Lillian nodded. She'd first envisioned dainty tables perched in front of the bay window, but Melanie's idea made more sense. They would enlarge the kitchen, bringing it into what was now the dining room. "What about opening up a dining area in the back of the house as well? A place for people to linger on sunny days?"

Melanie had created such a beautiful garden back there, and Lillian loved eating out of doors. Others likely would as well.

"Oh, yes." Melanie tapped a finger on her chin, a smile blooming. "We could serve tea and those fancy little sandwiches. Maybe serve a few simple meals, if the notion suits us."

A matching smile tugged at Lillian's own lips. "I'd thought the same."

Melanie beamed, and a sobering thought gripped Lillian's heart. She'd spoken as though she meant to stay. Permanently.

Truth be told, she liked it here and could easily envision herself making friends with the locals as she recommended books and served coffee. A simple life devoid of the pressures of trying to scale Atlanta society. The vision of herself moving happily around the bookshop felt more real and far more palatable than the vision of Reginald's quiet wife—a lonely woman tucked away in a grand house, hosting pretentious parties. Here, she felt alive.

Melanie chattered about some fancy new kitchen cabinets she'd seen in an advertisement.

Lillian gave her hand a squeeze and turned toward the doorway. "I'm going to finish those boxes, and then I'll be in here to help you with your . . . measuring."

"No need." Melanie gestured toward the floor. "I was checking to see how the bookshelves would look with the grain of the floor. Unless you think otherwise, I feel they should run with the length of the floorboards rather than against."

"That makes more sense with the long length of the room, so I agree," Lillian said. "Speaking of measuring, Rose mentioned she wanted to calculate how many yards of fabric we would need so that all of our cushions, linens, and curtains could match."

A gleam entered Melanie's eyes. "Did she? How wonderful that she's taking an interest. But I think her greatest excitement comes from sewing. I've been wanting—"

She was interrupted by a knock at the door. The women exchanged a look, and then Lillian went to open it.

A young boy, probably no more than nine, stood on the front porch, wearing an untucked shirt at least three sizes too large. His mop of blond hair stood in disarray as he swiped a bedraggled hat from his head. "Miss Lillian Doyle?" He shifted in his dusty boots worn clean through at the toe.

"Yes?"

He thrust a crinkled letter toward her. "Mr. Carson sent this for you."

As soon as she took the paper, he whirled around and bounded down the front steps that, thankfully, Jonah had already repaired. She poked her head outside, taking note of the straight post and the no-longer-drooping shutters. When had he accomplished those tasks?

Shaking her head, Lillian closed the door. Mr. Carson had sent a letter. Did that mean he'd finished transferring her father's estate?

But instead of masculine handwriting, Mother's flowing script across the front of the envelope greeted her. Lillian's heartbeat quickened. While she'd known reprimand would be short in coming, she nonetheless shuddered at the moment's arrival.

How she hated the tremble in her fingers as she popped the seal.

Only words on a page. She could certainly handle that. Drawing a quick, fortifying breath, she began to read.

Lillian,

Whatever foolishness has overtaken you, I suggest you regain your senses immediately. Since I can sympathize with the situation you find yourself in, I've decided to give you a measure of grace and ignore your telegram. You are feeling overwhelmed, that is all. I've included a ticket for you to return home, along with a letter to the solicitor outlining instructions for him to take care of whatever else there is left to do with Mr. Jackson's estate and then forward all the funds to the bank in Atlanta.

Lillian groaned, her fingers crinkling the paper. Of course Mother would choose now to take it upon herself to try to handle the situation. Anger swirled in eddies through her heart. Had Mother done so in the first place, then—

She brought the thought to a halt. If Mother had come, then Lillian wouldn't have had the opportunity to realize her forgotten hopes or to let herself step out from under the shroud of disapproval that had blanketed her for so long.

Resolve swelled to encompass her anger, bringing the ire from near boiling to a more manageable simmer. Lillian focused once more on the page.

Of course I have not worried the Montgomerys by mentioning your lapse of judgment. Mrs. Montgomery expects you here by week's end for the gown fitting, so as soon as you are in receipt of this letter, pack your things. I will take care of everything. No need for you to worry.

No need for her to worry? Two weeks ago, she would have loved for Mother to take care of everything. Now she was glad Mother had never come. Glad she had this house.

She couldn't leave. Not now. Not yet.

We will speak on this no more. It's my fault for letting you go on your own. Don't fear any reprimand when you return. We shall go on with our plans as before.

Mother

Lillian stared at the words. *We shall go on with our plans.* Those plans had never been hers.

She crumpled the paper into a wad and shoved it into her pocket. "Melanie!"

The woman appeared from around the corner, broom in hand and eyes wide. "What? What's the matter?"

"I have to go to the solicitor's office."

"Oh." Confusion crinkled Melanie's brow. "All right then."

Lillian's hand skimmed the bulge in her skirt pocket. "And perhaps the telegraph office." She hesitated a moment, then lifted her chin. "Would you like to accompany me?" Heaven knew she could use a dose of moral support, even if Melanie had no idea what they were doing.

Melanie drew back, nearly dropping her broom. "You want me to go with you?"

Why did she sound so surprised? "If you don't mind. I know you're busy, but . . ." She sighed, her voice dropping as the admission slipped out. "I could use a friend."

Melanie's bright smile felt like warm sunshine on a winter day. "That, my dear girl, I will most gladly be." She propped the broom against the wall. "Off we go then."

Lillian chuckled. "Perhaps we should get our hats and gloves first?"

"If you insist." Melanie smiled playfully, then scuttled toward the kitchen, where they'd been stowing their personal effects. She returned a moment later with hats and gloves. Once properly attired, they stepped outside.

"What are we going to the solicitor for?" Melanie adjusted the ribbons on her old-fashioned bonnet, fingers deftly folding the faded ribbon into a perfect bow.

"To undo the mess my mother caused."

Melanie's mouth made a little O before she smacked her lips together.

Lillian hadn't meant for the words to sound so snippy. But she didn't regret them either.

Melanie cleared her throat and lengthened her stride to match Lillian's brisk pace. "She's not happy with your plan to stay and open our shop."

Lillian nodded.

Melanie wiggled her fingers in the air. "A shop which still needs a good name, by the by."

Bless the woman for wanting to speak of happier things, but Lillian didn't let her veer them off track. She had a mind to speak her piece, and if Melanie truly wanted to be her friend, she wouldn't begrudge hearing it. "My mother wants me to come home immediately, have Mr. Carson transfer all the funds to her account, and see me swiftly married to Reginald."

Melanie stopped. "You're getting married?"

"No." Lillian kept walking for a few paces, but when Melanie didn't continue, she stopped and turned back. "My mother wants me to, and she and his mother have been making plans, but I already told her I wasn't getting married. There's no need now."

"No need now?" Melanie's eyebrows drew together. "Does this young man know?"

He should already, but . . . Lillian withheld a groan. He didn't. Of course Mother hadn't told him. Would he be disappointed? Surely he could quickly find a replacement for her. It wasn't as though either of them had ever pretended theirs would be a love match. Still, Reginald was a decent man. He deserved to know the truth.

Lillian resumed walking. Delivering the news would be up to her. "He will soon enough."

"Oh my." Melanie hurried forward, and they resumed their pace. "So you told your mother you don't want to get married and you want to live here?"

"I told her I would return when I was able, there was plenty to do, and I wasn't getting married."

"Too bad we don't have a telephone." Melanie made a tsking noise. "I've heard you can talk to a person with one of those things, even over a distance."

Lillian had no desire to listen to her mother's lecture, be that in person or over a wire. "Probably best I send her a letter. Better than that, Mr. Carson can send her one."

"Careful there, young lady." Melanie heaved a breath as she wagged a finger in Lillian's direction. "Temper is often what gets us into trouble, and pride is what keeps us there."

Lillian bristled. The trouble this time was of Mother's making. And it was not pride that compelled Lillian now but rather a newfound confidence in herself.

She told herself this three times over, but Melanie's words still haunted her all the way to the solicitor's office.

CHAPTER SEVENTEEN

———✦———

L illian drew in a long breath, held it, and released the air slowly. She gave the solicitor a decisive nod. "Yes, sir. I'm certain."

Mr. Carson nodded—dare she say approvingly?—and passed a paper across the desk. "You'll need to sign here."

Temper gets us into trouble and pride keeps us there.

Lillian sent up a quick prayer that pride wasn't driving her to do something foolish. She didn't think so. Making this choice felt right. But her hand hesitated over the pen Mr. Carson offered.

All she had to do was sign her name, and she became controlling partner of an established and successful business, owner of her own house, and—much to her surprise—the recipient of a bank account padded with more money than she would have thought possible.

If her father had all of those assets, why had the house seemed in such disrepair? Yet truly only from the outside?

Questions without answers.

"Do you need a moment, dear?" Melanie placed a hand on

Lillian's arm, and only then did Lillian notice the pen between her fingers shaking.

She scrawled her name in one fluid motion. "There. It's done." She shored up her spine. "Whatever my mother told you about transferring funds back to Atlanta, please disregard. I will open my own account at the bank here in Dawsonville. Will I need your help transferring Mr. Jackson's funds into my account?"

Mr. Carson gathered the paper and two others she'd signed and tucked them inside a leather folder. "No, there won't be any issue. I already discussed matters with Mr. Grimly when we went over the settlement of the loan and the bank's assessment of the business assets." He pushed another paper across the desk to her and regarded her thoughtfully. "Mr. Grimly informed me that Mr. Tanner has offered to purchase the business from you." A slight lift of his eyebrows. "As well as Mr. Jackson's residence."

"He has. I've not yet decided on the company, but I will be keeping the house." A bubble of excitement rose above her nerves. "Melanie and I are opening our own shop on the lower floor."

Melanie grabbed her arm again and squeezed, her excitement nearly pouring off her.

Lillian's welling enthusiasm warred with trepidation. Was she truly ready to give up everything she'd ever known and attempt to start something she had no idea how to do?

She glanced down at the paper, and her heart stuttered. Doing some quick mental math, she realized that her father's portion of the company was worth at least six times what Mr. Tanner had offered.

"Interesting." Mr. Carson's words yanked her from her

STEPHENIA H. McGEE

thoughts. His tone held no indication of whether he thought the shop idea had merit. "I wish you the best of luck with your endeavor, Miss Doyle." He rose from his desk and buttoned his black jacket. "I believe our business is now concluded, but if you find yourself in need of my services in the future, feel free to call on me."

"Thank you, Mr. Carson. You've been most helpful." She rose and took the bank's assessment, then paused. "Oh my. I'm terribly sorry. What about your fee?"

A small smile tugged at the corners of his mouth. "Not to worry. Mr. Jackson stipulated my fee in his will, along with detailed instructions on matters of the estate. All debts against his remaining balance, including my own, have been claimed."

She thanked him again, and she and Melanie stepped out of the office. Then she turned back, some of Mr. Carson's words snagging her attention. "You said 'detailed instructions.' Might I ask what those were?"

An expression that edged close to amusement tickled his features. "Mr. Jackson was abundantly clear that all assets were to go to you and you alone, and that no funds of any amount were to be transferred to Mrs. Doyle."

So Mr. Carson wouldn't have sent the money to Atlanta anyway, no matter what Mother wanted. But why was her father so adamant that Mother not receive anything when he'd taken care of her all those years?

He seemed to have executed his will in great detail but had not left anything personal. She had so many questions, and while her father had planned for her care in the inheritance, he'd not addressed the need in her heart.

Lillian hesitated in the doorway. "Mr. Carson, did . . ." She

161

fiddled with the edge of her sleeve, then met the man's eyes. "Did my father leave any instructions for me?"

Mr. Carson's face brightened with the first real smile Lillian had seen. "Indeed he did."

Her heart quickened. Then why hadn't he—

"Then why didn't you give them to her?" Melanie asked the question before Lillian could, hand propped on her hip.

"Because, ma'am, those were his instructions. I was not to pass this along to his daughter unless she indicated a desire for personal contact."

Lillian stepped fully back into the office as Mr. Carson pulled an envelope from the leather folder on his desk and extended it to her.

She took it gently and ran her finger over her name in masculine text on the front. "Is this all? Is there anything more?" She met his gaze.

"Only the letter."

"No other questions I need to ask that I haven't thought of?"

Mr. Carson's smile turned wry. "You have my word. Mr. Jackson said that he wanted you to have all of the assets regardless. But he made sure I understood that if you gave any indication you wanted to hear from him, I was to give you the letter."

Lillian held the paper against her chest, more questions swirling through her. A great tempest of the unknown. She thanked the solicitor once more and returned to the street, the letter feeling like lead against her palm.

She struggled to regain her composure as she slipped the letter in her handbag. What might her father say after all these years when he'd never once written to her before?

Melanie tucked her fingers around Lillian's elbow, offering

another gentle squeeze. Words weren't necessary. An ache swelled Lillian's throat. How thankful she was for the friendship Melanie offered. How had two strangers come to so quickly care for one another in such an honest and genuine fashion? She patted Melanie's fingers and sniffled, not trusting herself to words.

They walked slowly together down the street, the gentle bustle of the town nothing like the swarms in Atlanta. Melanie greeted people as they passed, often asking about family members and receiving genuine smiles in response. She introduced Lillian to several people, and all of them greeted her with friendly smiles and words of welcome.

The people around here knew one another and cared about their neighbors. Lillian found the idea refreshing. By the time they reached the bank, she'd gotten a handle on her emotions.

She had two bank accounts open before the day was half spent—one as a personal account, and one from which she would begin conducting business for their shop. Feeling accomplished, she turned with determination back toward the house.

"Didn't you want to go to the telegraph office?" Melanie's question followed her for three steps before Lillian paused.

"No need." Now that she knew Mother couldn't take the money, there wasn't anything more to say.

Melanie harrumphed. "No ma'am. You need to let your ma know you're safe and that you've made plans to stay."

Lillian turned but didn't make a move toward the telegraph office. "I've already told her I want to stay." Well, she'd said she'd return when she was able. "And I also told her I wasn't getting married."

Melanie didn't say anything. She stood there in the street, staring at Lillian until her ears started to burn.

"She won't listen anyway." Lillian threw up her hands, sending her handbag swinging.

"Maybe so. But we are responsible for our own actions, not the responses of others."

Lillian clenched her fists so tightly that if she hadn't been wearing gloves, her nails would have made imprints in her palms. The two of them stood there in a stalemate, staring at one another. Melanie could be as stubborn as a goat, but Lillian was finding she was usually right.

"Best you keep your own side of it clean, yes?" Melanie turned out a palm, her question neither rebuking nor judgmental.

The air left Lillian in a huff. Fine. She stalked past Melanie without a word, and the woman had enough grace not to smirk as she passed. In fact, Melanie simply kept in step, her gait relaxed. She was opposite of Mother in so many ways.

Lillian's shoulders eased down a degree. "I'm sorry, Melanie. That was terribly rude of me."

"No apology needed. You've been through quite a bit for anyone to handle. Circumstances like yours are bound to make a person a bit prickly from time to time."

Lillian wasn't quite sure how to respond. Had she ever apologized for her behavior and had the gesture met with such easy forgiveness? Forgiveness that didn't bear a single taint of haughtiness or condescension?

"What should I tell her?" she asked.

Melanie thought a moment before answering. "The truth. As clearly as you can."

"I already tried that." Lillian tipped her chin in greeting

when Melanie spoke to an elderly woman they passed. "She responded by telling me she was ignoring my foolishness."

"Then you tell the young man that you don't want to marry."

The words hung between them. Right. She needed to do that as well. Coldness seeped through her. Mother would be livid.

A bell chimed over the door as they entered the telegraph office. Melanie waited near the door as Lillian selected two pages.

How did she tell Reginald she would no longer marry him because she didn't need his money anymore? No matter how she turned the words, the truth remained harsh. Finally, she settled on tough truth delivered as gently as possible.

```
Sorry for telegram
Circumstances changed dramatically
Will not return
I pray you find a good wife who will be
better suited than I
Will send letter soon
```

Reginald would need more than she could express in the shortened words of a telegram already expensively long. But at least he would know quickly. She selected the second paper and addressed it to Mother.

```
Letter received
Will stay
Informed RM no wedding
Resuming monthly stipend
Funds included
```

She included three months' worth of the allowance Mother had received from her father and would continue to send money each month. Mother would be cared for in the manner she always had been. Better, actually, since she would need to care only for herself now. The Montgomerys would be scandalized and Mother's social standing bruised, but that couldn't be helped.

She paid for the delivery of the telegrams and met Melanie at the door.

"Feel better?" Melanie arched an eyebrow.

Lillian couldn't help but chuckle. "Yes, actually. I do."

They walked arm in arm back to the house, enjoying the sunshine and the pleasant day. Lillian slowed as they neared the residence. "Jonah did a wonderful job. The house looks so much more inviting now."

The shutters hung straight and the porch step no longer sagged. Melanie had even planted a few flowers along the front, giving the hint of what the house could soon be.

Her new home.

Well, not a home. A business. This was Melanie's home.

Lillian released a sigh. She couldn't stay at the Watsons' house forever, much as she cared for them. And even though she hadn't decided if she would stay in Dawsonville permanently or just get the business started, she would eventually have to figure out her own living arrangements. She wouldn't return to living with Mother.

Melanie stood beside her, studying the house. "Your father's room is ready whenever you decide to move in," she said softly.

Had Melanie read her thoughts? Lillian supposed they would be rather obvious. She closed her eyes for a couple of heartbeats. Living together? How would that work?

"The girls and I can leave, if you'd rather."

Lillian was shaking her head before her thoughts even had a chance to form. She wouldn't push them out, especially since they had nowhere to go. Staying with others in a house couldn't be all that different from boarding in a hotel, could it?

"I'll ask Jonah to move my stuff when we come back in the morning."

Melanie smiled, and a feeling of rightness seeped into Lillian. She looked up at the house again as they moved through the yard. Her new home, at least for a time. A bit of her father that she could share.

The living arrangement easily settled, they stepped into the house. Knowing Lillian would need time alone, Melanie gave her arm a squeeze and headed toward the kitchen.

In the large room that would soon be her bookshop, Lillian settled on the floor in the curve of the bay window and pulled her father's letter from her bag. The handwriting on the front pronounced her name in blocky script. She tugged the seal open and unfolded a page filled with the same handwriting.

My dear daughter Lillian,

The line immediately brought tears to her eyes. His dear daughter? How dear could someone be whom you refused to meet? She blinked to clear her eyes.

There are so many things I want to tell you—things I should have told you years ago. It's too late now. I've made some changes that will not be taken well, and I doubt I will survive long enough to finally do the right thing by you. This letter, which I will place under the secure care of my solicitor, is the best I can do. I can only pray you can forgive me, as God has in his mercy.

Perhaps I should start from the beginning. As a young

man, I had more ambition than opportunity and often found myself in one sort of situation or another. It happened one night that I met an intriguing city woman with a coy smile who was far above my station. Our affair was a short-lived thing, one that should have never been.

When we discovered you would be born, Florence's parents disowned her. They would not accept me as a suitable husband and claimed Florence had been ruined. They cast her out with instructions never to see them again.

Florence was enraged, claiming that I should have been able to convince her father otherwise. I should have found a way to make myself respectable and marry her. I tried, but the only options that would bring us what we needed quickly were not entirely legal. And she would not marry me penniless.

Lillian breathed deep, trying to digest the words. Her grandparents had cast her mother out because of her.

I found your mother a house in Atlanta but had to immediately leave on an expedition in order to cover the debts I had incurred. What should have been months turned into three years. By the time I returned, Florence had created a life for herself and our child. She refused to let me see you. I cannot blame her. I would have only brought my troubles to my family.

She had found another man to love, one who she said would be able to care for her. At the time, I did not know he was also in the same organization that became my downfall. It is my fault he died, and Florence never forgave me for it. She threatened to expose my deeds and all the information she knew about my employer.

If only she knew how dangerous those threats were—to her and to you. So we worked out a deal that I would stay far from both of you and make sure you were both cared for. I'm sorry that has come to an end.

My last allotment of funds sent to your mother included a note explaining that I had determined to make drastic changes in my life and would no longer send her money. My deepest hope was to come to you as a reformed man and share these things in person. I wanted to have the opportunity to get to know you and care for you myself. If you are reading this letter, however, then that hope did not come to pass and my worst suspicions have proved true. I am sorry for all that we missed.

I can only hope by now you have grown to be a strong and independent woman. Maybe my own mother's fortitude flows in your veins.

Eventually the past catches up to all of us, and sooner or later luck runs out. All I can leave you is a business I have scrubbed clean and a home that is yours if you want it. I wish for you a happy and long life. I wish I could have known you. I always loved you.

Your father,
Floyd

Lillian clutched the letter to her chest and cried.

CHAPTER EIGHTEEN

———— ❧ ————

L illian had wanted answers. But as she dried her tears, she was no longer so sure. Answers didn't bring her peace. If anything, after reading her father's letter she had even more questions. Who had Mother been before meeting him? What would cause her parents to send their child away as though she meant nothing to them, leaving her to face a difficult situation alone? What kind of grandparents didn't want an innocent child?

What mess had her father gotten into, and what exactly did he mean about scrubbing the company clean? Did Mr. Tanner know?

Lillian pinched the bridge of her nose, a headache forming between her eyes. She tried to shake her head to clear away the wave of questions, but they kept coming, one right after another.

What had happened to the man her mother had loved after her father? He'd said he was responsible for that man's death.

Lillian groaned and leaned her head against the wall, fighting the ache in the back of her throat and the burn behind her eyes. Sunlight filtered through the bay window and caressed her cheeks, but its warmth didn't provide her with any comfort.

Perhaps it was better if she didn't know the details. She couldn't change the past or rectify any of the situations that had led to this moment. Knowing the sordid details of her parents' relationship wouldn't change the decisions she'd made.

Except . . . if her parents' past cast a shadow on her inheritance—on the company she now partially owned and was thus responsible for—she needed to know.

Lillian tucked the letter away in her skirt pocket for safekeeping and dug deep within herself until she located a pinch of fortitude. She pushed herself up onto her feet. One step at a time.

First, she needed to finish sorting through the last of her father's possessions. She settled on the floor again and unpacked the first crate from her father's study, looking for any clues about his secret life. She found documents of all sorts, including receipts, account ledgers, missives, and various calling cards for businessmen all over the state. All appeared legitimate, at least to her untrained eye. She didn't locate a single personal letter or anything that might suggest an item of sentimental value.

The second and final crate contained miscellaneous items like a shaving kit and cream, a man's comb, a pair of cufflinks, and a small notebook that contained nothing more than a few reminders for needed purchases.

Lillian sighed and tucked the business items inside the crate she would set aside for Mr. Tanner. The other items she gathered to take out to the front porch. Someone from the church was coming by today to collect the donations.

She brushed her hands down her skirt and rolled her neck

to release some of the tension. The task of going through her father's things, which she had considered nearly unsurmountable when they'd first started, had now been completed. The house and belongings had been sorted and organized, cleaned, and put to proper use.

Now on to the next step.

Lillian found Melanie in the kitchen, scrubbing a clean table. She glanced up as Lillian entered, took one look at Lillian's face, and scuttled over to wrap her in a hug.

How terrible must she look?

Overcoming her surprise, Lillian returned the embrace, soon finding herself melting into the offered comfort.

Melanie rubbed small circles on her back. "It'll all turn out all right, dear. You'll see."

The soft words unraveled the composure Lillian tried to maintain. She clung to Melanie for a long time, tears dampening the woman's shoulder. The letters, her father's belongings . . . the day had weighed on her even more than she'd realized.

She didn't know how long they stood there, but by the time she was ready to straighten herself once again, the loneliness that had so long encased her heart had begun to melt.

Melanie grasped her shoulders. "You're a good girl, Lillian. Kind, thoughtful, and you've got an independent streak buried in you that I can't wait to see find its way out." Her eyes brimmed with sincerity. "God has plans for you."

Lillian swallowed, her throat too thick to speak the gratitude simmering inside. But Melanie seemed to understand it. She smiled brightly and released Lillian's shoulders.

"Now then." She clapped her hands together. "I've made the bed in your room and took up some of your father's quilts. We need to decide which of the dressers you want, and of course you'll need that little secretary."

The words washed over Lillian in a rush, and she barely had time to nod along before Melanie launched into another flurry of hand motions and excited pronouncements.

"He didn't have a lady's dressing table, of course, but you can always get one of those later." She walked out of the kitchen, and Lillian followed her into the dining room. "I think you should take that big wardrobe there." She pointed to a heavy oak piece with sturdy construction and a man's penchant for straight lines and minimal frills. "Then keep this smaller one here for storing linens and things we will need downstairs."

Lillian lost all thoughts of the past as they dove into their future plans. She enjoyed mentally arranging her new living space and discussing how they would organize the remaining furniture for their new customers.

They set to work moving the smaller furnishings and scrubbing every inch of the dining room, even though Jonah would make another mess as soon as he picked up that hammer again. They planned to enlarge the kitchen and create a more usable divider between the public bakery display space and work areas in the rear.

Soon the light streaming through the window underneath Lillian's polishing rag turned dusky.

"What time is it?" She pushed a loose lock of hair from her forehead. "Wasn't Jonah supposed to be back this afternoon?"

Melanie frowned. "He must have had more to do at the farm than he anticipated." She glanced around, just now seeming to notice the late hour as well. "Without the girls coming in to remind me of the time, it completely slipped away from me."

Oh. Right. Lillian had forgotten all about the girls. How

terrible of her not to have even noticed their absence. "Where are they off to today?"

"They're staying the night with the McClellan family. Martha's got two girls about the same age, and tomorrow they're all going on a hike up to the Amicalola Falls." Melanie laughed when Lillian's stomach growled loudly. "We better get something in you before you faint clean away."

They fell into easy conversation about the local waterfall and how much the girls would enjoy the trip as they made their way into the kitchen and washed up. Melanie produced various vegetables for Lillian to chop while she readied the stove and filled a pot with water.

A thump sounded from somewhere in the house.

Lillian paused with her knife halfway through an onion. "Jonah must be back. I'll go light a lamp for him." She wiped her hands on her apron and bustled out the kitchen door. She grabbed the lamp Melanie kept at the base of the stairs and lit the wick, turning the knob to flood the foyer with inviting light.

The entryway was empty.

Odd. She could have sworn she heard the front door close. Lillian strode forward and opened the latch. Perhaps Jonah had been stomping around on the porch. The man could be as loud as a horse clomping up the stairs.

The porch and street beyond the yard stood empty, the cart and horse nowhere to be seen. The boxes she'd left for the church had already been carted away sometime earlier.

Perhaps she'd imagined the noise. Lillian closed the door and started back toward the kitchen when a scuffling sound came from the other room. Her heart quickened.

She lifted the lantern higher. "Melanie?"

"Yes?" Her reply sounded from the back of the house, in

the direction of the kitchen. Opposite from where Lillian had heard the sound.

The rapid pounding of her heart lurched into a full gallop. Was there someone in the parlor?

Lillian chided herself. This wasn't Atlanta. Dawsonville was a quiet, sleepy town full of well-meaning neighbors and friendly people.

Still, her nerves tingled as she took a step forward. Best to simply go see the cause. Otherwise she'd worry herself to no end.

Maybe something had fallen. Or a cat had slipped inside. The one she'd kept for a short time when she was a girl had been prone to jumping onto places it shouldn't be and making a ruckus.

Lillian lifted the light cautiously in front of her, trying to see around the corner.

Her body suddenly lurched backward. A scream ripped from her throat as the lamp flew from her fingers. Feet tangling in her skirt, Lillian landed on the floor, her head slamming hard.

She blinked as a dark figure darted around her. Her vision swam as an ache swelled in the back of her head.

Then everything went black.

CHAPTER NINETEEN

An entire day gone. Jonah stretched his stiff back and shifted on the hard wagon seat. It would be simpler to ride, but Lillian didn't care to sit on a horse. She would probably be spitting mad at him for being so late. He should have had her returned to the Watson house before dark. Now they would have to travel at night, and who knew what city ladies thought about something like that.

The wagon bumped over the rutted road, passed through the town square, then eased along the short distance to the Jackson/Doyle/Peterson residence. He shook his head. They really needed to straighten out those details.

Jonah reined Mist to a stop and hopped down from the wagon. With a business here, he'd need to put in a good hitching post. Maybe even take up a portion of the yard for a small stabling area. There wouldn't be any room for automobiles, but there weren't too many of those around anyway. Most people could leave their conveyances in town and walk.

Mist nickered as he passed by, and he gave the mare a good pat. She also preferred a saddle to a harness.

The front door swung open and a tall, lanky figure darted out.

What in the—

Before Jonah could finish his thought, shouts rose from inside. Ma's shouts.

He lurched forward, hurdling himself over the short fence as the figure leapt off the porch. Jonah lunged for him, but the man skipped sideways, landing just out of his reach. Jonah shouted and spun.

The black-clad man, a bandana tied over his lower face, let out a low curse as he stumbled, but he regained his footing and shot through the front gate.

Mist snorted and pawed the ground as Jonah ran past her in pursuit of the fleeing figure. The man was fast. He was already putting distance between them.

"Jonah!"

Ma's shout came from the house, pulling him to a stop. He growled as the intruder slipped around a corner, then he spun and darted back the other direction.

An unnatural glow flowed through the front door, spilling onto the porch. He stumbled to a halt, taking in the scene in a glance.

Ma stomping out small flames.

Lillian sprawled on the floor.

A broken lantern.

He leapt into action, swinging his jacket off his shoulders and throwing it over a sputtering flame. After a moment, he had the threat squelched. Scorch marks marred the surface of the wood floor and smoke tinged the air, but the damage was minimal.

Ma knelt beside Lillian's crumpled form, gently rubbing her shoulder.

"What happened?"

Ma startled at his barked words but kept her gaze on Lillian. "She said she heard you at the door. Next thing I know there was a scream and pounding footsteps. When I got here, she was on the floor, the lamp was broken, and the front door was open."

Lillian moaned.

"Are you all right?" Ma gently pushed the hair from Lillian's face as the younger woman groaned some kind of answer.

Ma waved a hand at him. "Go fetch Doc Andley."

Jonah couldn't tear his eyes away from Lillian. She looked so fragile. Tender and beautiful and . . . hurting.

He snapped himself out of the strange trance that had held him in place and turned toward the door.

"Wait."

He spun back at Lillian's word.

"I don't need the doctor."

Ma shook her head, cutting off Lillian's protest before Jonah could. "You hit your head."

"I'm all right." Lillian tried for a smile for Ma, but her lips trembled. "Truly."

Ma lifted her eyebrows in defiance, and Jonah turned back toward the door.

"It smarts, but I doubt the doctor can do much about that." Lillian's voice shook. "And . . . I'd rather you not leave right now."

Fury snaked through Jonah's gut, releasing venom and causing his muscles to bunch. Whoever had done this to her would soon regret it.

Lillian glanced toward the door, eyes shining with unshed tears. "Did you see him?"

"He escaped." The words came out of Jonah's throat in a growl. "I'll get the doctor. And the sheriff."

He'd made three steps toward the door when Lillian's voice stopped him again. "And leave us here unprotected?" Desperation clung to her words and raked across him. "Really, I don't need the doctor. And you can talk to the sheriff in the morning, right?"

He paused, the desire to protect her battling with the need to see her attacker brought to justice. He risked another look at her, and that single glance had the effect he knew it would.

Those wide, luminous eyes looked up at him. Scared. Vulnerable.

He couldn't leave her.

He gave a curt nod, struggling with the emotions raging within him. He had every intention of hunting down the man who'd hurt her. The man could stand to sport a few bruises of his own when Jonah hauled him to the sheriff.

Though he'd likely never catch him now. The thought that he'd let the blackguard escape clenched his stomach into a sour knot.

Ma helped Lillian to her feet and gently prodded the back of her skull with her fingers. When Lillian winced in pain, it took far more self-control than Jonah had thought possible to keep his feet rooted to the floor.

"You're sure you don't want Doc Andley to have a look, dear?" Ma spoke gently.

"If I'm not better in an hour," Lillian finally consented.

Jonah assessed the damage while Ma looked Lillian over, but he found himself unable to keep his gaze from returning to Lillian. He'd deal with the damage first thing in the morning and repair any reminder of the scare they'd had. He wanted them to feel safe. Which they probably wouldn't for the re-mainder of the night.

Ma gave a sigh. "If that's what you want." She lifted a finger. "But first sign I think something's wrong, young lady, and I'll have Jonah haul you right off to the doctor."

A ghost of a smile tickled the corner of Lillian's mouth. "Yes, ma'am."

"Once we are sure you're well," Jonah said, "we'll get you both to the Watson farm." Good thing the girls weren't here tonight. The situation would have been worse if they—

"We aren't going anywhere." Ma used that voice she directed at his sisters when she expected immediate obedience.

"He'll come back as soon as we're gone." Lillian's protest held a thread of angst.

Jonah's gaze darted between the two stubborn females wear-ing determination like armor. He would never understand women. They had both clearly been frightened, and Lillian was hurt. Why would they want him to protect them yet refuse his method of doing so?

"It's not safe." Didn't they understand that until he had the chance to alert the sheriff and find the intruder, he couldn't let them stay?

Ma stared at him with her hands on her hips, and Lillian crossed her arms, expression rueful. As though *he* was the one who didn't understand the nature of the situation.

"He's gone now." Ma scrubbed the toe of her shoe across the soot on the floor and frowned. "And he won't come back as long as you're here to keep watch."

"Yes," Lillian agreed far too quickly. "That's most likely the case."

He glanced between them again, but they apparently considered the matter settled. Lillian joined Ma in looking at the damage on the floor, the disappointment in her eyes another stab.

"I'd feel better if you stayed at the Watson farm." Why did his voice sound so gravelly? "And they are expecting you back."

Lillian's gaze slammed into him. She studied him a moment, then slowly shook her head. "There's no point going tonight. And besides, your mother and I have decided I will live here. In my father's room."

The statement took a moment to settle in. She planned to live here? For how long?

A topic of discussion for another time.

"I can't leave a houseful of women unguarded." He held up a hand to stay Ma's protest. "And I mean beyond tonight. I've never been comfortable with you and the girls this far away. Now that someone has broken in . . ." His jaw tightened. He didn't need to finish the statement.

Ma shook her head so forcefully that she loosened one of her hairpins and the pile of curls on her head toppled at an odd angle. "And you won't." Again she used that tone that brooked no argument. "You'll stay here with us."

He got the feeling Ma also meant something more permanent than tonight. She was probably right. He could talk to Lewis in the morning. If someone had broken into the house—which must have something to do with Lillian and whatever Floyd had been hiding—then he had no choice but to spend his nights here.

Jonah's gaze drifted to the parlor where they'd found the hidden book.

"You don't think . . . . ?" Lillian's voice said she'd come to the same conclusion.

"We need to keep that book safe until we figure out what it is."

"What book?" Ma asked.

"We found a book in the wall when Jonah widened the parlor." Lillian thumbed toward the kitchen. "I stashed it in the cupboard. It was filled with nonsense, but . . ." Lillian's words trickled away, and Ma paled.

Thankfully, Ma didn't demand to know more. Right now they needed to secure the house and make sure Lillian was all right. The intruder likely hadn't found the book hidden in the kitchen since Ma hadn't seen him there, but they'd check to be certain.

Lillian wrapped her arms around herself, and Jonah had the strangest desire to encase her in his own embrace. The sensation was so strong he took two steps in her direction before he stopped himself.

Tonight proved one thing. Lillian Doyle had firmly entrenched herself into his life.

Lillian's head pounded. Not that she would admit it and have Jonah leaving them to fetch the doctor. Or think her some sort of incapable damsel. Lillian liked her share of dime romances, but she certainly didn't fancy herself a helpless female in distress. Even if Jonah might make a striking hero.

In truth, she didn't want him to leave, and though she had a fierce headache, she didn't really need medical attention. She'd be fine.

She followed Melanie back into the kitchen while Jonah sputtered something behind them about needing to inform the Watsons and fetch her belongings, then something only slightly intelligible about the locks on the doors.

Melanie took Lillian's elbow and guided her onto a stool at their prep table. "Sit there while I make you a rousing tea, and then I'll get some soup in you."

A few moments later Melanie set a steaming cup in front of Lillian. Had she moved that quickly, or had Lillian been sitting with her head in her hands for longer than she'd thought?

"Chamomile with ginger root and clove. My mother swore it could cure any ache and ailment, but I think it works best for headaches."

"Thank you." Lillian accepted the offering and blew the steam from the top. "Do you think Jonah is upset with us?"

Melanie paused with a heavy wooden spoon over a steaming iron pot. "What makes you think that?"

Lillian took a slow sip, the tea plenty warm but not scalding. The taste was slightly bitter but still pleasant. "He didn't seem out of sorts to you?"

"Of course he is." Melanie stirred vigorously. "We all are. Someone sneaking around where they don't belong is plenty cause for concern." She tapped the spoon on the edge of the pot. "Men get snippy when they're angry, that's all."

Lillian wasn't so sure. Something about the way he'd looked at them suggested at least a portion of his ire had been directed their way.

Not that she had the energy to untangle the reason. She focused on sipping her tea. Men were unpredictable at best and rarely understandable.

Pounding sounded from the other room, and Lillian winced. Her pulse seemed to be trying to keep the rhythm, jarring in her skull with each sound. When the racket finally stopped, she breathed a sigh of relief. The pain in her head eased considerably with the quiet.

A moment later, Jonah stalked into the room. Every movement about him signaled a warning, almost like a wolf attempting to look tame but failing. From the tight set of his shoulders and jaw to the way his feet prowled across the floor, he exuded fierceness.

Perhaps not a wolf. Maybe a lion. The cat she'd hidden from Mother for a few weeks had also moved like that when it found a mouse.

Lillian forced her eyes to her tea. She was imagining all sorts of stories.

"I'll need to get a better lock, but for tonight I have the door barred, and I tacked down the lower-floor windows." Jonah paused, and Lillian could feel his eyes boring into her. She refused to meet his gaze, and after another heartbeat he spoke again. "I'll stay up and keep watch."

Melanie ladled vegetable soup into a bowl and lifted the steaming meal toward her son. He hesitated, but Melanie stood there until he finally accepted and nodded his thanks.

"No need to stay awake all night, Son."

His brows furrowed as though she'd lost her marbles. "Someone must."

Melanie heaved a sigh. "No, someone *mustn't*." She placed a funny emphasis on that last word. "You've secured the house. You need to sleep."

"It's my responsibility." His words were low. He leaned against the table, still holding the bowl of soup like he had no intention of tasting it.

He caught her watching him, and she looked away. Why had the intruder troubled him to this degree? They were all unhappy about it, certainly, but Jonah took the incident much harder than the women. Maybe because he begrudged the inconvenience of staying?

Thinking to set him at ease, Lillian summoned her most appreciative smile. "Yes, you have done enough. You can return to the farm. It's all right."

Jonah's eyes flashed.

Oh dear. That was not the reaction she'd expected.

"I will not abandon you." His nostrils flared. "And I will always see to it that my mother and sisters are safe."

She hadn't wanted him to leave. But she didn't want to feel like she was making him stay either.

Lillian slowly lowered her tea to the table and regarded the man across the kitchen—the dutifully responsible son who clearly loved his mother and sisters. Tonight she'd witnessed the intensity of his loyalty. And having him blanket that same kind of concern over her warmed her insides. This fierce protectiveness brought out something warrior-like in him. He would do anything to defend those he loved.

"Of course you'll stay." Melanie stirred the simmering pot. "I do wish we could send word to Alma, though. She will worry."

Lillian's heart pounded. She barely registered Melanie's words as her and Jonah's gazes remained locked. No matter how she tried, she couldn't look away. Was this what it felt like to be cared for by a man? For him to want to do anything in his power to shield her from harm? She'd always imagined it to be something a father would do. A brother too, perhaps.

But . . . she was no sister to him.

I will not abandon you.

The statement clung to her in a way it should not. Swallowing hard, she managed to break the strange intimacy of their eye contact and focused on her tea.

Lillian purposely kept her eyes off Jonah as Melanie spooned another two bowls of soup and set them on the table. After a moment of silence, her voice carried over them. "Father, we thank you for protecting us tonight. For the fire doing little damage. For Lillian being mostly unharmed. Thank you for my loving son, who does so much for those under his care. Bless us, that we may honor you with our lives each day."

Strange tears burned Lillian's eyes, and when she lifted her gaze she found Jonah staring at her.

Heaven help her, but she could have sworn she saw something almost yearning in his gaze. But as suddenly as the look blazed, it vanished beneath hooded eyes cast toward the table.

Lillian's heart lurched, and she had the distinct feeling she'd never look at Jonah Peterson quite the same again.

CHAPTER TWENTY

L illian wasn't quite the delicate flower Jonah had imagined. Nor was she too prissy to dirty her hands. She successfully hammered in her third nail, and Jonah smiled, pride in her accomplishment swelling.

Four days since the incident and she showed no signs of lingering head injury. She hummed to herself as she selected another nail and carefully placed it in the center of the wood plank as he'd taught her.

Something had changed between them that night. Something he couldn't quite describe and yet found himself constantly looking for. A sly glance his way. The twitching of her lips into a genuine smile. Bit by bit he'd watched her shell fall away and something truly beautiful emerge from within.

Lillian looked up, catching him watching her.

He held her gaze, surprised that he didn't feel embarrassed at having been caught staring. "You're getting good at that." He chuckled. "Pretty soon I can leave all the construction to you."

Her sweet laughter echoed through the room. "Hardly. I'd pity the person trying to place a book on a shelf built by my hand." A playful gleam entered Lillian's eyes. "Besides, I already have you."

The words slammed into his gut and caused his breath to snag.

She meant she had him for building projects. He knew that. Still, the sentiment wedged inside him and lodged there.

He loved his mother and adored his sisters. Had always wanted to protect and provide for them. Yet deep inside he'd longed for that duty to lessen to the degree that he could follow his own path. His own dreams.

Why, then, did he find himself wanting to apply that same duty to Lillian? Only, with her it didn't feel as much a responsibility as a longing. A desire to shelter her under the umbrella of his care so that she could grow and bloom.

The feeling surged within him, and he caught himself shaking his head.

"What? You don't plan on building for us anymore?" She cocked her head to the side. "Despite what you said, you really are quite good at it."

Best if he let her think that was where his thoughts had gone. "Maybe you're right." He offered a tired grin.

Lillian returned his smile, though hers held a wariness. She didn't resume humming as she steadied her nail.

The night the intruder had broken in had shaken him in a way he still didn't understand. And since that night, he'd made a sleeping space in the front parlor. The Watsons had hired a temporary man to work in his stead, and he'd spent every moment here.

With her. Growing comfortable occupying the same living space. Working side by side. Sharing amused glances whenever Betsy said something silly or Ma made one of her predictions about what the future would hold.

Lillian bumped her shoulder into his, and his eyes shot up from where he'd been dumbly staring at his hammer. When had she gotten that close? The subtle scent of something floral—jasmine, perhaps, or honeysuckle?—mingled with the earthy aroma of the sawdust.

"I think Melanie is making those turnovers you like so much for tonight," she said.

Jonah forced himself to think about something other than Lillian's sweet aroma. Or the way that one stray lock of hair fell across her cheek. "My stomach is rumbling just thinking about it."

Lillian playfully squeezed his arm. "Mine too."

He was staring at her again. Lillian turned her face toward him. Only inches away. Her eyelashes fluttered.

"Did you make any more of that bread?" Jonah stepped back, searching for something else to say before she noticed emotions that he wasn't ready to share warring inside him. "I've never had any like it." She managed to make the loaf light and fluffy with a bit of nutty flavor.

Lillian watched him with a strange look.

He threw out another set of pointless words. "Those are going to sell well."

"I did make more." The playfulness in her tone melded into something more. "Just for you." She tilted her head back, her lips parting slightly.

The desire to kiss her nearly overtook him like a scorching fire in his chest. "Lillian—"

"That man's here again!" Betsy's voice sliced through the air, breaking the intensity of the moment.

Lillian blinked, perhaps coming out from under the same

spell. She stepped back, her hands twisting nervous folds in her dress. Had she wanted the kiss as much as he had?

Jonah could punch whoever had come to the door at such an inopportune moment. More so if it was that slimy Mr. Tanner again. Lillian had already turned down his offer for the house.

"It's Mr. Tanner!" Betsy's voice came from the front door, cheery as always.

Jonah and Lillian shared a look. She appeared as pleased at Mr. Tanner's arrival as he was.

They walked to the door together, Jonah taking deliberately long breaths to try to tame the heat inside him. Outside, the very man he'd hoped not to see stood on the porch, thumbs hooked through his suspenders and a straw hat tilted back on his head.

"Afternoon, Miss Doyle, Mr. Peterson." Mr. Tanner nodded to them in turn. "Fine day, isn't it?"

Betsy ran down into the yard where Ma was planting flowers. Seemed Lillian had found a bucket of some kind of purple bloom the two of them liked. Lord only knew from where.

"It is." Lillian closed the door behind her. "How can we help you?"

Mr. Tanner smiled broadly. "I've come with a final offer for you. One I believe you will find more than fair."

"No thank you. I won't be selling."

Jonah inwardly cheered at Lillian's quick answer.

"Not even if the sum gives you enough to purchase a much larger building right in the center of town?" Mr. Tanner rocked back on his heels, clearly pleased with himself. "I've made all the arrangements. It's far better suited to your venture."

Lillian hesitated, sharing a look first with Jonah and then

seeking Ma's gaze. "I'd have to discuss it with my business partner, but my inclination is to stay." She gave a small shrug. "I like it here."

Mr. Tanner's eyes tightened around the corners. Why was the man so determined to get this house? Were there more secrets hidden inside, or was he after the book they'd found in the wall?

He turned to Jonah. "Surely you see the wisdom in more money and a larger facility. Women can be too sentimental for business, don't you agree?"

"I say the lady can put her business wherever she chooses." He shrugged. "That's her decision."

Lillian favored him with a warm smile that caused another round of heat in his chest. It faded as she faced Mr. Tanner again. "You're quite intent on purchasing the residence."

"Sentimental value, of course." Mr. Tanner nodded emphatically.

Jonah almost didn't contain the laugh that tried to jump from his throat. Which of them was too sentimental for business now?

From Lillian's suspicious expression, she thought the same, but she kept her tone professional. "I have, however, decided to sell you my father's portion of the shipping business—"

"Splendid!"

Lillian held up a hand. "With stipulations."

"Stipulations?" A crease formed above Mr. Tanner's nose. Perhaps he hadn't thought a woman capable of coming up with any sort of condition on his offer.

"First, according to the bank's assessment, my father's portion of the company is worth at least six times what you offered."

Mr. Tanner's face clouded.

"I ask for the four thousand you offered for the house for my part of the company. Still a deal for you and a better one for me."

After a slight hesitation, Mr. Tanner nodded.

"And second, I wish to maintain ten percent of the ownership, so I'll be selling you fifty percent, not all sixty." Lillian's spine hardened into that perfect posture she still used on occasion.

What was she up to? Jonah shared a look with Ma, but she seemed as confused as he. Betsy tugged on Ma's skirts, trying to get her to go look at a butterfly.

Mr. Tanner scoffed. "You cannot think to have any controlling say with so little a share."

Lillian laced her fingers in front of her. "I will not interfere in the daily affairs and have no interest in voicing a say. I merely want ten percent of the share of profits."

Clever girl. Not only would she receive a sum up front, but she would continue to have a stipend after. She would do far better in business than Jonah had imagined. Certainly had a better mind for it than he did. What would a simple farmer be able to offer her?

The thought clawed into his growing swell of affection for Lillian, and he had to force it down.

Mr. Tanner's eyes narrowed at Lillian. "And if I refuse?"

Lillian shrugged. "That's your choice, of course. Just as it's my choice for who to instate to run Mr. Jackson's share of the company. Or who else I might sell it to, I suppose."

Ha! Jonah wanted to cheer. He caught Ma's strangled snort of laughter, and she quickly turned away. Mr. Tanner didn't seem to notice. He focused on Lillian with eyes now mere slits.

Then, as quickly as a hare darting from a shrub, Mr. Tanner's features turned friendly once more. He thrust out his hand. "You are your father's daughter indeed. We have a deal."

Face impassive, Lillian took the man's hand and shook it. "Excellent. Mr. Carson has offered his services should I ever need them, so I'll head to town first thing tomorrow to ask him to draw up the necessary legal contracts."

"Contracts? When we've given a word and a handshake?" Mr. Tanner frowned.

"Which all parties will honor, I'm sure." Jonah pushed off the wall where he'd been leaning. "I do believe Miss Doyle's idea will make things easier, though, especially given she won't be involved in the business's affairs."

The gleam Jonah had been looking for flashed across Mr. Tanner's eyes. He didn't want Lillian poking around in the business. Why? Merely a matter of pride? Some men thought women had no place in business. While Mr. Tanner was likely of that ilk, Jonah sensed there was something more.

That greasy smile pulled over the man's features again. "Quite so. A simple matter. I have no objection since it will make the lady more comfortable." He tugged his hat over his brow. "And you are certain that you don't wish to part with the house, Miss Doyle?"

She drew a breath. "Yes, sir."

He shook his head as though she'd made a poor choice. "Very well. Good day to you." He nodded to Jonah, the merest acknowledgment.

Betsy waved at the man as he exited the yard, then she and Ma returned to the porch. Ma's eyes sparkled with victory, her gaze telling Jonah she'd been right all along.

Jonah couldn't help but share in the sense of victory. Maybe, for once, the circumstances thrust upon him would turn out to be something he enjoyed after all.

She'd handled that well.

Lillian swept back inside, satisfaction dancing through her. With the funds from Mr. Tanner, she'd be able to order them a large stove. Two, possibly, as well as the iceboxes. And with the steady income from the business, she wouldn't have to worry over spending so much of the money up front. If nothing else, she would always be able to use her portion of the company to care for Mother, leaving the shop entirely to herself and Melanie.

Lillian paused in the doorway to the large room that would be her bookshop. The necessary floorboards had been repaired, and she could hardly even tell where the much smaller door had once been. Jonah had done a wonderful job creating a large cased opening that made the two rooms feel much more like one.

The entire back wall would be for bookshelves, and then of course there would be a few freestanding ones throughout. She tapped a finger on her chin, planning out where to arrange the shelves so that they created a couple of cozy little nooks, with a chair inside for young girls to curl up in their own little worlds.

"Have it all mapped out?"

Jonah's voice behind her snagged her from her thoughts. Her heartbeat quickened. From being startled, or something else?

"Almost." Lillian let her gaze roam the room. "I can still

scarcely believe it. This isn't at all what I'd planned when I came to Dawsonville."

"Ma always says that God already knows the plan. Best we get on board." He chuckled, a deep sound that came from his chest and made Lillian want to place her fingers there to feel it.

"I admire her faith," she said. "I don't know if I would have remained as hopeful as she with so many trials."

Jonah nodded slowly, something churning behind his eyes. "I admire her as well, even if I often have a hard time understanding."

They stood in silence a moment, each in their own thoughts. Lillian inched toward him, the draw something she could no longer deny. Her already thudding heart picked up a staccato rhythm. Before Mr. Tanner came to the door, there had been something happening between them.

"Jonah?" She shifted her feet. Words she wanted to ask felt like molasses in her throat, taking too long to trickle out. "Do you . . . do you think she's right?"

Jonah's lips thinned into a line, and he took a moment to answer. "About what? Following heavenly plans or her idea that you and this shop are meant to be?"

"Both, I suppose."

"I don't know."

Disappointment flared, surprising her with its intensity. She'd been looking for him to say that he believed this was where she was meant to be. Here in this house. With his family.

With him.

Lillian swallowed, forcing the emotion down. She wouldn't fault him for honesty. The trait made him trustworthy, and she wouldn't disregard something just because it hadn't been what she wanted to hear.

She gave a tight nod and turned back to their building project. A little time focusing on a task would help her clear her thoughts.

They started back to work, him sawing boards and her hammering together brackets in the way he had shown her. These would be used for the shelves along the wall. The work was tiresome, and at the end of the day her back always protested, but the labor brought a certain sense of satisfaction.

Nine brackets later, her thoughts finally detached themselves from Jonah and settled on Mr. Tanner. His interest in the house had nothing to do with care for her father. More likely, he wanted the house because he knew about the ledger hidden in the wall.

But then, was the ledger so important that he would be willing to buy the house to get it? And if he was willing to do that, then . . .

Lillian lowered her hammer. He'd probably also be willing to break into the house to steal it. If he'd known where to find it. Lillian pinched the bridge of her nose.

The sound of Jonah's saw ceased.

Words popped out of Lillian's mouth as soon as quiet prevailed. "Do you think Mr. Tanner wanted this house because of that book we found in the wall?"

"I've considered it." Jonah rolled his shoulders, muscles bunching underneath his shirt.

Heat warmed Lillian's cheeks. "I've studied those pages several times, but I can't make any sense of it. And there wasn't anything in the rest of my father's belongings that helped."

Jonah nodded, face thoughtful. He rubbed the back of his neck, gaze glued to her. Too bad she couldn't read the thoughts behind those ocean-blue eyes.

The words of her father's letter swirled through her mind. All of it was connected. Maybe if she told Jonah about the letter, he would have an insight she'd missed.

Lillian studied the hammer in her hand, noting how her palms were starting to resemble its toughness. "My father left me a letter. In it, he said he had scrubbed the business clean." After a silent heartbeat, she met his eyes. "I don't know what that means."

A crease formed between Jonah's brows. "You think he was doing something illegal?"

"I can't find any evidence, but the letter also mentioned him doing things 'not entirely legal' in his past." She rubbed at a callus forming on her hand. "Do you think it was a bad idea to keep a portion of the company?"

He shook his head. "Just because we found a book we don't understand and your father referenced something vague doesn't mean you have anything to worry about."

Maybe. Lillian breathed out, wanting to feel relieved. The sensation refused to take hold.

"Maybe he meant he made things more efficient or got rid of endeavors that drained profit." Jonah's voice took on a smoothness, and Lillian appreciated his efforts to make her feel better. Even if they didn't work.

As much as she wanted to hold on to the scrap of love offered in the letter, the truth remained that her father had also alluded to criminal activities he'd been involved in. Apparently for most of her life. Maybe for most of his. Who was to say Mr. Tanner hadn't been as well? Perhaps still was.

The crunch of wagon wheels drew their attention to the window. Jonah strode over and peered outside.

"Are Alma and Edith here? I want to talk to Edith about

some of her recipes for the shop." Lillian ambled in Jonah's direction, glad for a diversion from the thoughts plaguing her. "We're considering serving a few simple meals during the day, and I . . ." She trailed off at Jonah's frown. "What? Who is it?" She tried to peer around him, but his wide shoulders blocked her view.

"I don't know. Fancy-looking lady."

Coldness poured through her. No. It couldn't be. Lillian grabbed Jonah's arm and tugged him aside.

The breath lodged in her throat.

Oh no.

Mother.

CHAPTER TWENTY-ONE

Lillian had turned to stone. Jonah put a hand on her shoulder and she jumped.

She sucked in a sharp breath. "This isn't good."

Jonah followed her gaze to the woman departing a two-wheeled carriage. He didn't see any of Lillian's features in her round face and sharp nose, but from Lillian's reaction, the woman could only be one person. "Your mother?"

"Yes." She scarcely breathed the word.

Was she truly so terrified of her own kin?

She fanned her face, mumbling something about regaining composure and cleaning herself up. He took her hand and she stilled.

"Lillian." He waited until her gaze fully settled on his. "You're capable and smart. I'm sure you and your mother can work out any differences between you."

Something flickered in her gaze. Hope? Along with a dose of skepticism. He squeezed her fingers for good measure. "I'll stall her for a few moments, if that helps."

The muscles in Lillian's neck tightened as she swallowed, then she nodded. "Thank you."

He released her hand. "Do you want me to keep her on the porch?"

Lillian's eyes widened in horror. "Oh, no. She'll insist on coming in." Her brow scrunched as she surveyed the room, clearly dismayed they lacked a seating area.

"It's a good day for sitting out back."

She brightened. "Yes. Lead her around the side of the house. I'll prepare a refreshment and be out presently."

Why did she suddenly sound stiff and formal? Jonah tried for an encouraging smile, but she had already turned and scuttled out of the room. She made a mad dash up the stairs just as a knock sounded at the door.

Jonah didn't bother hurrying. He casually pulled the door open, revealing a stout woman in a vivid blue dress. The breezy fabric pulled a bit too tight against her chest and shoulders, then fell in long drapes to her toes. The hat, however, demanded the most attention. He'd never seen one quite that wide. Or with so many flowers.

The woman glowered at him, not even a hint of friendliness smoothing the harsh lines of her face. "I'm here for Miss Lillian Doyle."

She spoke as though she'd come to fetch a wayward child who'd escaped chores. Jonah bristled. He almost yielded to the temptation to tell the woman Lillian wasn't there.

"Are you just going to stand there?" Dismissive eyes swept over him. "Let her know I've arrived."

The woman barked orders like she fancied herself royalty. Rebelliousness welled within him, and he had to practically seam his lips together before he told the woman to be on her way. But that would cause Lillian more trouble later, and Ma would likely try to swat him.

He unclamped his jaw. "Good afternoon, ma'am. I'm Jonah Peterson."

Her gaze raked over him as though he was beneath decent manners. She tilted her chin in a haughty way. "Mrs. Doyle." Another assessing sweep of dark brown eyes. "Are you under my daughter's employ?"

"No." At least, not in the manner she implied.

Mrs. Doyle's eyes narrowed. "They why are you here?"

"I'm helping with the construction."

"Construction?" She yelped the word and then fanned herself as though Jonah had said something scandalous. "Is this not the former home of Floyd Jackson?"

"It is."

"Does it now belong to my daughter, Miss Lillian Doyle?"

"It does."

Frustration boiled from her haughty features. "Then what sort of construction are you performing on my property?"

"Yours? I thought the property belonged to Lillian."

Red seared through the woman's cheeks. Apparently he'd just made an enemy.

Ma would say to love his enemies, and that thought alone had him forcing the closest thing to a patient smile he could muster. "Lillian asked me to escort you to the seating area on the back porch while she prepares a refreshment. I'm sure she can answer all of your questions."

"Fine then." She gave a little sniff. "Be on with it."

Insufferable woman. He gestured behind her. "It's around that way."

"Not through the house?" Confusion melted the hostility, and Jonah glimpsed what had probably once been a beautiful face. Then she scowled at him again.

He stepped out, forcing her to move back. "Construction, remember?"

She pinched her lips together. The expression made her look like she'd eaten a lemon. No wonder Lillian had reacted as she had to this termagant's arrival.

He led the woman around the side of the house and underneath the maple dividing this property from the elderly Mr. Ratliff's. He should put in some paving stones here for muddy days, in case Lillian wanted to take an outdoor path to the rear garden or allow her customers the option. He opened the gate at the back corner of the house and waited for Mrs. Doyle to pass inside before securing the latch behind them.

"And where am I to sit?" She looked around the space as though there weren't two rocking chairs on the porch, two tables set with six chairs each, and two benches surrounded by one of Ma's flower designs near the fence.

"Take your pick, I reckon." He gestured at the abundance of seating.

She sniffed again in a manner he doubted had anything to do with the fragrant flowers and lifted the edge of her skirt to mount the porch steps. She slowly lowered into one of the rockers, sitting so close to the edge Jonah wondered if she might fall off.

"Lillian will be here soon." He nodded as politely as he could and then hurried back to the gate.

The path around the side of the house would take longer, but it also kept him farther away from that bulldog of a woman. He slipped back inside the front door and waited. A few moments later Lillian descended, face scrubbed clean of any evidence of this morning's work.

She wore the dress she'd donned for church the past Sunday—

a cream-colored frock with long sleeves and a high neck. Bits of lace dotted the ends of the sleeves and the bottom third of the skirt.

Jonah's chest tightened. She was beautiful. "Sunday best?" A ridiculous question, but he couldn't seem to form anything else to say.

"She's on the porch? What did she say?" Lillian ran her hands down her skirt like her palms were sweating. She must have noticed his gaze. "I couldn't find my gloves. She won't like that." She tucked her hands behind her back as though he cared whether she wore gloves. She looked more nervous than a cornered mouse. "Did you tell her I would bring refreshments?"

"Yes. She's waiting on the rocking chair."

"Did she seem upset?"

Uppity and rude. More angry than anything. But he didn't want to fluster Lillian further. "She asked a lot of questions."

Lillian's eyes flew wide. "What did you tell her?"

"That you would answer."

"Very well. Thank you." She sucked in a sharp breath and marched toward the kitchen.

Stop being a coward! The self-admonishment did nothing to stiffen Lillian's spine. Her hands still trembled as she gathered the pitcher with iced tea and two glasses.

Lord, guide me in the thin space between honoring my mother and following this path I believe you've placed before me.

She opened the door and crammed as much cheer into her voice as she could. "Mother! What a surprise that you've come for a visit."

"Visit!" Mother sprang from her precarious perch on the rocking chair. "Don't play the little fool with me, Lillian Grace Doyle. You know precisely why I'm here."

So much for a veneer of pleasantries. Mother must be truly undone.

"I am not a fool." Lillian's voice was strong and steady.

"You are that and more." Mother stepped close, tilting her head back to glare at Lillian. "How dare you telegram Reginald and make a mockery of me."

Lillian stepped away from Mother's glower and placed one of the glasses on a small end table before pouring sweetened tea into the other. She offered the glass to Mother, who refused it with a scowl.

Lillian took a slow sip before answering. "Reginald needed to know I didn't intend to marry him." If Mother had told him on her own, none of this would have happened. Of course, that would have been the coward's way out. Even the short letter Lillian had written him, doing her best to explain her desire to stay in Dawsonville—at least for a time—and dissolve their relationship, had been a convenient way to avoid having to tell him in person.

Mother sputtered something about Lillian's complete lack of sense, and Lillian held up a hand. Shock rendered Mother quiet. Something that had never happened before.

"You're correct," Lillian said. "I should have come home and spoken to everyone instead of sending letters. For that, I am sorry, and I regret the problems my reluctance to do so garnered."

Mother opened her mouth to spout something more, but Lillian wasn't finished.

"I'll send for someone to gather my things. I won't be returning to Atlanta."

Crimson tinged Mother's cheeks, making her look like she'd spent too many hours in the sun. "After all I've done for you, this is how you treat me?"

The words raked across Lillian's heart, scratching and tearing at tender places that yearned for her mother's affection. "I made arrangements for you," she said softly. Every ounce of her being struggled to hold fast to her composure. "You will receive the same monthly allowance from me that you had from my father."

Mother pointed a finger. "While you take the rest for yourself?"

Hurt and anger grew in equal swells, and Lillian struggled to keep them at bay. "As my father intended."

"Why, you insufferable—"

"Take care with your words," Lillian snapped, "lest you find yourself not only without a portion of my inheritance but without my generous allowance as well."

Mother stared at her, mouth agape. When Lillian refused to be cowed, Mother gathered her skirts and stormed down the porch. "Don't bother sending after your things," she flung over her shoulder. "A rich heiress such as yourself has no need of any reminders of the life she's turning her back on."

Was she truly that angry? Because of Reginald or . . . ?

"I will visit, Mother. You won't be alone." The words raced after Mother's retreating form, but she didn't even pause.

Lillian sank into the chair, glass of warming iced tea still clutched tightly between her hands. Mother's anger would subside. She'd grow used to Lillian's newfound independence, and eventually they would find companionship again.

Perhaps.

The door opened a moment later, and the heavy tread of boots announced Jonah's presence. "Are you all right?"

The warm words glided over her. How long had she been sitting here staring at her glass? She looked up at him. "Not entirely. But I suppose I will be. With time."

He eased into the other rocking chair. "I'm sorry you don't have the support from family you deserve."

"Don't I?" A tiny smile tugged on her lips. "Edith and Alma are plenty supportive." And she'd come to think of Melanie and her beautiful girls as part of her extended family as well.

"They are. And you have us." He cleared his throat. "For what that's worth."

His support was worth more than he could know. So much had changed in such a short time. She had been gone from Atlanta merely two weeks, yet she felt like a new person. This town—these people—had opened up places within her that she would never again try to ignore.

"Thank you, Jonah." She searched his face, looking for a hint of the affection she'd seen swimming in his gaze on rare and special moments. "For all you've done. You've accepted a stranger into your life and trusted her with your mother and sisters. You've worked tirelessly to help us, even though you don't want to be here."

"What do you mean, I don't want to be here?" A crease formed between his brows, but there was a knowing look in his gaze.

"You had plans of your own that didn't include me. You wanted to go to electrical school and follow a different path. My coming here and my father's will changed all of that." She lifted her shoulders to let him know she understood. "Even so, you've given this venture your all, and for that I am exceedingly grateful."

No matter what twists and unexpected turns she found on the next steps of this adventure, she knew one thing. She would no longer face her challenges in fear. She wouldn't let her notions of how things *should* be make her desperate to control everything around her.

Lillian drew a deep breath of perfumed air and rose from her chair. "Now that that's settled, let's get back to work." She gathered the pitcher and glasses and tried not to let the heat of Jonah's lingering gaze make her wish her life's new direction headed straight into his embrace.

CHAPTER TWENTY-TWO

———————

S he thought he didn't want to be here.

Jonah laced his fingers together and stared at the calluses on his palms, Lillian's words repeating over and over in his mind. The statement was both accurate and as far from the truth as possible.

Before the fire, Jonah had been ready to finally take his chance at university. The girls had gotten old enough to help Ma more, and he'd saved up enough money to ensure their care. He'd wanted to learn the electrical trade and find work that would make sure Ma and the girls had all the things they deserved.

His sisters would have beautiful weddings.

Ma wouldn't have to work so hard.

The fire had taken that option from him, incinerating his dream along with the cabin his father had built. Then Ma had declared the house in town a blessing in disguise and said with the land and cabin gone, she could make a way for herself with her talent for baking and confections.

Jonah hadn't really known what to think of that.

He leaned back in the rocking chair and watched the

breeze play with the blooms along the fence. So much had changed since then. Nothing had gone as he'd planned. Or wanted.

A gentle tug on his spirit brought a sigh. That wasn't true. Ma had a house she'd fallen in love with. A wealthy heiress had provided all the trappings he could not.

Jonah closed his eyes, a realization coming to the surface and wounding him in a way he never would have expected.

They didn't need him anymore.

Why did the idea make his chest tighten and his stomach turn sour? Is that not what he'd wanted all this time? For Ma and the girls to have a better life, to step out of poverty and enjoy life a little more?

He'd always pictured himself providing that freedom for them. Not a spirited woman who had upended everything in their lives.

"You don't want to be here."

Lillian's declaration played on a loop through his mind. These past days spent working with her on the house had been more satisfying than he could have ever imagined. Certainly more so than his time working on the farm.

He rose from the chair. He had work to do. A bakery to start.

Then what?

They wouldn't need him anymore. The thought persisted, pushing down on him with unexpected weight. He'd be free to do as he wished.

Funny thing was, leaving no longer seemed as appealing.

Jonah rounded the house, thoughts peppering him like buckshot. The only answer he could garner for his reluctance to leave or chase the dream he'd always wanted contained no logic at all. He suddenly found himself wanting more than anything to be the kind of man Lillian Doyle deserved.

He returned to the front of the house to find Ma, Betsy, and Rose standing with Mrs. Doyle just outside the fence.

What in tarnation?

Jonah cut a glance at the house. If Lillian knew her mother remained, she didn't bother making herself available. Knowing Ma, she would try to force the Doyle women together and insist they work through their problems until one or both of them broke.

He didn't dare approach for fear Ma might force him to fetch Lillian. He'd as soon snag a kitten and deliver it to an alligator than make Lillian face Mrs. Doyle again today.

As he watched from his place near the maple tree, Ma and Mrs. Doyle finished speaking. With the slightest nod that could scarcely be considered polite, Mrs. Doyle mounted the rented carriage and steered the horse back toward town. Ma turned back to the house.

And spotted him.

Ignoring the churning in his gut, Jonah smiled at Rose and Betsy as they hurried through the yard with the energy of children and made their way inside. Ma waited for him on the front porch steps, her expression far too placid for someone who'd had to face the wrath of Mrs. Doyle.

"What happened?" Jonah rubbed the back of his neck in a vain effort to loosen the tension.

The smile lines that usually creased Ma's face sagged, making her appear more tired than he'd seen her in a while. She blew out a breath. "That woman makes loving your neighbor a challenge." She made the pronouncement with such exasperation that Jonah couldn't help but chuckle.

"I had a time myself." He pointed a thumb toward the house. "Lillian spoke with her, but I don't know much about it."

Ma placed a hand on his arm. "Be gentle, Son. She's like a turtle."

He hated when Ma said strange things. Did she want him to be gentle with Lillian or her mother? One would most certainly be easier than the other. But what did that have to do with reptiles?

Jonah followed Ma inside the house. "A turtle?"

"Mm-hmm." Ma grabbed a broom to sweep a kitchen floor that didn't require the job. "Lillian might have a tough shell, but inside, everything's delicate."

Leave it to Ma to come up with the strangest comparisons. Jonah moved a stool so she could sweep underneath it. The work likely had more to do with keeping herself busy. Ma never could stand idle, not even when having a conversation.

He replaced the stool underneath the table. "No wonder she has a shell, with a parent like that."

"We all have our challenges, Son, as you well know." Ma tsked. "Each of us faces different trials." She worked the broom under the preparation table. "And each of us receives different blessings. Oftentimes the blessings go with the sorrows."

Jonah nodded. "You mean finding the good in the bad." Today he'd been thinking along those same lines himself. If they hadn't endured the fire and loss, would he have met Lillian?

"There's that, yes." Ma poked the broom under the edge of the cold stove, where three loaves of Lillian's bread and some kind of pie rested on top. "But I mean that we are shaped by the misfortunes we face. Often they create hard places within us. Then comes the blessing, one that seems to fit in just the right way to ease that hurt." She straightened, and the broom stilled as she met his gaze. "Others who haven't gone through that trial wouldn't recognize the blessing in the same way."

The wisdom his mother possessed often surprised him. She was right, he supposed. His thoughts returned to Lillian as Ma took up sweeping again, seeming to know he needed to process her words.

The death of Lillian's father must have been difficult for her. But it also brought with it a blessing of independence. Would she have appreciated and needed that gift in the same way if her relationship with her mother had been different?

When Jonah's family lost their home, his employer and friends had provided one for them—something that had nicked his pride. But it was still a blessing, since any other house would have been more than he could afford.

He'd considered Lillian's arrival a disruption, but instead she had blessed them with a house for which they no longer had to front the expense. And she'd proven herself a valuable addition to Ma's dream—taking something simple and turning it into a business he truly believed would thrive.

"Thoughts are churning awful hard behind those eyes," Ma said with a smirk. "What's got that brow of yours furrowed so deep?"

Jonah sighed. "Thinking about Lillian and all the unexpected things that have happened lately."

She chuckled. She'd put away the broom while he'd been lost in thought and had started taking stock of ingredients. "Unexpected to you, maybe. I knew a bit of the plan, and of course God knew all of it."

He couldn't help but laugh. He pulled Ma into a hug and

kissed the top of her head. "I better get back to work if I'm going to get Lillian's shelves finished anytime soon."

She returned his squeeze but kept a hold on him when he tried to ease back. "Don't be so busy working on what you think you need to that you miss the blessings in front of you."

He nodded once, throat tight.

They both knew she wasn't talking about bookshelves.

What had she done? Lillian paced a circle around her bedroom—her father's room—and replayed the conversation with Mother over and over in her head. What could she have said differently? Why hadn't she tried to prepare herself for the possibility that Mother would come looking for her? If she had been more prepared, would she have handled the visit better? Would Mother really refuse to see her ever again?

A knock sounded at the door. She wiped her eyes and struggled to regain her composure. "Yes?"

The door creaked slowly open.

"Rose?" Lillian had expected Melanie, not the quiet child who hardly gave her a passing glance. "Are you all right?"

The dark-haired girl stepped in and closed the door behind her. "I heard you crying."

"Oh." Lillian pressed her fingers to her cheeks in an attempt to cool them. She hadn't realized she'd disturbed anyone.

"Sometimes when I've been crying, Ma says I should close my eyes and think about as many good things as I can." She gave a tentative shrug. "Maybe that will help?"

Sweet child. Lillian's heart squeezed. "Thank you. That's wonderful advice."

Rose pulled her lower lip through her teeth. "I wanted to say . . ." She blew out a breath. "Well, I'm sorry I haven't been nice to you."

Lillian blinked. The girl had been quiet and somewhat distant, but Lillian hadn't found that unusual. "That's all right. I know me coming here wasn't what anyone wanted."

Rose shook her head emphatically. "That's not it." She met Lillian's gaze again, large eyes brimming. "I was mad that we lost our house. Lost everything that I had left to remind me of my pa. I didn't want to come to this house. I thought I would hate it forever. Then you came." She looked at her fingers. "Now my ma is happier than I've seen her in a long time. Jonah smiles more. And I—" Her tears overflowed. "I think your bookstore is the best idea in the world."

Before Lillian could stop herself or think better of what an impulsive move might mean, she gathered Rose in her arms. The girl smelled of sunshine and lavender.

"When I was your age," Lillian said against the top of Rose's head, "there was a little bookshop in town. Whenever I got the chance, I would slip in and find a cozy chair and a new story. Everything else in the world faded as soon as I entered the fictional world."

Rose clung to her tightly, her arms encircling Lillian's waist. "And you want to make a place like that here? In our house?"

Our house. "I do." She eased back to look into Rose's face. "Would you like to help me?"

Rose puckered her lips. "Ma doesn't know much about books. Betsy is just a girl, and Jonah hates reading." She wrinkled her nose. "I don't think I can do it on my own."

Releasing the girl, Lillian stepped back. Why did she think she'd be doing it on her own?

Rose shook her head. "It's just another idea we won't get to keep."

Lillian pressed a hand to her heart in a vain attempt to stop the ache blooming there. "What do you mean?"

"Because you're going to leave. Jonah said so." She shrugged. "Every time we get something nice, it doesn't last long."

A quiet longing stirred in Lillian's heart, then swelled to a tempest, pushing out the lingering doubts. "I'm not going anywhere." She gave a nod, solidifying the pronouncement. "I'll stay as long as your family wants to have me."

Rose crossed her arms. "Jonah said you might still make Ma buy the house. Or you'll leave us with the work and go somewhere else."

A sharp stab sliced through her. She hadn't thought of her indecision in those terms but could certainly see how Rose would. And Jonah.

"I was scared." Lillian's shoulders rounded as the truth leaked out of her. "I came to a new town not knowing anyone. My father—who I never got to meet—left me a house already claimed by other people. Just my being here ruined everyone's plans. My mother wanted me to sell everything and give her the money, and I just . . . I didn't . . ." Tears welled and she struggled to keep them at bay. "I wasn't sure what to do."

"I know what that feels like. The part about not knowing what to do." Rose squeezed Lillian's hand, and the sweetness of the moment nearly undid her. "Ma says God only gives us one step at a time, and all we can do is try to make that step with faith."

Lillian chuckled despite the ache in her throat. "Your ma is very wise."

Rose nodded solemnly, as though such a fact had never

come into question. "Sometimes I have trouble doing that, though."

"Me too." Lillian wrapped an arm around her shoulders. "But I think it helps to have people around who are also trying. Maybe doing it together will make it easier."

A large smile covered Rose's face. It was contagious, and Lillian found herself matching the expression.

She offered her hand to Rose. "Jonah taught me how to make some brackets for our new bookshelves. Would you like to help me? It will go faster with two."

Rose's smile could have lit a room at midnight.

Hand in hand they stepped out of Lillian's room and started down the stairs. For the first time Lillian could remember in a very long time, she felt perfectly at home.

CHAPTER TWENTY-THREE

Lillian could scarcely believe how much progress they'd made since Mother's unexpected visit. She wiped her forearm over her perspiring brow and stood back to admire the work. In only two weeks, they'd managed to build an entire row of shelves all the way across the back wall of the bookshop room, as well as four shorter shelves that they would soon position into little nooks.

The bay window now housed a beautiful built-in bench, and as soon as Rose finished sewing the cushion, it would be the most perfect reading spot. Rose had skill with the needle and loved fabrics and sewing. Lillian had already discussed purchasing the girl a foot-pedal sewing machine with Melanie. They planned to surprise her on her fifteenth birthday next month.

Lillian made a circuit around the room, fingers trailing along the newly painted shelves waiting to be filled with books of every kind. Sunlight streamed through the windows, filling the space with light and hope.

"Looks great, doesn't it?"

Lillian turned toward Melanie's voice. "I can't wait to fill it with books." She pushed a loose lock of hair back into the coil on top of her head. "Have you heard anything about our shipment?"

"Jonah says he'll check at the station in Dahlonega. The new stove should be here. Icebox is planned for next week."

Everything was coming together. With the bookshop nearly ready, they could start on the kitchen expansion. Lillian had purchased two sets of McDougall kitchen cabinets, one for each side of the room. The large cabinets featured drop tables for additional working space as well as bins designed to hold flour, sugar, and salt. She'd paid out a hefty fifty dollars each for them, and they were coming all the way from Indianapolis by train. From there, the delivery wagon would haul them to Dawsonville's general store. Mr. McClure said Dawsonville had never seen the like.

Lillian smiled to herself. What would the shopkeeper think when her combination gas-and-coal stove arrived from Detroit? It was another massive expense, and one she'd hesitated to make, but the advertisement in the catalog had won her over. The time and labor they would save using gas and coal rather than chopping and storing wood to keep the bakery going would be worth the expense. They would simply have to adjust to the new way of cooking.

She and Melanie made their way out of the bookshop room, across the foyer, and to the second set of rooms housed on the lower floor, where the dining room connected to the small kitchen in the rear.

"Should be able to get this wall down in the next few days, don't you think?" Melanie gestured toward the wall between her kitchen kingdom and the dining room.

Lillian nodded. "Jonah said we could build a new wall

here"—she pointed to a place near the center of the dining room—"then open the current kitchen wall to create the expansion. We can't remove it entirely, since he says it supports the second floor, but we can leave large posts for support." She studied the area, mentally calculating the layout of the new cabinets, icebox, and stove. "It won't be as open as you wanted, but we'll still have the space."

"Whatever y'all think is fine by me." Melanie turned in a small circle, probably also trying to judge the placement of the new amenities and how they would fit around the support posts. She suddenly flung her arms wide. "Well! Don't see why the two of us can't get started now."

"You mean start swinging hammers? Us two women?" Lillian chuckled. She doubted they would get far. Neither of them possessed the strength Jonah wielded to topple walls.

Melanie laughed. "Why not? I take it there isn't much skill involved in destruction, is there? We won't bother with the support posts, just the wallboards."

After a moment of hesitation, Lillian nodded. They could give it a try. "I'll get the hammers."

A little while later, both women were wrapped in sturdy aprons, pairs of Jonah's work gloves encasing their hands.

Melanie grinned. "Ready?"

In response, Lillian pulled back her small hammer—she wouldn't attempt to lift that hefty sledge Jonah wielded—and heaved it against the wall. The heavy metal head bounced back and knocked her in the shoulder. She yelped, dropping the tool.

Onto her foot.

She yowled in pain and crumpled to the floor, Melanie squawking like a flustered hen over her. Lillian curled her legs under her, grabbing her throbbing toe.

"Oh, honey. Are you all right?" Melanie reached for Lillian's injured foot. "Let me see."

They unlaced her boot and got her foot free in a joint effort that had tears streaming down Lillian's face. Melanie leaned over her foot, obscuring her view.

"Just bruised, I think. Nothing looks broken. Hit right on the tip here." Melanie touched the end of Lillian's big toe and Lillian screeched. "Sorry." She patted her knee. "That toenail will probably turn black and nasty, but there's no real harm done."

Lillian begged to differ. The throbbing gave all the proof of harm she needed. Her shoulder ached, but hardly compared to her foot. She sat on the floor sniffling until the worst of the pain receded, Melanie fussing over her the entire time. Part of her wanted to shoo the other woman away to let her ache in peace, but in truth she cherished Melanie's genuine concern.

Finally, Lillian replaced her stocking and boot. Standing, however, proved to be more than she could handle, so she promptly returned to the floor.

How humiliating.

Melanie removed her apron and collected their hammers.

"What are you doing?" Lillian asked.

"Putting these away, obviously." Melanie cocked an eyebrow toward Lillian's foot. "We'll wait for Jonah."

She didn't want to wait for Jonah. She could do this. It simply required a little practice. "Give me that hammer."

"No ma'am." Melanie shook her head. "You'll get yourself a trip to Dr. Andley for the trouble, and I'm not having that."

Lillian extended her hand and wiggled her fingers, which looked ridiculous in the oversized gloves. "I'm determined, Melanie."

After a slight hesitation, Melanie handed over one of the hammers. "What are you going to do with that thing, sitting down there on the floor?"

"Approach the problem from a new angle."

The small hammer was intended for farriers removing horseshoe nails, but it would work for her purpose as well. She scooted herself closer to the wall. Here in the kitchen, the wallboards were free of decorative paper and molding, making it easier for her to locate the nails.

Melanie crouched beside her, watching. After a few tries, Lillian got the hammer's claw underneath a nailhead. Bending the hammer back, she pried the nail free. The next one followed, and after a moment she had the end of the board loose.

She grinned. "There!"

Melanie chuckled. "It's going to take you an entire day to get the boards off like that. Why not wait for Jonah?"

Because she had nothing else to work on today. And she hated admitting defeat. "We can help him by doing a little of the work ourselves."

With a sigh, Melanie knelt beside her, and together they pried nails and boards free, creating a hole in the wall. Lillian shifted to her knees, the throbbing in her toe having lessened by a degree. She wedged her hand underneath a board that seemed newer than the others and grunted. It was hammered in more firmly too. She tugged and struggled until finally the board popped free.

Hay poured out of the opening, followed by a burlap-wrapped package.

"What in the world?" Melanie dropped her hammer and scooted to Lillian. "What is that?"

Lillian had no idea. But after the ledger, she feared it wouldn't be anything good. She untied the twine on the package and pulled back the layers of wrapping. More hay filled the inside, insulating three large, corked glass bottles that contained deep amber liquid. Lillian brushed aside the hay and then lifted one to examine it. A faded label clung to the front.

Melanie gasped. "That's whiskey."

Georgia had passed a law in favor of the temperance movement something like five years ago, banning the sale and purchase of all liquors. But as far as Lillian understood, it wasn't illegal for people to consume liquors they already owned in their homes. So why hide them?

She exchanged a look with Melanie, the same thought showing in the other woman's gaze.

Bootleggers.

Without another word, Lillian and Melanie set to work opening up more of the wall. Two hours later, they'd uncovered forty-seven whiskey bottles of various makes and types along with nearly two dozen unlabeled bottles of numerous sizes and shapes, mostly filled with a clear liquid.

"Goodness," Melanie said on a long breath. "What are we to do with these?"

Lillian examined the collection of bottles they'd placed in rows across the kitchen floor. "Do you think this is why Mr. Tanner wanted the house?"

Melanie grunted. "Fair probability, I'd say. He sure didn't want it for any sentimental reasons."

A mysterious ledger and a wall full of illegal liquor. Lillian sighed. "And here I was beginning to hope I'd found the last of the trouble my father left behind."

What were they going to do?

Jonah returned home to find his mother and Lillian stand-ing amid a sea of glass bottles. He stepped into the kitchen. "What in the world?"

Ma put her hands on her hips. "Look here at what we found in the wall. If we'd been swinging those hammers like a man, we would have busted liquor all over the place." She scrunched her nose. "Would have taken ages to get rid of that smell, it soaking into the floors and whatnot."

Jonah stared at her, trying to make the strange pieces fit. Ma and Lillian had taken it upon themselves to work on the wall, but rather than busting through it they'd . . . what? He frowned at stacks of wallboards haphazardly scattered about. They'd taken the wall apart piecemeal?

And had found an entire hoard of alcohol.

He shifted his gaze to Lillian for explanation. She lifted slim shoulders. "We pried the nails out to remove the boards."

That didn't explain *why* they'd done so. He scooped up one of the bottles and examined it. "This is whiskey."

Both women nodded.

"Whiskey you found boarded up inside the wall."

They nodded again.

Jonah's fingers tightened on the neck of the bottle. The led-ger. Jeffery Tanner's insistence on buying the house. "We need to get rid of these."

Ma nodded her agreement, but Lillian frowned.

"Why?"

"Because it's illegal." Didn't she know that? "And I have a feeling this is what Mr. Tanner wanted from this house." Not to mention what the intruder had been after. As long as they kept possession of what had to be a fortune of moonshine and whiskey, his family wouldn't be safe.

Lillian lifted her chin. "Selling liquor is illegal. Having it already in your house is not."

Jonah set the bottle down and studied Lillian's stiff shoulders. She had that look again, the one that meant she'd become determined but wasn't exactly comfortable about it. What did she want to do with dozens of bottles of hooch and home brew? "It came from somewhere. Therefore, it's still illegal."

"As soon as this stuff leaves the house, someone is going to know about it." Lillian's gaze bore into him. "Before that happens, I'd like to see what else we can find."

"You want to tear into more walls?"

Lillian appeared to waffle, and a crack formed in her stubborn streak. "Maybe. But that's not what I mean. I need to know what my father was doing and if the company still has anything to do with it."

Ma put a hand on Lillian's arm. "This could be dangerous. I say we dump it all out and get rid of the bottles in secret." She looked back at Jonah. "I don't want anything to do with devil's brew."

The look in her eyes knifed him.

Pa had been a good man. Loving to his wife and children. But there'd been some hard times in his later years when he would turn to a drink to soothe his body's aches. They hadn't liked the man he became on those days.

"I have a few of those crates left," Jonah said. "We'll package this up so the girls don't see it." Then tomorrow he'd have to figure out what to do about these bottles that would satisfy both women.

They set to work placing the bottles in the crates, packing them in with the scattered hay so they wouldn't rattle when moved. They filled five crates before the last of the cache was safely tucked away.

Jonah stacked the crates in the corner of the kitchen. "They can stay there until we decide what to do."

Ma removed a heavy work apron—where had she gotten that from?—and draped the stout fabric over the crates in a vain effort to get them out of sight. "I need to fetch the girls from Sarah." Thankfully, Rose and Betsy had been playing with a friend a few houses down the street and hadn't been present for this discovery.

Left standing alone in the kitchen with Lillian a few minutes later, Jonah thumbed toward the mess. "Why'd you do this without me?"

She stared at the dissected wall. "We thought we could help by getting a start."

Stubborn woman. How was he supposed to take care of her if she didn't want to let him?

When did you decide she was yours to protect?

He searched for words but found none. Lillian looked up at him, eyes luminous in the late afternoon light. They were beautiful, those eyes. They spoke every emotion she often kept from her face. Told truths she tried to conceal.

Like now.

Her face remained smooth. Impassive. But those eyes . . .

He took a step closer and she tilted her head back, watching him. Lately he'd figured out how to read her. Decode the messages hidden in the depths of that gaze.

"I'm not trying to reprimand you, Lillian." His voice dipped low, carrying with it the undercurrent of longing her nearness incited. Her lips parted in surprise. Warmth spread through him. "You want to know what your father was involved in and if it will seep into the company you now benefit from."

Lillian nodded slowly, wonder swimming in those pools of velvet brown. He dared another step closer. Just to see.

As he'd hoped, something new surfaced. Something he suspected mirrored whatever escaped through his own expression.

His fingers succumbed to the temptation of feeling the smoothness of her skin. They inched up the side of her neck and trailed the edge of her jaw. So soft.

Lillian pulled in a breath but didn't move from his touch. He eased his palm along her jawline and slid his fingers into the silk of her hair. Gently, slowly, he closed the distance between them until he could feel the rapid rise and fall of her chest. Desire stirred, a torrent of heat within him.

A flicker sparked in her gaze that warmed him further until he could no longer help himself. He leaned close, his lips an agonizing fraction above hers.

She didn't move. Then fluttering lashes closed over the simmering depths, and it was all the permission he needed.

The first taste of her erupted something inside him. Something that wanted to hitch his life to hers and never let anything snatch her from his embrace. She melded into him with a sweetness that nearly undid him, opening up a yearning to protect that preciousness from anything that sought her harm.

Lillian stirred beneath him, her gentleness finding a boldness he didn't expect, and he allowed the kiss to deepen. To further open himself to a feeling he'd never thought to experience.

Nearly breathless, he pulled away.

Her eyes fluttered open, and he was met with glimmers of fascination. A sentiment he shared.

Childish giggles erupted behind them. "Oh wow!"

Lillian leapt out of his arms, stumbling before she righted herself. The loss of her jarred him, and he took a deep lungful of air before he could compose himself enough to face his baby sister. It certainly hadn't taken her and Rose long to return. He hadn't even heard the door open.

Betsy stood in the doorway, hand clamped over her mouth and eyes wide.

Lillian turned a bright shade of pink, but he couldn't manage to feel the proper embarrassment at having been caught. If Lillian Doyle would let him, he'd kiss her every day. And he didn't care a whit who saw.

Betsy bounced on her toes. "Does this mean you're going to marry her now?"

A tiny squeak escaped from Lillian before she managed to excuse herself and dart away. Betsy watched her flee, clearly confused.

Jonah took his sister's hand. "How about we get you back to Ma?" She'd likely run ahead, beating her mother and sister home by a fair pace.

Her lip poked out.

"She might let you go with me to the train station tomorrow."

Ma had said nothing of the sort, but the distraction worked.

"Truly? I've always wanted to see the train!"

Her smile warmed him. It would be a quick dash to claim their shipment and arrange transportation for the heavy items, but Betsy's company would bring a bit of fun to the errand.

Jonah led his sister from the kitchen as she chattered happily, and her question filled his mind.

"Does this mean you're going to marry her now?"

CHAPTER TWENTY-FOUR

*O*h *my heavens and stars above.* Lillian pressed her fingers to her lips and leaned against the wall on the back porch. Reginald had chastely kissed her once, in celebration of their engagement, he'd said. Good gracious. Jonah's kiss had been nothing at all like that.

Her pulse thrummed, vibrating through her veins with an erratic energy. And the way she'd responded . . . was that even proper?

Probably not. She'd kissed him as freely as though they'd shared vows. He must think her far too forward. But then, maybe she didn't care. He hadn't seemed to mind.

She fanned her face. Of course he wouldn't mind. What man would?

Still, she'd sensed his kiss went beyond desire. There had been something else in his eyes. A blaze of endearment. The promise of something deeper.

While she had the tendency to encourage unfounded hope on occasion, she didn't think this particular instance fell under that umbrella. Something *was* starting between them.

And she didn't want it to stop.

Evening shadows blanketed the yard before Lillian's temperature returned to normal and she no longer feared her flush would give her away. Not that Melanie wouldn't know soon enough. Betsy couldn't keep a thing to herself.

The night creatures commenced their barrage of sounds, filling the air with a strangely soothing chorus. Another thing she never expected to like about the country.

The back door opened and light spilled out onto the porch. "Lillian?" Rose poked her head outside. "Are you back here?" She turned her head and spotted Lillian still slumped against the wall like a woman in a stupor. "Oh, there you are. Ma says it's time for supper."

Already? How long had she been out here mooning over a man? Embarrassment crept up her neck. But if Rose knew anything about the kiss, she didn't let on.

Lillian came inside to discover that Jonah had moved a table into the dining room, positioning it toward the front of the room farthest from the partially demolished wall. It had been set with flickering candles and mismatched china.

How utterly charming.

"I figured we could eat inside again now that the bugs are getting worse." Jonah gestured toward the humble offering, a tinge of embarrassment in his tone.

Didn't he realize she found the cozy setting where they would all share food and laughter the most perfect place in the world?

"I thought this a good spot," he continued, appearing adorably sheepish. Had their kiss flustered him as well? His gaze sought hers across the room. "We need somewhere to eat as a family, even once the store opens."

Lillian's brain snagged on the "as a family" part, and she

could only nod. Would this be her life? Days spent in the company of the townsfolk, serving coffee and recommending books? And evenings here with her new family?

Jonah stared at her intently, and her pulse trembled. My, but the man had an effect on her.

Betsy bounded into the room, breaking the spell. She scurried to the table with a basket of rolls, tripped on her own feet, and nearly lost the rolls.

"Whoa now." Jonah gently grabbed his sister to steady her. Lillian's already fluttering heart sputtered again. He would make a good father someday.

Melanie and Rose brought out more food, and Lillian turned to retrieve a pitcher of iced tea from the kitchen. They settled in for a good meal as soon as Jonah asked a blessing from his place at the head of the table.

"Jonah said he's going to take me to see the train tomorrow!" Betsy spoke around a mouthful of yeast roll, excitement in every muffled word.

Melanie paused slicing a section of ham. "What now?"

To Lillian's left, Jonah cleared his throat. "No reason she can't ride with me and look at the trains while I settle the shipment."

Melanie lifted her eyebrows. Before she could respond, Rose brightened. "May I go too?"

Surprise flickered over Jonah's face. "If you'd like."

Rose turned to Lillian. "Dahlonega is much larger than Dawsonville. I bet they have a better selection of fabrics than what Mrs. McClure has in that tiny shop."

A crease formed in the center of Melanie's brows.

Rose sucked in a quick breath before her mother could object. "I could help you, if you want, pick out some fabrics for the curtains."

The hopefulness in her gaze snagged Lillian's heart. "That's a wonderful idea, Rose. But—"

"And we can pick out matching cloth for the window seat. Oh, and we need to decide on the right flatware and crockery for the bakery, right?" Rose swept her bright gaze to Melanie. "We want to make sure we have plenty so that we can serve a host of customers should they converge on us all at once."

Melanie's features softened. "I'm sure we can plan a time to do that soon."

"Why not tomorrow? Jonah has to go anyway, and he already said he would take me and Betsy, so why can't we all go?"

The adults shared a look, and Melanie shook her head. "Perhaps another time." Her expression grew closed as she picked up her fork and stabbed at her food.

"We could all go, Ma," Jonah said. "Just for the day."

Melanie set her fork down and leveled a heavy gaze on her son. "And leave everything here?"

There was no mistaking her meaning. Lillian shifted. It had been more than two weeks since the intruder, and Jonah had secured the house well. Whoever had been looking for the book—if that was what they'd been after—hadn't made any further attempts.

"I'll make sure everything is locked up tight," Jonah responded. "And having everyone with me might be a good idea anyway."

Rose and Betsy beamed, having no idea about the dangers. Melanie shifted her gaze to Lillian, something flickering in her expression. "While that would be nice, it's probably best if you go alone this time. It will be faster that way."

"But I wanna see the train!" Betsy's lower lip poked out. "Jonah said I could when I saw him—"

"And you can," Jonah said quickly.

So that was it. He'd used the train to distract the child. A bubble of laughter welled in Lillian's stomach, and she had to hide it under the guise of using her napkin.

"I would like to go into Dahlonega too, Ma." Rose glanced between her mother and brother. "You're always saying we'll do things later, when circumstances are better." Her gaze lowered. "But then we never do."

Mother and son looked at one another for a loaded moment.

Jonah drew a long breath. "It will only be for the day. As long as we make preparations . . ."

Melanie watched Rose push her food around on her plate. "How would you take all of us?"

The mode of transportation hadn't occurred to Lillian. Jonah usually rode Mist and had started keeping her at the livery in town. The Petersons didn't own a wagon. The livery owner, however, kept two.

"A carriage ride would be splendid," Lillian said. "And a day in town would be a well-deserved break from all our hard work. I'm sure Mr. Blake has something to accommodate five."

The grin Rose sent Lillian's way pushed out her doubts. A day out wouldn't hurt. They couldn't very well spend their entire lives in this house.

"Hiring a carriage that big is an unnecessary expense," Melanie replied, but the resolve in her argument disintegrated. She shot a questioning look at Jonah.

An expectant silence settled over the group for several heartbeats. Jonah looked at each of them, then smiled conspiratorially at his sisters. "But an expense we can afford. We'll make a day of it."

Rose beamed and Betsy cheered. Melanie, however, watched Lillian closely, penetrating eyes digging past Lillian's smile.

She looked away before Melanie could mine too deeply.

After supper, Lillian helped Melanie wash the dishes while the girls got ready for bed and Jonah gathered wood for the morning's fire.

"I've been thinking about that book you showed me," Melanie said, handing a plate to Lillian to dry. "I wonder if the letters connect to those." She flicked her eyes toward the crates in the corner.

Lillian stacked the ceramic plate on top of the others. "How so?"

"RM could mean rum, and MS moonshine."

"Maybe. But there are lots of letters in there."

Melanie nodded and handed her another plate. "Numbers too, which is what got me to thinking. What if it means something like three bottles of whiskey to, or maybe from, a person's initials? I've heard plenty of rumors about moonshiners up in the hills. Somebody's got to be sending that stuff into the cities."

The rag in Lillian's hand stopped its trip around the edge of the plate. That made sense. Too much for comfort.

As soon as they finished drying the dishes, Lillian fetched the book and spread it open on the table. Jonah came back inside just as Melanie lit the wick on the lamp. Without a word, he came to peer over their shoulders. Lillian had to force herself to focus on something other than his nearness.

She ran a finger down the first column. "You may be right. Look at this here." She pointed at the entry *3HWW*. "That could mean three bottles of Henry Watson whiskey. We found several bundles of three bottles each of that." She skimmed her finger down a few more entries. "There are several of this same notation."

Jonah leaned closer, and the scent of his aftershave, which reminded her of cedar and sage, muddled her senses. "Could be." He pointed to another entry. "This here—*18WLMcD.*" He leaned back. "What do you bet that's eighteen bottles of McDonahue's white lightning?"

Melanie peered at her son. "What do you know about white lightning and those fools who brew it?"

"Men talk, Ma. All you have to do is listen."

Lillian ignored whatever Melanie mumbled under her breath and flipped through another few pages. "That makes sense. There's several other entries with *WL* listed behind a number. These entries must list liquor he stored."

"And those notations over on the other line are probably where they were going," Jonah said.

The three of them stood silent a moment, the implications of what they'd figured out settling on the room. Floyd Jackson had been some kind of smuggler of illegal liquor, and they'd just discovered his stash. And the entire list of where it was supposed to go.

A very dangerous combination.

CHAPTER TWENTY-FIVE

This was exactly what they needed. Jonah relaxed under the gentle sway of the carriage, the girls' excited conversation peppered with Ma's patient responses. Ma and Lillian had been stressed about their discovery in the walls, and a trip through the countryside proved to be the cure to ease worry lines and tempt smiles. He'd hidden the crates and secured the doors and windows. For today, at least, they would leave Floyd Jackson's troubles behind.

Lillian sat perched beside him, dressed in a fetching pink dress and a straw hat that shaded her face from the sun. She'd tied a gauzy swath of material over the hat and under her chin, causing the brim to bend just enough that she might not notice how often he glanced her way.

"I'm glad we're going." Lillian tipped her hat, giving Jonah a glimpse of eyes that sparkled with delight. "The girls will enjoy the outing, and a larger town will give us more options for purchases."

"I'm pleased you are pleased," he drawled, enticing the chirp of laugher he'd been hoping for.

"Well pleased indeed, sir."

They settled into silence as the breeze played with Lillian's hat and the horses bobbed their heads in a steady rhythm down the road.

"And that's when I saw them hugging with their faces all smushed together," a sweet voice trilled. The words broke free of the pleasant murmur behind them and latched on to Jonah's senses.

Oh no.

Lillian sucked in a breath but kept her eyes forward. Tension poured off her. Embarrassment he expected. But was it because of the situation? Or of him?

Jonah pushed the notion away. He may be a country bumpkin and she a city socialite, but there'd been no denying her response to his embrace. The memory kicked up a spurt of heat in his chest.

"Are you serious?" This from Rose. "They were kissing in the kitchen?"

Leave it to a fourteen-year-old girl to sound both thrilled and mortified at the same time.

Lillian went completely rigid, her spine so stiff if he hit a hard enough bump she might go flying off the seat.

"Hush, girls," Ma chided. "We don't speak of such things."

The humor in Ma's voice didn't surprise him in the least. He risked a glance at Lillian, spotting only reddened cheeks beneath the fold of her brim. Her head turned back ever so slightly. Jonah suppressed a smile. Cared to know what Ma thought of them together, did she?

Now he sounded like a smitten schoolboy. Jonah gripped the reins tighter and forced the mirth from his lips. Of course she would care. A relationship could complicate all the women's plans.

Or fit in perfectly.

He ignored that last thought as Betsy's voice rose again. "But why not, Ma? They both looked pretty happy, so what's the problem with talkin' 'bout it?"

"It's not polite, my dearest." A thinly disguised chuckle filled Ma's voice.

Jonah dared another peek at Lillian. Her face resembled a beet. Best he save them while he could.

"First we will go to the train." He raised his voice to be sure everyone could hear. "That way Betsy can get a good look."

She clapped her hands together. "Jonah's taking me to see the train 'cause I saw him smushing lips with Miss Lillian."

Lillian groaned and lowered her head.

So much for the distraction. Defeat lowered his eyes for a moment while he filled his lungs.

"Betsy Ann Peterson. You hush with that talk." Ma's voice came more firmly now.

"But why, Ma?"

"Because I said, and that's all you need to know about it."

Betsy sighed, and the rear of the carriage fell into silence. Jonah could only imagine the look on Ma's face. She'd probably started picking out wedding cake recipes.

Lillian remained a frozen sculpture next to him for the remainder of the ride into the gold boomtown of Dahlonega. The town had grown in bounds back in the gold rush of '29. Even after the miners moved on, a community had remained. It was far shy of the metropolis in Atlanta that Lillian was accustomed to, but still a larger community than Dawsonville.

Jonah reined the carriage to a stop at the local livery and helped the women down from the conveyance. Excitement filled their expressions, and even Ma seemed to have forgotten the earlier awkwardness. Still, he hurried to speak before she decided now would be a good opportunity to polish one of her pearls of wisdom.

"I'll take Betsy with me to see the trains while you ladies have a look at the shops. Then we'll have our dinner at a nice restaurant."

Betsy cheered and even Rose looked pleased, a girlish exuberance returning to her features.

"Really, Jonah." Ma sidled up to him, speaking low. She sent Betsy to Rose to retie her bonnet. "You know we can't afford what a meal like that is going to cost."

"We can, Ma. Or have you forgotten that money I'd saved up for the house?"

She shook her head. "You need that money for your schooling." She cut a glance at Lillian. "Or perhaps other things."

He let the comment pass. "One luncheon won't hurt, Ma. Our family has been through a lot, and there's plenty to celebrate." He squeezed her shoulder. "Enjoy the day."

She regarded him thoughtfully for a moment longer and then finally gave a nod. "All right then. If you're sure."

He watched the smiling women gather and discuss where to start their shopping, then took Betsy's hand when she scampered back to him, bonnet tied and face bright.

Lillian caught his eye and smiled. Her eyes already spoke, but her lips mouthed "thank you" anyway.

Jonah winked at her and enjoyed every bit of the pink that bloomed on her cheeks.

That man. Lillian couldn't tear her eyes away as Jonah smiled down at his chattering little sister.

"He'll make a good pa someday," Melanie noted, taking Lillian by the elbow.

The heat already climbing up her neck intensified. "Melanie, I—"

"No need, dear." She gave Lillian's arm a squeeze. "Whatever is blooming between you and my son is between the two of you." She leaned closer, her voice dropping to a whisper. "I'm just hoping it leads to a church soon enough."

Melanie's acceptance tingled through her, and Lillian returned the woman's squeeze, words unnecessary.

Being the person most used to the crowded streets of cities—though one could hardly call Dahlonega more than a modestly sized town—Lillian took the lead while Melanie and Rose trailed behind.

Rose chattered excitedly. "Oh. Look there! That store has windows even bigger than the one in Lillian's new bookshop." And a few breaths later, "Do you see that? We've passed two restaurants already!"

Every architectural detail and crowded walkway proved an adventure for the girl. Even Melanie seemed fascinated by the taller buildings and abundance of people. When a sleek black automobile rumbled past, Lillian thought Rose would squeal with excitement. She might have, if her gloved hand hadn't quickly covered her mouth before she exhibited too much glee.

They neared a dress shop, and Rose's eyes filled with longing as her steps came to a halt in front of the window. Two gowns hung on display, one a more modest ensemble with a high neckline and long, tapered sleeves, the other an elegant evening gown.

"Isn't it beautiful," Rose breathed. "Look at that beadwork." The green fabric of the gown fell in shimmering folds from a straight neckline and tapered waist. The shoulder-length sleeves had been gathered with golden ribbons, matching the elaborate gold beadwork covering the front panel and bottom third of the skirt.

"Perhaps when you're older you will have an event when you can wear a dress like that," Lillian said.

"Maybe." Rose shrugged. "But what I really want is to *make* dresses like that."

Lillian squeezed her shoulder. "I have no doubt you can. You're skilled with the needle already." And as soon as she started with the new sewing machine, Rose could prove to be a talented seamstress. Lillian could scarcely wait to share the gift. She nodded down the street before the temptation to spill the birthday secret got the better of her. "I have no doubt you will be the best seamstress in all of Georgia. Come now, let's catch up with your mother and choose some fabrics, shall we?"

Melanie had already wandered at least half a block away from them, her head tilted back as she examined the multiple shops. Lillian and Rose hurried to catch her, but they needn't have rushed. Melanie came to a sudden stop much the same way Rose had in front of the dress shop. Unsurprisingly, the older woman had been caught by a bakery.

"Should we go in and see how they've arranged their shop?"

Lillian smiled at Rose. "I could stand to have a bit of sugar to fuel our adventure, couldn't you?"

The girl nodded, and the three stepped inside to the heavenly aroma of fresh breads and iced cakes. Would this be what their home would smell like? Coffee, books, and confections. There could be no better aromas than those. Except perhaps sage with hints of cedar.

"Oh, look at this display." Melanie bustled forward, her attempts at hiding her excitement forgotten. "They have glass cabinets!"

Rows of confections, cookies, and candies lined the shelves enclosed in glass. Lillian resisted the urge to reach out and touch the display. "We could order one of these, I'm sure."

"Shipping glass isn't like that stove you ordered." Melanie shook her head. "No, we would need someone to build one."

A man in a white apron emerged from a doorway behind the counter. "Anything strike your fancy, ladies?"

Melanie chose a lemon square, Rose picked a cookie filled with chunks of chocolate, and Lillian selected her favorite, maple walnut fudge. She paid for the treats, even buying them each a Coca-Cola in a glass bottle. They settled at a table by the storefront.

"Do you suppose they will let us look at their kitchen?" Melanie whispered.

Lillian chuckled around a bite of fudge. "What for? We already designed ours." After the way Melanie had reacted to the glass display cabinets, Lillian didn't want her becoming discouraged if the shop here had more than they'd be able to have at home. "I see no reason to compare our plan to theirs."

Melanie drew her head back a fraction. "You're right, of course." She cast another glance at the kitchen, then focused on her small plate.

After finishing their treats, they continued on to the large mercantile.

"Have you ever seen the like?" Melanie's eyes widened as she took in the store easily four times larger than the general store in Dawsonville.

Lillian had seen Rich's and other two-story department stores in Atlanta, so she merely smiled her response.

By the time they'd chosen several yards of fabric to make matching curtains, seat covers, and tablecloths, the hour had grown late.

"We best hurry. Poor Jonah and Betsy will think we've gotten lost," Lillian said, tugging Rose from a display of glass vases. She paid for the fabric and requested the bundles be packaged and held until Jonah could come back with the carriage.

As they made their way to meet him, Lillian's heart soared. This had been the most perfect day she'd ever had.

CHAPTER TWENTY-SIX

o. Oh no.

Lillian gripped the packages stacked in her arms, her heart hammering. Melanie had been right. They never should have left their house unattended.

You are a fool, Lillian Doyle. A woolly-headed ninny who forgets her responsibilities to go gallivanting off and—

Jonah let out a low sound from his chest, his form crowding in behind Lillian after she'd come to a sudden stop in the front doorway. He looked over her shoulder.

"What? What's wrong—" Melanie stopped short when Jonah barked some kind of command Lillian could scarcely hear over her own rapid breathing.

All that work . . .

Jonah gently took her shoulders and eased her back. "Stay outside. All of you." He set the packages of wrapped material he'd been carrying by the door and stalked inside.

"What's wrong?" Betsy lifted onto her toes, doing her best to see past Melanie into the house.

Lillian dropped her packages on the porch and gripped the bridge of her nose. The pressure did nothing to hold back the tears. Her lip trembled. "The shelves. They destroyed the bookshelves."

Splintered wood littered the floor in the bookshop room, thrown in heaps and discarded. She had no idea if the rest of the house fared better.

"Destroyed?" Melanie gripped the doorframe. She poked her head inside and gasped.

"Outside, Ma," came Jonah's clipped response. "Until I make sure there's no one in here."

Melanie pulled her head back and wrapped her arms around Betsy, who now clung to her skirts.

"Why would somebody take down Miss Lillian's bookcase, Ma?" Betsy's sweet little voice was filled with confusion.

Melanie stroked the girl's golden hair. "Sometimes people do bad things, darling." She met Lillian's gaze over the top of Betsy's head.

Her expression matched the regret clawing through Lillian's heart. They'd been reckless to leave, even for one day. Someone had broken into the house—despite Jonah's extra locks—in search of the hidden liquor. Just because they hadn't found more bottles during their construction didn't mean other illegal stores didn't exist.

Would there be a wall left undamaged?

"Do you think there's more?" Lillian whispered.

"More what?" Betsy poked her head out from behind Melanie's skirt.

"She means more things those bad men tore up." Melanie patted the girl's shoulder, lifting one of her own in silent response.

Rose swung her gaze between her mother and Lillian, clearly aware they'd veiled their conversation. Thankfully, she didn't voice any questions. The four of them waited in tense silence until Jonah finally stepped back outside.

"I didn't find anyone hiding." He blew out a breath, all signs of the delighted man who'd treated them to a wonderful meal at a fancy restaurant now hidden beneath a mask of frustration and anger. "They did a great deal of damage, so prepare yourselves."

While Melanie and the girls turned toward the kitchen, Lillian made a beeline to the parlor. She tried to heed Jonah's advice, but no amount of mental preparation could stop her heart from plummeting at the scene she found. The bookshelves had all been demolished save for the standing ones in the center of the room. She stepped over the splintered wood.

Her beautiful window seat. Ruined.

Tears burned up the back of her throat.

Strong arms wrapped around her shoulders, pulling her close. "We will rebuild." Jonah's featherlight kiss stirred the hair at her temple.

Lillian nodded, her throat too thick for words. For several moments she soaked up his comfort. Then she stepped out of the protection of his embrace to find that the rest of the rooms on the lower floor had fared no better. Broken boards littered the floors, jagged edges snarling at her like vicious teeth.

Lillian stared at the ruins, fists clenching and unclenching with equal swells of hurt and anger.

"They did much the same upstairs." Jonah's quiet voice came from behind her. "I'm sorry, Lillian. I shouldn't have taken everyone away."

"This isn't your fault." She moved to where he stood in the center of the room, head bowed. "They eventually would have found a way to come after what they were looking for. We couldn't stay in this house forever." She drew a shaky breath. "Maybe now that they've gotten what they want, we can live in peace. It's probably best we weren't in their way."

Jonah stiffened. "I moved the crates early this morning while everyone was readying for town." His eyes searched her face. "I didn't like the thought of that in the house, so I hid them out back."

Lillian's mind scrambled. Then the intruders hadn't gotten what they'd come for. "Do you think they discovered more in the walls?"

"I don't know." The muscle in his jaw pulsed with anger. "Doesn't matter, I suppose."

It did matter. If they hadn't found what they wanted, they could come back.

"We need to go to the sheriff." She stepped away, fingers tightening on her skirt. "I should have looked more closely into what my father was doing. Shouldn't have been so quick to dismiss his underhandedness." Tears burned again, and she angrily swiped them away.

All their hard work destroyed, their beautiful day ruined.

And for what? A few bottles of whiskey and moonshine? Was the bootleg liquor really worth so much?

Enough that Mr. Tanner had offered double for the house. Surely he would know they suspected him. But how could she prove anything?

Jonah stood shaking his head. Her insides twisted.

Whatever it took, she would see the men responsible brought to justice.

Jonah prowled the shadows in the front of the house, too furious to sleep. If anyone dared come near the house tonight . . . He clenched his fists. He wouldn't let down his guard again.

The damage would take weeks to repair, not to mention the expense. But the worst of it had been Lillian's tears. The fear in Rose's eyes. The disappointment in Ma's. Why was it that every time Jonah thought something was going right, everything went wrong?

The squeak of the front door sent a surge of energy spiking through him.

"Son? Are you out here?"

Jonah stepped out of the shadows surrounding the porch. "Here, Ma."

"Come, sit with me on the steps."

She didn't ask why he stalked in the dark, nor did she demand he come inside. She simply offered to sit with him in the quiet of the night. Muscles twitching, he sat on the front step next to her. Ma shifted her faded robe—one of the many things donated to them by the kind families of the town when the cabin had burned—and tucked her bare feet beneath her. The crickets sang out in swells, their lives untouched by the events of the house they surrounded.

The two of them sat there for a time, until Jonah's breath slowed and the tension coiling in his shoulders released.

"Why does everything always go wrong?" He probably shouldn't ask, knowing Ma would only point out all the things they'd been blessed with. But the question had festered in him a long time, tainting every hope he dared feel. "No matter how hard I try, nothing works out like I plan."

"I have to wonder," Ma said after a moment, "if maybe

when everything is going wrong, that perhaps we're doing something right."

Jonah shifted to try to see her in the dim light. The moon cast silvery rays over her face, making her look more aged than she should. "That doesn't make the first lick of sense, Ma."

"Don't you think that if we're doing something good or following a path or a direction God's given us, there might be opposition?"

Jonah tilted his head back and stared at the stars. Ma had her convictions, and he was happy she had something to get her through the hard times. But the bitterness within him roiled, souring his stomach. "Were we doing something right when Pa suffered a long, wasting death? Or when my infant brother suddenly died? Or what about when the cabin burned?" He pushed up off the porch and stalked into the grass. "How about those times, Ma? Or what about all those times when I worked my fingers to bleeding to make sure you and the girls had something to fill your stomachs?"

Ma didn't answer. This time, no bits of wisdom painted in unyielding hope could stand up to the tempest.

He should stop. He would never want to hurt Ma. But the questions demanded release and pushed out of his mouth despite his better judgment. "Or how you had to age yourself beyond your years trying to coax a life out of ground that refused to yield crops?" He pushed his fingers through his hair.

Ma rose, wrapping her dressing gown around her. She regarded him for a moment, and when she spoke again, her tone remained gentle. Understanding. "I said sometimes, Son. Not always. Tragedy befalls everyone in one form or another. No one glides through life without trouble."

Jonah pulled in a lungful of summer air laced with the

scents of flowers and grass. He knew everyone had disappointments. Dashed dreams and hardships. Alma desperately wanted children. Instead, the Watsons had four tiny markers behind their house in memory of the babies who had never been born.

"Just this once," Jonah said softly, "I really thought everything would work out."

"We can build again."

He wanted to be like her. Focus on the steps they could take and move forward rather than gnawing on a past he couldn't change.

"It will just take us a little longer." Ma joined him in the moonlight, her hand resting gently on his arm. "This is still what we need to do." Her voice held hope and determination, and Jonah loved her for it. But he couldn't muster the words of encouragement she wanted to hear. Couldn't produce an agreement he didn't feel.

"In this life there will always be trouble," Ma said. "You make it harder when you try to face it alone."

Jonah set his jaw, still feeling like that boy terrified of the massive responsibility of the lives of his family. Every decision he made, every trouble he faced, affected not only him but those he loved most.

And time after time, he'd failed them.

Now he'd failed Lillian as well. Her assurance otherwise did nothing to quell the bitter taste of guilt. Maybe it would be best for them not to need him anymore. What good did he do anyone?

He tried to push the thoughts away, knowing self-deprecation wasn't healthy, but they remained like claws sunk into his skull.

"Come inside when you're ready." Ma gave his arm another

squeeze. "You aren't alone, and you don't have to carry this weight you seem so intent on handling."

Jonah stood in the center of the yard and watched her shadowed form climb the steps and disappear inside the house. A house he hadn't been able to protect.

He worked his hands into fists, frustration mounting. He had a good idea exactly who'd been behind the intrusions. Who'd been responsible for destroying their home and for the hurt in Lillian's eyes.

He drew long breaths and willed his anger to cool. Heaven help Jeffery Tanner if Jonah couldn't get control of himself come morning.

The tempest roiled through him, until in desperation he did the only thing left he could do. In the cool of the night, with darkness swelling like a living thing around him, Jonah dropped to his knees and prayed.

Lillian stared at the ceiling, thoughts too tangled to sleep. Whoever had broken into the house had done a thorough job of searching. At least through the walls. They'd neglected looking in the kitchen cabinets behind the bags of flour, however, where her father's ledger remained.

Without the book or the crates Jonah had hidden, had the intruders gone away empty-handed? If so, would they consider the venture a failure and leave the house be?

Or would they be back again?

She threw back the cover and scooted out of bed. Her window looked out onto the moonlit rear yard. Where could Jonah have possibly hidden five large crates? Her gaze rose over the fence and to the shadows beyond. An expanse of land stretched between their row of houses and the next street over. She couldn't make out the shapes of the buildings in that direction. Surely Jonah wouldn't have placed the crates outside of the fence.

First thing in the morning, they needed to go to the sheriff. Turn in the evidence and have Mr. Tanner questioned.

Except she didn't have any proof.

Lillian paced in front of the window. If she were to go see Mr. Tanner first, would she be able to root out his involvement? Could she demand to see the books for the company?

No, that wouldn't matter. If anything in the company wasn't on the up-and-up, she wouldn't find evidence clearly written in the books. Her father had been too smart for that. Mr. Tanner would be as well.

Lillian leaned her head against the cool windowpane.

Why did her father have to be a criminal? Why was it that each time she thought things would be better, another snare reached out to grab her?

She stared out the window deep into the night, praying for guidance.

But no answers ever came.

CHAPTER TWENTY-SEVEN

J onah breathed in the fresh morning air, his entire being feeling lighter than he could ever remember. He'd taken Ma's words to heart and spent the majority of the night in prayer. He'd had little sleep, but the time had been well worth the loss.

He felt whole again. A new man with a new purpose.

Out in the front yard, a squirrel chased its fellow across the grass and up the maple tree, their excited chatter making him smile. Even the sunshine felt brighter, the air cleaner, the critters more jovial.

His circumstances hadn't changed. Merely his perspective. He remembered a story in the Bible where a demon-possessed man was healed. Jesus sent the demons into a herd of pigs, freeing the man. The man begged to follow Jesus.

But Jesus had other plans.

The notion had wrapped around Jonah's insides, tugging him toward a hard truth. What he wanted wouldn't always be God's plan. And maybe a bit of his own struggles stemmed from him always resisting the path the Lord laid out before him.

The front door opened and footsteps sounded behind him. Soft and slow. Lillian.

He nodded toward the playing squirrels, thinking their antics would elicit a smile. "Beautiful morning."

"I brought you coffee." Lillian's tone said she'd had little sleep as well, and her words carried an undercurrent of disappointment and weariness.

Jonah accepted the steaming mug. "Thank you." They stared out over the yard for a few moments before he broke the silence. "We will rebuild what they destroyed, Lillian. You have my word."

She remained silent for a long time. Frustration replaced the weariness in her voice. "They'll just keep coming. Keep destroying until they have everything they want." She shook her head. "I'm going to Mr. Tanner and getting all of this out in the open."

"I don't think that's a good idea." He turned to look at her. She was already dressed for the day with her hair perfectly styled.

Her eyes flashed. "I'm tired of hidden plans and dishonesty."

He had the feeling she meant more than merely the bootleg liquor. "We need to take everything to the sheriff."

Lines tightened around her mouth. "You told the sheriff about the first intruder. He did nothing."

He couldn't refute her. The sheriff had said they were looking into the incident, but without a better description, they really had no way of knowing who had snuck into the house that night. "There's a lot more happening now."

"I want proof first." Conviction steeled her tone. "I want to leave no doubt that man belongs in jail."

"What did you have in mind? We have the liquor and the ledger."

"Which only point to my father." The steel in her voice rusted a little. "We need evidence of who destroyed the house."

"How are we going to get that? Mr. Tanner isn't going to confess to anything."

"What if we catch him?"

Jonah didn't care for the glint in Lillian's eyes. "You want to use the whiskey as bait." He shook his head. "Then what? We aren't lawmen. This is something the sheriff needs to do."

After a long moment, Lillian finally said, "Very well."

She left him on the porch to contemplate his options. By the time he'd finished his coffee, he had at least one part of a plan in mind.

After rinsing his mug and pulling on a pair of sturdy work gloves, Jonah hauled broken boards and debris out the back door, through the yard, and out the rear gate. Along the back of the fence, five crates sat in a neat row. Undiscovered.

He carefully stacked the broken boards, concealing the crates with each trip from the house.

Lillian tucked a stray lock of hair under her blue straw hat, secured her bundle under one arm, and headed for the door.

"Where are you going?" Melanie's startled voice followed Lillian through the foyer.

"Out." She didn't look back.

"Clearly." A huff of air. "Out where, exactly?"

Lillian bristled. Melanie wasn't her mother. She didn't owe her an explanation. A tingle of guilt tried to work its way into her heart, but Lillian pushed it away. "I'll be back soon." Without waiting for Melanie to protest, she scrambled out the door and onto the front porch.

She had to hurry before Jonah caught sight of her. Not that she had any reason to hide from him. She simply didn't want to be delayed in her task. She exited the front gate and turned toward town.

Oh no.

Lillian clutched the package tighter. A two-wheeled carriage rumbled down the lane, headed straight for her and carrying two people who would most certainly delay her. Lillian dipped her head in greeting and quickened her pace. Perhaps if she hurried along—

"Lillian!" Alma's voice carried on the clear air. "Lillian!"

She pulled up short. Her sour mood gave no excuse for rudeness. She forced her lips to turn up into a friendly smile.

Alma tugged the reins and pulled the horse to a stop.

"Heavens, child. What's got you in such a dither?" Edith leaned forward to look around her daughter, bright eyes sweeping over Lillian. "You look madder than a wet hen."

Clearly, her attempt at passive politeness had failed. "Good morning, Edith, Alma."

Edith's sharp eyes flicked to the package tucked under Lillian's arm. "And where is my spirited little niece headed off to on this fine morning?" She cocked an eyebrow underneath her old-fashioned bonnet and cut a pointed glance at the bundle again.

Despite herself, Lillian shifted the package. "A bit of business, is all."

Alma smiled sweetly. "We've come to help Rose with the new curtains today. Could your business wait?" She gestured toward something on the floor. "We brought a lovely picnic, and I'd hate to miss your company."

A fire sparked in her center. "We won't be hanging curtains

today. Someone destroyed the house while we were away in Dahlonega."

Alma sucked in a breath. "Destroyed?" She glanced at the house, confusion tugging on her features.

"They broke the new shelves and took a hammer to the walls."

"But why would anyone do something like that?" Alma stared back at the house and shook her head.

Edith's eyes narrowed. "Something to do with that brother of mine, I take it." She pulled the reins from Alma's hands. "Down you go, dear. Go help Melanie with the mess. I'll accompany Lillian."

Accompany her? "Thank you, but that's not necessary."

Alma gathered her skirts and stepped down from the carriage in a sweep of floral fabric. She grabbed the picnic basket and looped it over one arm. With the other she snaked a hand around Lillian's shoulders and leaned close, her voice low enough for only Lillian to hear. "No sense arguing with her. She'll get her way in the end. Besides, from the looks of things, you might need her help. Two formidable women are better than one, yes?" A light sparkled in her eyes as she gave Lillian a squeeze and walked toward the house with a gentle sway.

"Well, let's get on with it." Edith jiggled the harness and the mare bobbed her head. "Where to?"

Lillian measured the lines of determination etched across Edith's brow and decided it best to heed Alma's advice. She scrambled into the carriage and settled the bundle on her lap, fingers clutching it tightly.

Edith guided the horse back toward the center of town. "All right. Out with it. I need to know what we're facing."

After only a slight hesitation, Lillian sighed. She had no reason to keep anything from her father's sister.

Family.

"We found bootleg liquor in the walls." She tapped the wrapped bundle. "And this ledger, which seems to be a record pertaining to that liquor."

Edith's lips puckered. "Best start at the beginning."

As the horse slowly clopped into town, Lillian recounted finding the ledger, their suspicions about what the first intruder might have been looking for, the bottles in the kitchen wall, and finally the destruction they'd encountered yesterday. "I think they were looking for either the whiskey we found or other bottles we didn't discover."

Edith was quiet for a moment as the horse neared the livery. She handed the reins down to a lanky stable boy who hadn't yet grown into his ears, and the two of them dismounted. Once the horse and carriage disappeared inside the barn, Edith took her arm. "Off to Mr. Tanner, then, are we?"

The woman was keen. "I thought if I confronted him with the ledger, he might make a misstep. Let loose some sort of information." As she said it aloud, the plan seemed as flimsy as a pair of threadbare shoes. Since signing the contract with Mr. Tanner, she now only owned ten percent of the company instead of the majority share. What could she really do with so little power?

"Why not go to the sheriff?" Edith guided them around a pile of horse droppings and onto the brick pavers. "That is his job."

"He didn't do anything about the man who sneaked into the house and knocked me over." Lillian resisted the urge to rub at the place on her head that had held a bump for days.

"Not much to go on, I reckon, since none of you had a good look at him and he didn't steal anything."

The same thing Jonah had said. The frustration still nagged at her. "We have no evidence this time either. Which is why I am going to Mr. Tanner."

Edith nodded, her wide-brimmed bonnet dipping. "Excepting, of course, that you will tip your hand."

Would she? Lillian adjusted the burlap-wrapped book under her arm. "I'm not a detective, Edith. What else am I supposed to do? The sheriff has no evidence, and talking to Mr. Tanner—who clearly has a motive, I might add—is the only thing I can think of to find any."

"Push a bad man into a corner and he comes out fighting." Edith tightened her grip on Lillian's arm as they neared a squatty building forlornly tucked between two happier structures. "Maybe he got everything he wanted out of the house and you'll do nothing but stir trouble."

The heat that had started to cool swirled again. "So you propose I do nothing?" Lillian shook her head. She was finished ducking her head and letting others take advantage of her. "If Mr. Tanner is involved, he deserves justice."

"That he does."

Something about the way Edith spoke gave Lillian pause. They lingered outside the building belonging to Jackson and Tanner Distribution. She should have visited before now, but she'd been too occupied with getting the money to really look closely at her inheritance of her father's company.

A scandalous inheritance, by all accounts.

"What a mess." Lillian's voice cracked on the last word, and she clutched the ledger tighter.

"Let's leave that thing, shall we?" Edith tapped the ledger. "That might be the very thing he's after."

Feeling foolish, Lillian groaned. "Let's just go home."

Edith took the book from her hands and turned her around. "I say we take this to the bank for safekeeping before we have a little chat with Mr. Tanner. Discreetly, of course. Then we will stop by the sheriff's office."

Leaving the book at the bank was a fine idea she should have thought of herself.

Edith turned to walk in the other direction toward the bank. Lillian considered and dismissed a half dozen ways to approach Mr. Tanner. None of them were likely to get her anywhere. By the time they'd secured the book in the bank's vault and returned to the street, she had no better ideas.

"If it's not stepping on your toes," Edith said as they trekked down the street, "I'd like to have a go at Mr. Tanner. He's of the same cloth as Floyd, and I daresay I know a thing or two about such men."

Lillian frowned. "Like what?"

"They are charming, but underneath is a cunning spirit that is always looking for one angle or another. They have a dozen schemes going at once and can map out their moves far in advance."

What kind of man had her father been? From what he'd said in his letter, he'd been involved in criminal affairs, but by the way Edith spoke, perhaps she could help Lillian understand a little more of what had happened between her parents.

All these years she'd thought herself a widow's daughter. Turned out she'd been a swindler's heiress instead.

Lillian pulled to a halt. "Perhaps you were right. We need

to go to the sheriff first. Then they at least know to be suspicious of Mr. Tanner."

"Whatever you think is best, dear."

The smile in Edith's voice drew Lillian's eyes up from the bricks passing underneath her feet and straight to the swinging sign announcing the sheriff's office. She grunted a laugh.

They entered an office that smelled of woodsmoke, tobacco, and unwashed men. Lillian wrinkled her nose as the door behind them closed, cutting off both the fresh air and the majority of the light.

"Morning, ladies. Can I help you?" A man with out-of-fashion muttonchops rose from a squeaking chair positioned behind the desk in the center of the room.

"Sheriff Whittle, if you please." Edith lifted her chin. "Tell him Edith Hampshire wishes to speak with him."

A few moments later the muttonchops man returned with a thick-necked fellow in a sturdy suit and functional hat. With his gray beard that brushed the top of his collar, Lillian guessed him to be around sixty.

A smile shifted the hair around his mouth. "Why, Mrs. Hampshire. What a surprise to see you here."

"We've suspicious activity to report." She gave a decisive nod. "As I'm sure you've heard, this is my niece, Miss Lillian Doyle. Someone has vandalized her house."

The sheriff's gaze darted to Lillian for a half breath. "You want to file a report?"

"Naturally." Edith chuckled. "Why else would we have come?"

The muttonchops man rummaged around in his desk and produced a small pad and pencil, which he handed over to the sheriff.

"It's the strangest thing, Fred. Must be some boys bent on mischief, best I can tell." Edith made a tsking sound.

Lillian cut her eyes at Edith. What was she talking about?

"Doesn't make a lick of sense. They busted up all the walls. Now why would anyone do a thing like that?"

A glint flickered in the sheriff's brown eyes. A fleeting look, but one Lillian didn't miss.

He overexaggerated a shrug. "No call for boys to be damaging property, most certainly." He hovered the pencil over the pad. "Was there anything missing from the house?"

"Missing?" Edith scoffed. "What could possibly be missing from inside the walls?"

There it was again. That glint.

A ball of ice formed in Lillian's stomach. Whatever was happening here, she feared it went deeper than Floyd Jackson and Jeffery Tanner.

CHAPTER TWENTY-EIGHT

———— ⟡ ————

L illian swept the floor like a madwoman, as though moving dirt could scrub the anger from her heart. Horrible men. They'd destroyed out of greed. Taken away the dreams of others without the first compassionate thought.

"You're going to work those bristles clean through the floor." Melanie put a hand on Lillian's arm, stilling her furious movements.

Lillian moved away and resumed her task. "We have a lot to do."

"Yes, but working yourself into a tizzy isn't going to make the job any easier."

She stopped sweeping to face her business partner. "It might make it go faster."

Melanie shook her head, a rueful smile on her lips. "You're a sweet girl. But every time someone says something you don't like, your back goes up straighter than a new broomstick."

Even as a protest swelled on her lips, Lillian forced her posture to relax. "Isn't it better if I channel my anger into something productive?"

Melanie shrugged. "Maybe. But you'll also work yourself

into as big of a mess as you're trying to sweep up." She tilted her head, a gentle smile coaxing Lillian to deflate a little more. "I know you're angry. We all are. But all we can do is make the best of the situation we've found ourselves in. Keep being faithful and keep moving forward."

Should she tell Melanie about what had happened at the sheriff's office this morning? A feeling wasn't much to go on. "At least it gets the energy out."

With another gentle smile, Melanie left Lillian to her sweeping and headed to the other part of the house to help Alma and Edith.

If Edith said something, then Lillian would add in her thoughts on the matter. But if all she had to go on was a look . . . well, she'd misjudged looks before. She worked the broom harder, then paused to cough as the dust cloud she'd stirred settled in her lungs.

Could the sheriff know about the bootleg operations? Did he condone them? Good thing they hadn't gone to Mr. Tanner with that ledger. Problem was, Lillian still had no idea how they were going to bring the man to justice.

An hour or so later, Lillian had made far more progress on her task than she'd anticipated. Jonah and the others were gathered in the bookshop, an area she still couldn't bring herself to enter. Perhaps when all the debris had been removed, she could look at the room as a blank canvas once again rather than a depiction of dashed dreams.

She walked through the dining area, her footsteps falling on floors cleaned free of the debris. She'd righted the table and chairs and dusted the sideboard. As long as she ignored the walls, she could pretend she'd merely been tidying the room and readying it for their company.

The sounds of laughter drifted on the air. At least the others kept their spirits up.

Despite her determination, Lillian's eyes drifted to the walls. They all stood bare—strange stick posts with jagged teeth formed by the missing wallboards. The effect made the room feel poised to gobble up more secrets.

Lillian suppressed a shudder. At least she knew there weren't any more illegal bottles in the house.

She moved to the kitchen, where Melanie would soon arrive to start on the evening meal. The furniture had all been moved to the center of the room so Jonah could remove the debris. Lillian set to work with her broom, working her way around the wall.

Strange.

She paused at the back wall, inspecting the floor that had once been underneath the prep table. The boards didn't quite match. She dropped the broom and knelt close. This looked like . . . She placed her fingers underneath the edge of a board and lifted.

A trapdoor!

"Jonah! Melanie!" Lillian leaned closer and peered into the musty darkness.

Rushed footsteps sounded behind her, followed by the rich timbre of Jonah's voice. "What's happened? Are you—" The words cut off as he gained her side.

"What is it?" This from Edith, who slipped around Melanie and lowered herself to peer into the opening. "Looks like a cellar."

Jonah took Lillian by the elbow and lifted her. "I'll get a lamp and check it out."

Lillian nearly protested, except she didn't truly have any

desire to climb down into a dank cellar. Probably filled with more of her father's illegal liquor.

Alma gathered Rose and Betsy, who were both excitedly chattering about hidden treasures. If they only knew. Their voices disappeared up the steps a few moments later, and Lillian let out a breath of relief. She didn't want the girls to be part of whatever they might find.

Brushing her hands on her skirt, Edith stepped back from the cellar opening and met Lillian's eyes. "I think Alma and I should get on home before dark. And I sure could use two energetic girls to help me make supper tonight."

Melanie swung her gaze from Jonah, who had returned with a lamp, to Edith. "What? Oh. Yes. That would be lovely. I'm sure they would enjoy it." She gave a nod. "I'll pack their things for the night."

Edith gently squeezed Lillian's elbow and turned to walk with Melanie. Bless the woman for knowing exactly what to do.

Lillian tried to mentally prepare herself as Jonah swung his legs down into the opening. What would they find now? Just more liquor? Or perhaps weapons this time? Or a skeleton of someone who had crossed Floyd Jackson?

Lillian shuddered. Why couldn't her father have been a decent man? A respectable merchant who hadn't wanted to acknowledge his mistress's daughter would have been preferable.

She held her breath as Jonah disappeared beneath the floor.

Jonah placed a finger under his nose to stifle a sneeze. The cellar was deeper than he'd anticipated, leaving a good foot of clearance over his head. He lifted the lamp to illuminate the space that spanned half the width of the kitchen. Shelves lined all four walls, the only break allowing for the small ladder he'd used to descend.

"Well? How bad is it?" Lillian's pinched voice shot through the square of light above his head.

Jonah stepped to the nearest wall. "Mostly empty save a few bottles."

Floyd hadn't kept canned vegetables and potatoes in his cellar like any normal person. Of course. Jonah was not at all surprised that the cellar had been used as another storage place for the bootlegger.

How big an operation had the man been running? And how had the neighbors never noticed?

Lillian's face appeared. "That's all? Just more bottles? Nothing . . . else?"

He squinted into the light. What did she think he'd find? Before he could ask, she disappeared. Voices came from above, followed by the sound of footsteps. Must be Alma and Edith leaving with the girls.

Jonah made a slow trip around the space. Six shelves wrapped the room, each coated in a heavy layer of dust. A few broken bottles littered the floor, along with scraps of straw and a few remnants of burlap.

Had Floyd packaged and moved his stash from here and hidden it in the walls? Why? Had he planned to hide the bottles long-term? It would certainly be easier to move them from the cellar than the walls.

Jonah set the lamp on the floor and plucked a dusty bottle from the nearest shelf. The wax seal covering the cork and the French writing on the label gave him his answer. Wine. The next two bottles he inspected were similar. Apparently Floyd hadn't worried about hiding bottles of French wine. Only the white lightning and hooch.

Jonah replaced the bottle and turned toward the ladder. At least down here there wasn't any more of the liquor he'd need to store. He still had to figure out what to do with those crates. He'd planned on going to the sheriff today, but they'd been so busy cleaning that he hadn't had the chance.

It could wait until morning. And if someone found the hidden crates, he couldn't say he'd be all that concerned. Having the stuff out of his possession would be—

A noise sounded from above. Followed by a crash. Screams.

What in the—?

Jonah dashed for the ladder.

CHAPTER TWENTY-NINE

J onah's feet slipped on the bottom rung of the ladder, found
purchase, and launched him toward the light above. A
woman shouted. Men's voices followed. He scrambled
out of the cellar and gained his feet.

The bookshop. Jonah sprinted through the kitchen and
grabbed the doorframe to pivot himself into the foyer. A shadowed form lingered just inside the next room.

Jonah slammed into the figure, and the two of them hit the
ground. The compression of his lungs forced the air out, and
he sucked in a quick breath just in time to dodge a punch. He
twisted to heave his body over the other man, gaining the better position. They grappled, and Jonah landed a solid punch
to the nose of a face he'd never seen before. A face scarred
from the pox with eyes that shouted hatred.

Behind him, the women screamed.

The man thrust his shoulders off the floor and slammed his
head into Jonah's right eye. Stars erupted in his vision and his
eyes watered. He tilted backward. Blinked.

"Jonah!"

Lillian's panicked voice clawed at him, and he shook the

blurriness from his sight. He managed to hold firm and force the fellow's arms beneath his knees. The miscreant struggled, a string of obscene words flying from his lips along with his spittle. But Jonah had him now. Pinned beneath—

Pain exploded on the back of his skull. He swayed. The man beneath him heaved up, and Jonah felt himself slip sideways. Darkness crowded his vision. Ma shouted his name. Then a curtain as dark as midnight slid over his senses and everything went quiet.

Jonah's head throbbed. He drew slow breaths through his nose, hoping to quell the sickness churning in his stomach. His head felt like an axe landed at the base of his skull with each heartbeat. Two breaths. Six more. The sickness started to quiet.

Slowly, he opened his eyes, only to be met with continued darkness. He blinked. Twisted. Found his hands held securely behind him.

Awareness returned in a flood. Men in the house. Ma's and Lillian's screams. The girls. Where were the girls? He shifted, struggling against the binding. He had to find them all. Save them from . . . from whatever was happening here. He drew deep breaths, willing the throbbing to subside and his thoughts to clear.

"Jonah!" The sharp whisper stilled him. "Jonah, are you all right?"

Lillian. Here in the dark with him. He groaned, the best answer he could muster. Blast. He'd failed them. Failed to protect them when they needed him. Again.

"Where's Ma? The girls?" Each word scraped out of his throat with effort.

"I'm here. The girls left with Alma and Edith. They're safe."

Only Ma could sound calm in a situation like this. He pulled in another slow breath and stared into the darkness, seeking to find their figures. "Are you tied?"

"Yes." Lillian spoke somewhere to his left. "We both are. But we're otherwise unharmed. Mr. Tanner and two of his men are still upstairs. You've been unconscious for a long time."

Tanner. Jonah shifted against the restraints, but the cold metal of a sturdy chain dug tightly into his skin. He jiggled his hands. They'd used a chain to secure him to the ladder. Bitter defeat soured his tongue. "I knew I should have gone to the sheriff."

"Yes, well, about that."

Jonah stilled. What had Lillian done? He breathed slowly, waiting. Each breath sent more spikes of pain through his skull.

"Edith and I went to the sheriff this morning."

"That's where you took off to?" Ma huffed. "Why didn't you tell me?"

Lillian ignored the question. "Edith told Sheriff Whittle that some boys had vandalized the house. Asked him why anyone would tear up walls."

Why had she gone to the sheriff without him? Had Lillian not told Edith their suspicions, or had the woman been playing a ruse? "Explain."

Even in the darkness he sensed Lillian bristle. "I took the ledger. I was going to go talk to Mr. Tanner, see if I could dig up any evidence."

Ma sucked in a breath. "And reveal that we know about the bootlegging?"

A sharp huff of air. "A bad plan. I know that now. And not one I followed through on. Edith convinced me to stash the ledger at the bank and go talk to the sheriff. We told him about the damage." Lillian hesitated. "I can't be sure, but there was something about him when Edith told him about the walls. He asked if we found anything, and when Edith asked why there would be anything in the walls . . . well, it was this look he had."

Silence settled. Surely Lillian didn't suspect Sheriff Whittle. "What did he say?"

"That he'd look into it." She gave a derisive snort. "Just like the last time." When he didn't respond after a few heartbeats, she spoke again. "What did you tell the sheriff after the first intruder?"

Jonah grunted. "That someone sneaked in and knocked you over."

"Did you say anything about the ledger?"

"No," he said slowly, trying to think. Had he mentioned anything else? "I told him we were undergoing some construction for Ma's bakery." A sense of unease wormed through his gut. "I mentioned something about wondering what the man was after. That we'd found this strange compartment in the wall."

Lillian groaned. "We can't trust that sheriff."

Had this been his fault? Had telling the sheriff he'd found the compartment led to the men tearing through the walls? Jonah dropped his chin to his chest.

"What I don't understand," Ma said, "is what they are doing here now. They already searched the walls. They already took all the liquor."

Jonah shifted his feet. "Not exactly."

"What do you mean, *not exactly*?"

271

He tilted his head back, and the throbbing subsided a blessed measure. "I hid the crates. Until we knew what to do next."

Ma's long sigh knifed through Jonah. Another failure.

"Then I reckon that's what they're after," Ma said.

"But what are they going to do with us?" Lillian's soft words hung between them in the darkness.

Jonah tested his bindings again, but no matter how hard he twisted, the pressure of the chain never lessened. He had to get out of here. Make things right. There might be a mole in the sheriff's office, but Jonah simply couldn't fathom Sheriff Whittle a part of this scheme.

"We need to get—" Jonah let the words die as the sound of footsteps neared above them. He stiffened. If those men came for the women, he'd . . .

He'd what? He couldn't get loose. Fat lot of good he'd done protecting them.

"Ain't none of it here, boss." A reedy voice.

"It has to be somewhere." A deeper voice, belonging to the man he'd fought. "I told you, I been watching this house all week."

Someone cursed. Jonah stiffened. Tanner.

"Floyd couldn't have moved it all. He kept that last shipment for himself. I know he did. It has to be here." Boot steps that had to belong to Tanner pounded closer. "You took it, didn't you, girl?" The words reeked of desperation as Tanner flung them into the cellar. "Not enough that I had to buy my own business, eh? Or that you were too uppity to accept a fair price on the house." A dark chuckle. "But no wonder. You really are his blood. Soon as you found out about what he'd hidden for you, you planned to cut me out. Just like Floyd." His shadow blocked what little light filtered through the opening. "This is all your fault, missy."

When none of them responded, Tanner cursed again and kicked dirt at the opening. Bits of debris rained down on Jonah's head.

He had to break free. Find help. Tanner no longer sounded like a man who could be reasoned with. And men who couldn't be reasoned with were dangerous.

"What are you going to do about Samuels?" This from the man with the reedy voice. "We sent the last of everything we had to Grayson so you could pay back that loan and—"

"Shut up!" Tanner's boots thumped across the floor.

"It's here somewhere," the other man said. "Ain't never going to make it on the jug train, though. We'll have to get the trippers. You know how much they cost, boss. Are you gonna need another loan so we can—"

"Shut up, both of you!" Tanner spat.

Jonah rolled the terms around in his still-struggling mind. The trippers ran the roads from the distilleries to the cities, usually at night and fast enough to outrun the law. He'd even heard of a few with automobiles. He wasn't familiar with the jug train, but the name seemed simple enough. Illegal train cars loaded with white lightning headed for the speakeasies and blind tigers in Atlanta. An entire underworld taking advantage of the prohibition and temperance laws and making hefty sums on homemade hooch. No wonder he'd heard people referring to real whiskey as liquid gold.

And Floyd Jackson had a fortune's worth.

Tanner growled and approached the hole again. "I'll not let a dead man get the better of me. You hear? I didn't have him killed just so he could swindle me from the grave."

A small intake of breath from Lillian. Jonah squeezed his eyes tight and lifted a desperate prayer. If they didn't find a way out of this, Tanner would kill them to cover his tracks. The man would never let them take that confession to the law.

"Samuels said he'd kill us all if we don't get it there by Friday," the reedy man said.

"I said shut up!" Tanner's voice swelled with a string of curses.

So that was it. Tanner had promised a shipment to someone. Probably in Atlanta, and likely worth a lot of money. Floyd must have hidden the goods, keeping Tanner from making the sale. For whatever reason, they must not be able to get more. At least not in time.

"There could be a fire, boss. The bodies burned up inside." The laughter in the man's words sent a cold chill down Jonah's spine. "Nothing left but bones. That'll serve him right for messin' up my nose."

"We're not going to risk burning up any of the stash, you fool." Tanner mumbled something Jonah couldn't hear, and the voices moved away from the opening, fading into the distance.

Suddenly Lillian gave a small squeak.

"What?" Ma's voice sounded strained. "Are you hurt?"

"No." A shuffling sound. "I cut through the rope."

She'd escaped? Jonah strained to see in the dark. "How did you—"

"There was glass on the floor. I grabbed a sharp piece." A shadow separated from the others, and soon Lillian was next to him. She leaned close, her body pressing into him as she reached around him.

"Can't," Jonah grunted. "Chain. Not rope."

Lillian leaned back. "But there must be a way to—"

"Cut Ma free," he said. "You two escape."

"You think this old woman can outrun those men?" Ma huffed. "Lillian, you're going to have to sneak out. Go to the sheriff. Taking me will only slow you down."

Jonah opened his mouth to protest, but he couldn't think of another option. One person would have a better chance than two, and Ma wouldn't be able to run as fast as Lillian. As much as he hated it, he couldn't see another way. "You can do it."

"What? No." Lillian leaned close, her voice in his ear. "How do you think I'm going to get up that ladder and out the door without anyone seeing me?"

"We'll create a distraction."

"How?"

He had no idea.

"And then what? I go to the sheriff? What if he's in on the whole thing?"

Another point he had no answer for. Jonah leaned his head back against the ladder. *A little help, Father. Please.*

"We get them down here in the dark," Ma said. "And then she can sneak up the ladder."

"They'd notice." Jonah shook his head, a plan forming. "You need to go to Sheriff Whittle, Lillian."

"But I don't know if—"

"We have to take that chance."

The voices moved closer again.

"Trust me," Jonah said in a harsh whisper. "Get back against the wall where they can't see you and wait. I have an idea."

Lillian hesitated only a moment, then shifted away from him, disappearing into the shadows once more.

"Hey! Tanner!" Jonah tilted his head toward the opening above him. "Let's make a trade!"

A few breaths later, the man appeared above him. "You're in no position to be making demands, farm boy."

Jonah craned his neck to get a better view. Where were the other two? "That so? Well, seeing as how I'm the only person who knows where to find your stash, I'd say otherwise."

Tanner growled. "Where is it?"

"Not so fast. I want assurances. Promises the women will remain unharmed. Let them go and I'll tell you where it is."

"No deal." Tanner knelt closer. "No one leaves until I have what I want."

"Then I'll go with you. Show you where it is. Once you have it loaded, you leave. No harm to the women."

"Of course." Tanner chuckled. "I wish no one harm. Only want what's mine." He hesitated. "But what's to say they won't double-cross me first chance they get?"

Jonah's mind whirled. He had nothing to offer as collateral. "You won't get any trouble from us. You leave us be, and we won't breathe a word to anyone about what you do. Lillian will turn over everything to you."

Tanner sucked his teeth. "See, I trusted a man's word once on nothing but blind faith, and that left me with this situation here. So you'll understand if I'm not keen on making that mistake again."

"I have the ledger." Lillian's voice, clear and strong, filled the silence. "If anything should happen to us, I'm sure there will be lots of questions about the nature of that ledger . . ." She let the implications dangle.

Brilliant. If anything happened to Lillian, the banker would have to go through her belongings in the vault, including the ledger.

Tanner cursed. "Fine. We all go our ways. Tell me where you've hidden my property."

"You'll have to release me so I can show you," Jonah said. "Telling won't do much good." He'd take a twisted route. Give Lillian as much time as possible.

Silence stretched for several moments. "There'll be a gun at your back every step, Peterson. So don't think you can get away with anything."

Footsteps sounded on the ladder.

"They'll kill you as soon as you show them." Lillian's harsh whisper sliced through him.

But she and Ma would be safe. "Then you better run fast."

CHAPTER THIRTY

urry! Lillian grabbed Melanie's wrists as soon as the men's footsteps faded. The bit of glass nicked Lillian's palm as she sawed, making her hand slick with both sweat and blood.

"Don't waste time on that." Melanie leaned away. "You need to hurry."

Lillian snatched Melanie's arm and grabbed the rope. Thank goodness the ruffians hadn't used chain on the women like they did on Jonah. "I'm not going to leave you. The more time you spend resisting is less time we have to escape." And save Jonah.

Melanie mumbled something incoherent that Lillian took as agreement, and she sawed faster. "Let me know if I cut you."

After a few breathless moments, the rope frayed, then snapped, freeing Melanie from where she'd been tied to a sturdy post. She rubbed her wrists.

Lillian grabbed her elbow and heaved. "Come on."

The older woman scrambled to her feet, and they felt their way to the ladder.

Lillian took Melanie's hand and guided it to the first rung. "No, wait. Let me make sure they've gone."

She made her way up the ladder, slipping twice. Slowly, she eased up until her eyes cleared the opening.

The kitchen stood empty. Quiet.

Thank you, Lord.

But there was little time to celebrate small miracles. "Come on."

Once she heard Melanie on the ladder beneath her, Lillian crawled onto the kitchen floor and crouched, her body on high alert. An eternity later, Melanie scrambled up out of the cellar.

They tiptoed across the floor and paused to listen. No sounds came from the house save Lillian's own erratic breathing. They crept the rest of the way through the kitchen and past the dining table.

Lillian stopped again at the doorway into the foyer. Would they have left a man guarding the door? She poked her head out.

Empty.

She breathed another sigh of relief and one more quick prayer of thanks.

They scooted through the foyer. The front door opened without protest, and the welcome scent of outdoor air caressed Lillian's face. The yard dripped in shadows, but none of them proved more nefarious than that of shrubbery.

As soon as they cleared the gate, they broke into a sprint toward town.

This wasn't how Jonah had expected to die—with the cold metal of a pistol jammed between his shoulders as he led a trio of bootleggers on a wild goose chase. What would it cost him when they finally realized he'd only circled back to the rear fence?

It didn't matter. He needed to buy time.

"Get moving." The barrel dug deeper. The man to whom Jonah had given the broken nose to go with his pockmarked face gave a dark chuckle. "Slow steps ain't going to change your fate."

Jonah stopped. "If you're going to shoot me anyway, then why should I show you where it is?"

"Because." Tanner's voice snaked over his shoulder. "You know if you don't, nothing will save your mother and that sassy little city gal." He sucked his teeth. "Or those two little girls you sent to the Watson farm. It would be such a shame if that farm were to burn, don't you think?"

Jonah clenched his jaw and stepped forward. Had Lillian made it out of the house yet? He lifted a prayer for her safety and for protection for Ma.

They continued the slow trudge down the residential street, in the direction opposite town. At the next intersection, he turned left.

If God had mercy on him, someone would be up at this hour of the night and would notice the man with a gun in Jonah's back and the death parade marching down their street.

But as house after house passed in slumbering ignorance, his hope dwindled.

Somehow he managed to make two more turns before Tanner finally snatched him to a halt. "You're leading us in circles." When Jonah didn't respond, he barked an order to the man with the reedy voice. "Dan, go back to the house and get the old woman. Farm boy here needs some motivation."

Jonah's stomach twisted. "Wait." He nodded toward the turn just up ahead. If he remembered correctly, it would lead them down the road that ran parallel to Floyd's property and would take them to the crates stored on the back side of the fence. "The last turn is just there. You have my word."

Tanner grunted, but a second later the barrel in Jonah's back jarred again and they were moving forward. Their boots crunched as they walked, causing an eerie cracking noise that grated on Jonah's already frayed nerves.

A couple hundred feet down the road, Jonah paused. He gestured with his shoulder toward an empty lot. "It's that way."

Tanner scratched his chin, his lean features barely visible in the half-moon's light. "Through that field?"

The fact that this patch of land directly behind the house remained empty was the main reason he'd chosen this location. "There's a fence at the back of the property. That's where I hid the crates."

They turned off the road and past two sleeping homes unaware of the evil creeping between them.

When they reached the fence, Jonah gestured toward the pile of debris. "Everything we found is under there."

Tanner took the gun from the other man. He made a half circle to stand to Jonah's left, keeping the barrel aimed at Jonah's head. "Start looking."

Jonah took a step forward as both of the goons rushed to the pile.

"Not you," Tanner said to Jonah. His eyes drifted toward the men throwing splintered boards on the ground. If they made any more noise, someone might come out of one of those houses to investigate.

Please, God, let it be so.

If Jonah could create enough of a distraction, maybe he could escape.

"Got 'em, boss." The reedy fellow Tanner had called Dan tapped the top of one of the crates.

The larger goon grunted as he toppled several boards. "Looks like four more under here."

A smile entered Tanner's voice. "It better all be there."

Jonah grimaced at the dark greed curling around the words. "Every bottle we found in the wall is in those crates." When Tanner didn't respond, Jonah hurried to add, "I have no idea if that's everything or maybe even more than what you thought, but that's all we found."

Tanner grunted an incoherent response, and the gun dipped from Jonah's head to his hip. A moment later Tanner moved forward to peer over the crates.

Jonah tensed. If he ran, how far could he make it before getting shot?

He took a step back. Two more.

The men focused on the crates, pulling out bottles and exclaiming over the contents.

Three more steps. Five.

Jonah turned and ran. His legs pumped, his feet gaining ground. He listed to one side, off balance with his hands bound behind him. Only a few more feet to the nearest house. To help. He opened his mouth to shout.

A pistol shot cracked in the air, and Jonah's world exploded in pain.

Lillian's breath came in great heaving gulps. A stitch in her side made her droop, but she kept running. There wasn't enough time. Finally, the courthouse came into view. The sheriff's office stood just down the street from the large building. Gas streetlamps illuminated the empty sidewalks. Not a single deputy out on duty.

Melanie had fallen behind some time ago. Lillian could only pray the woman remained safe while she fetched the sheriff.

She forced her legs to move faster. Her skirts twisted around her legs, hindering her stride. She hiked them up over her knees and jumped over the low brick wall surrounding the courthouse, taking a shortcut through the yard to the sheriff's office. Her feet churned in the soft grass and launched her toward the beckoning light filtering through the small building's windows.

Lillian hit the door with the full force of her momentum. Her shoulder screamed in protest as she righted herself and pounded on the door.

Shouts rose from within. A moment later, the door swung open.

Lillian clutched her side. "Help." She stumbled forward, losing her balance as her legs trembled uncontrollably. "Please . . ."

Gasping for breath, she collapsed.

CHAPTER THIRTY-ONE

W hat in the dickens?" A man's gruff voice filled the room. Footsteps came closer.

Lillian struggled to get her feet underneath her. A massive paw gripped her elbow and snatched her to her feet.

"What's happened? Are you harmed?" Sheriff Whittle's face hovered over her, wide-set eyes simmering with both alarm and concern. In a sleepy town like Dawsonville, women probably didn't often burst into his office in the middle of the night.

Lillian gulped air. "Help . . . please . . . house." Her lungs burned as she forced them to give her enough air to form words. "Going to . . . kill him . . . please."

"Who? Kill who?" He shook her elbow, but that did nothing more than send Lillian off balance.

She sucked more air. "The bootleggers!"

Sheriff Whittle's eyes widened. "Coleman! Get the horses."

A burst of activity erupted around her as the sheriff's two deputies scrambled into action. Lillian focused on her breathing. She had to get enough air to speak.

A few moments later, the sheriff guided her to a bench near the door. "Wait here."

"No!" Lillian refused to sit. "I'm going with you."

The sheriff frowned. "This is hardly—"

"Horses are out front, sir." A man hurried past her, and the sheriff released her arm.

Lillian scrambled after them, her feet snagging on the hem of her skirt. Her legs felt as firm as hot butter, but she managed to make it out the front door and into the night air. The three men swung into their saddles with practiced ease and turned their mounts toward Lillian's house. Hooves pounded on the pavers. In an instant, they disappeared into the darkness.

Lillian hiked her skirts once more and ignored the trembling in her legs. Lamplight bathed the street in front of the courthouse, and she negotiated with her body to take her as far as the first lamppost. Then the next.

When she reached the fourth island of light, a feminine figure emerged from around the side of the courthouse.

"Lillian!" Melanie scrambled toward her. "I saw them ride by." She gained Lillian's side, her own breathing labored. "You made it."

Time would tell. She may have done nothing more than send men to Tanner's aid. Not Jonah's.

Please, God.

Lillian's lungs still heaved, so she gave a simple nod that would have to suffice. The two of them turned and trotted back through the center of town at the quickest pace they could manage. She hadn't even told the sheriff where Jonah had hidden the crates. What if they didn't find him in time?

She lengthened her stride, ignoring all protests her legs tried to wield. Melanie kept pace with her past the mercantile, but when they reached the bank, she snagged Lillian's sleeve and bent forward, fingers clutching her side. "You go. I'm right behind you."

Lillian wanted to argue, but urgency pounded through her with each heartbeat. She gave Melanie's arm a quick squeeze, prayed her friend would be safe, and forced herself to run again. Skirts at a scandalous height, she stretched her legs to their full length. By the time she made it back to the house, her lungs were aflame and her vision had started to swim. Still she pushed herself through the gate, up the front steps, and into the house.

Fire seared through Jonah's leg like swarms of burning insects chewing away at his flesh. Behind him shouts erupted, followed by another shot. He flattened himself on the ground, trying to conceal his body in the ankle-high grass. He wouldn't stay hidden long.

Working his elbows beneath him, he belly-crawled toward the nearest neighbor's house. His vision swam, and the lower left part of his body weighted each of his forward propulsions. He focused on the structure before him. He could reach it.

Must reach it.

The rear door of the brick house flew open, and the light of a lamp held high beckoned Jonah nearer. A little closer. The toe of his boot dug into the soft earth, forcing his weight forward. He clawed with his fingers, willing himself nearer the beacon of hope.

"What in tarnation is going on out here?" A woman's voice rang out in the night, followed quickly by the distinct click of a loaded shotgun.

"You men there!" A man's voice this time, gruff with sleep but loaded with steel. "What are you doing?"

Jonah collapsed, his face pressed against damp ground, and willed his vision not to leave him. Not yet. Fresh earth filled his nose. The relief of unconsciousness begged him to surrender. He had to call out for help.

But his head pounded and his thoughts felt as slow as cold molasses. He opened his mouth. Filled his lungs. Words wouldn't come. His fingers sought the tender flesh on his hip. Warm, thick liquid coated his hand.

Alarm spiked through him, pushing out some of the fog. "Help!"

The weakness in his voice fueled another surge of desperation. He refused to lie here unconscious, his blood fertilizing the ground while Ma and Lillian faced danger alone. He would not fail them.

Not again.

"Help!" He pushed the word out with the last of his strength, then let his face fall back against the grass.

Footsteps pounded near, followed by blessed light.

Empty. Lillian paused in the silent foyer. Where was the sheriff? His deputies? They should be here, searching the house.

She skidded down the hall and through the kitchen. The crates. Maybe God had been merciful and even now the sheriff would be on his way to where Jonah led the men to the illegal liquor. Maybe she'd made it in time to save him. Lillian tugged on the doorknob and wrenched open the door. She surged outside.

Lantern light glowed beyond the rear fence. Someone shouted.

A gunshot ripped through the air and sucked what little air Lillian had from her lungs. She grabbed for the post on the back porch, holding on as the world swam. More men's shouts.

Hoofbeats!

The sheriff. Lillian scrambled down the steps and dashed through the yard.

"Thank God you're here! I've caught them!"

Lillian froze. Jeffery Tanner.

The despicable man shouted again, presumably to the sheriff. "Uncovered an entire operation that Floyd Jackson kept from me."

How dare he! Lillian thrust open the back fence gate and stepped into a scene of chaos. Lanterns bobbed wildly around the open field. Two gun barrels swung her direction. One from a deputy and the other belonging to her elderly neighbor.

Mr. Thatcher held a shotgun, his wife a raised lantern. Lillian's gaze slid off them, passed the sheriff, and barely snagged on Mr. Tanner's reddened face. Where was Jonah?

"There!" Mr. Tanner pointed at Lillian. "She's her father's daughter all right. The little swindler." He gestured at the crates. "An entire bootleg operation, I tell you."

Lillian's jaw dropped. Her? Surely no one would believe such nonsense. But none of that mattered right now. "What did you do to Jonah? Where is he?"

The sheriff gestured to his deputy. "Take them all in for questioning."

Ignoring Lillian's protests, the deputy gave a tight nod and waved his gun barrel at the broad-chested fellow Jonah had grappled with earlier.

Pain tangled in heaving knots through Lillian's chest. She stepped toward Mr. Tanner, each word cold and measured. "Where is Jonah?"

Mrs. Thatcher held up a hand and moved closer, as one might toward a spooked horse. "He was shot. My Luke got him inside while we came after these ruffians." She gestured toward the house behind them, where light spilled from an open doorway. "Emma will tend him while Luke fetches the doctor."

Shot? The word bounced through her heart, finding the tender places that yearned to call Jonah her own and flinging them wide.

Lillian swayed. She hadn't made it in time. She had to see him. Had to—

"Come with me, Miss Doyle." The sheriff's gruff voice pierced her spiraling thoughts. Once again his large hand wrapped around her elbow. "I have quite a few questions."

Questions for her? Lillian pulled against the vise holding her in place. "I have to get to Jonah."

"I must insist you return to my office. Everything can be sorted from there."

Was the man mad? Lillian fought against the urge to scream, jam the heel of her boot into his foot, and free herself from his grasp. But rash action would gain her nothing, as good as the emotional release might feel.

Lillian forced herself to calm. She met the sheriff's hard gaze. "Surely you don't think I had anything to do with this."

His cold silence clenched Lillian's stomach.

"I am the one who came to you!"

His eyes narrowed, and he tugged her arm. "If you will not come peacefully, I'll have no choice but to place you in handcuffs."

Her eyes darted to the faces around her, finding compassion nowhere except mingled with the confused expressions of the Thatchers.

Tanner. Lillian's gaze sought his as the sheriff turned her toward the deputy. A wicked gleam in his dark eyes sent spikes of terror through her.

Would she end up like her father? Thrown in prison until someone could come silence her permanently?

She twisted in Sheriff Whittle's grasp. "Unhand me!"

The sheriff's grip only tightened. "Coleman, take this lady into custody." He released his hold so quickly Lillian stumbled. "And get all of these men in handcuffs."

Mr. Tanner stuttered a protest. "Wait now, Sheriff." He showed his palms. "There's no call for that. You know me. I've never broken the law."

The snake!

"I'm sorry, miss," the deputy, a man not much older than herself, said in a grave tone. "This will go easier if you comply."

Despair fought with panic, both ravenous wolves seeking to devour her. Yet she stood motionless. Too numbed by the injustice to do anything more.

Tanner continued to argue with the sheriff as his two men were also bound. The fact that he also was in custody was the only spark of hope Lillian had that truth might yet win out.

"Mr. and Mrs. Thatcher." Sheriff Whittle watched as his deputies bound the two ruffians and tied them to his horse. "I'd like you to come back to the station for questioning too."

"What for?" Mr. Thatcher scratched his tousled gray hair with one hand while still balancing his shotgun against one hip. "May and I heard a shot. We got up to investigate. Found young Jonah Peterson bleeding in our yard and calling for help. Y'all rode in right after."

Lillian clasped the fabric at her throat. *Oh, Jonah. Please, God.*

After a moment of hesitation, Sheriff Whittle grunted. "I'll have more questions for you in the morning." He cast a pointed look at the crates stashed within sight of the Thatchers' back door.

Mr. Thatcher shrugged. "I'll come by first thing." He took his wife by the arm, and they turned back toward their house.

Lillian took a step after them. She just needed to see Jonah for a moment. Make sure he would be safe.

"You're coming with me, Miss Doyle." The sheriff's voice left no room for argument.

Lillian tried anyway. "I must check on Jonah."

Bushy eyebrows rose. "You a nurse?"

She shook her head.

"Doctor?"

Lillian glared at him.

The look had no effect. "Then there's nothing more you can do."

The sound of protesting hinges snagged his attention, and he turned toward the gate.

A feminine figure emerged, shoulders heaving with labored breaths. Melanie.

"Oh, thank the good Lord." Melanie put her hand to her heart, her chest rising and falling rapidly. "You've captured them."

The sheriff's eyes roamed over the group, lingering on each person, including Melanie and Lillian. "So I have."

The pounding of hooves brought another mounted deputy.

Sheriff Whittle thumbed toward the Thatcher house. "Reynolds. Keep an eye on Jonah Peterson. Don't give him the opportunity to escape."

Escape?

A ball of ice formed in the pit of Lillian's stomach. Melanie's protests fell on deaf ears as she was herded in with the rest of them. It didn't matter that they had gone to the law. The truth might not even matter, given the way the sheriff refused to listen.

She'd been right all along. The corruption went deeper than Floyd Jackson and Jeffery Tanner, plummeting all the way into the hearts of the very men who'd sworn to uphold truth and justice.

CHAPTER THIRTY-TWO

⟡

Morning light seeped through the bars separating Lillian from the break of a new day. How long had she been in this cell? She drew her knees up beneath her on the hard cot that made for the only furnishing in the small room.

They hadn't even put her with Melanie for company and comfort. They'd thrown her in this tiny, dark room with as much compassion as a vulture had for a field mouse. She'd passed the hours reliving every moment since she'd first found out the father she'd thought long dead had instead recently died and left her with this wretched inheritance. She evaluated every decision and mistake that had landed her here.

Why, Lord? Why bring me here for it to end like this?

Had she not tried to surrender her own ways to follow God's prompting? Had she not worked to be a stronger, better woman? Why, then, did he punish her so? Dark thoughts plagued her, weighing her heart. Tears no longer welled, having been spent some hours ago.

Lillian leaned her head against the wall, closing her eyes against the new day.

Sometime later, a key scraped against the lock, jarring her from fitful dozing. The door opened, revealing a short, stocky fellow with a shock of red hair and a nose almost long and thin enough to serve as a blade.

"Let's go." He gestured toward the door. "Sheriff's got questions for you."

And she had a few for him. Lillian straightened, indignation giving her the strength to push back against injustice. She was not "her father's daughter." No matter what it took, she would prove it so.

She held her head high as she passed through the door. The deputy led her out into a short hallway and past three other closed doors. Did one of them hold Melanie? Mr. Tanner and his men?

The door at the end of the hall stood open. The deputy waved her inside, then shut the door behind her. This room looked similar to the one she'd just left, save a little more space and a table that replaced the cot. The same hard, unyielding floor. The same cold stone walls broken by only one small window striped with bars.

Two sturdy chairs sat on opposite sides of a scarred table with a surface that looked like it had once served as a butcher's block. The one window faced the rear of the building, but nothing stood beyond it except a few scraggly trees and some struggling grass that stretched toward the nearby woods, longing to reach its more vibrant fellows.

Lillian leaned against the wall and stared out the closed window, wishing she could at least get a breath of clean air. Her legs still ached from running, but she refused to sit and wait. Standing somehow gave her a measured feeling of control, and she held on to it with fervor.

A few moments later, the door opened and closed, and a man's boots crossed into the room.

Lillian whirled. "Where is Jonah? Is he all right?"

The sheriff gestured to the table. "Join me, Miss Doyle. We need to clear up a few things."

A few things? She should say so. Lillian clenched her hands, and her nails dug into the tender place she'd sliced in her palm. The pain fueled her resolve. "I'll not discuss anything with you until you tell me how Jonah fares."

The sheriff held her gaze, unflinching. "He's with the doctor."

"And?"

"And that is what I know. He continues in the doctor's care."

That meant he was still alive. She could be thankful for that, at least. "And Melanie?"

"Awaiting questioning." He gestured to the table. "Please sit, Miss Doyle. We have several things to discuss."

"I couldn't agree more." Lillian fisted a hand on her hip. "Starting with why you hauled me in here like a criminal after I ran all the way to town to fetch you in the first place."

The sheriff opened his mouth, but once the words started, Lillian couldn't hold them back.

"I reported an intruder to you not only once but twice!" Her voice rose in pitch, throat tightening in fury. "And you did nothing. Then I came for you—after having been captured and thrown into a cellar, mind you—only for you to side with the very criminal responsible for the entire affair."

"Miss Doyle, that is—"

Lillian stepped toward the table, which served as a wall separating her from where the sheriff stood by the door, a set of papers clutched in his hand. "Are you proud of yourself?

A man sworn to justice but so corrupted by greed that you would let the innocent bear the crimes of the guilty?"

Silence fell on the room. He stared at her, the emergence of a vein across his forehead the only indication that she'd struck a nerve.

The sheriff cleared his throat and gestured to the table. "Have a seat, Miss Doyle."

The man's insufferable calm further stoked the fire in her belly, but she saw no other option than to plop herself down into the chair and glare at the man who seated himself across from her.

"What do you know of the business left to you by Floyd Jackson?"

Lillian laced her fingers together on the table, willing herself to calm. A lady conducted herself with poise. She needed him to see her as a lady and not a criminal. She tried to school the ire still insisting on tainting her voice but succeeded only in part. "Very little, other than what the banker and Mr. Tanner told me. It is a shipping business of some sort, moving goods from warehouses to stores. Though it seems that the business was also, at least in part, a front for distributing illegal liquor."

He nodded, leafing through the papers. "And what of your mother's enterprises in Atlanta?"

"Enterprises?" Lillian shook her head. "The only enterprise my mother is involved in is obtaining invitations to functions held by those in social stations beyond hers."

Sheriff Whittle plucked a page from his stack and pushed it across the table to her.

Lillian scanned the top. Sucked in a sharp breath. The short set of words could have reached out and slapped her.

This couldn't be.

"You'll see here a letter that names one Mrs. Florence Doyle as the contact point between her late husband's business and his partners in Atlanta."

"She was never his wife." The whispered words seeped out as Lillian stared at the page in front of her. It was a detailed description of a shipment and the contacts with whom her mother was supposed to meet. She didn't recognize the hand-writing. It didn't match her father's, at least.

Her nerves tingled. Mother's name. Right there on the page.

"Were you aware that Mrs. Doyle planned and organized the sale and distribution of illegal moonshine and whiskey to various blind tigers around the city?"

Lillian could only stare at him. Mother had a way with words, yes, but she couldn't have been involved in such a scheme.

Could she?

Lillian shook her head again, loose curls that had long since come unpinned swaying against her neck. "That's not possible."

He pulled out another paper and placed it on the table between them. Some other letter she didn't bother to try to read. "Where do you suppose Mrs. Doyle got the funds to pay for her residence and lifestyle without any sort of employment?"

"My father sent her . . ." The words died. He'd sent her an allowance. A way to care for Lillian. Or had it been something more? Payment for her part in his schemes?

Her father's letter had mentioned another man Mother had loved. Had he been involved? Included Mother?

Lillian's throat ached. She wanted to vehemently deny the possibility, but she knew far too well how silvered Mother's tongue could be.

Sheriff Whittle met her gaze, expression unreadable. "According to the documentation we uncovered, Mr. Jackson and Mrs. Doyle were involved in an intricate organization that ran a substantial bootlegging business from Dawsonville to Atlanta. Mr. Tanner became aware of inconsistencies in the business finances and confronted his partner."

"Is that why my father went to jail?"

"Mr. Jackson was arrested on charges of drunkenness in public." He tapped a finger on the table, studying her. "He died of a heart apoplexy the next day."

Lillian pulled her lower lip through her teeth. Her palms itched with sweat, the cut stinging. She thought her father's stipend stopped because he'd determined to do better, planned to care for her himself, and cleaned up the business, as his letter claimed. But had the money actually ceased because Mr. Tanner had uncovered the operation between her parents and brought it to a halt? How coincidental did it seem that her father would end up in jail on unrelated charges and suddenly die of a failed heart?

"I heard Mr. Tanner say he killed my father."

He merely watched her, waiting for more.

"I was trapped in the cellar—where Mr. Tanner put me, tied and bound, need I remind you—while he was searching out the liquor his partner said they had to find and get to a Mr. Samuels." Lillian fixed him with a pointed glare. "When they couldn't find it, Mr. Tanner said specifically, 'I didn't have him killed just so he could swindle me from the grave.'"

They sat in silence for several heartbeats, gazes locked in a stalemate. Would the sheriff ignore her evidence as he had the intruders they'd reported?

"Do you have any proof?" he asked.

"I have two other witnesses who were tied up with me who also heard what he said." Her heart wrenched at the thought of Jonah. "One of whom is currently under a doctor's care because Mr. Tanner or one of his men shot him." Lillian emphasized each of her words. "After they made him show them where he'd hid the liquor."

He plucked another page from his stack and pushed it across the table to Lillian. "Is this the letter left to you by your father?"

She scanned the now-familiar words. "It is."

"So you were aware of his criminal activities."

"Not until I read this letter." And found the ledger. And the bottles. Lillian pinched the bridge of her nose. "The letter also says he cleaned up the business."

"Yet the contraband was discovered in his house. The one he left to you, his partner's daughter." His eyes speared her with accusation.

"I'm not his partner's—" Oh. He meant her mother. Lillian shook her head. "You have that all wrong."

The sheriff settled back in his seat and regarded her a long moment. "There are a lot of pieces to this puzzle, Miss Doyle. Ones I intend to examine until I discover how they all fit."

Lillian placed her hands on the table and leaned forward. "Please do. In the end you will discover a picture that points to the treachery of Jeffery Tanner."

She could only hope this man hadn't become involved in the schemes and wouldn't let greed outweigh his oaths of justice. *Please, Lord. Let the truth come to light. Let justice win out.*

The sheriff's features never changed. Never twitched. Though Lillian could swear she saw doubt swimming in his eyes.

He gathered the papers and tapped them on the table to straighten them, then rose from his chair. "I suppose we shall see, won't we?"

Without waiting for her response—not that Lillian could work past the dryness in her throat to create one—he strode from the room and left her alone once more with her thoughts.

CHAPTER THIRTY-THREE

e had to get out of this confounded bed. Jonah ground his teeth against the sharp pain and swung his legs over the edge of the fluffed mattress. He breathed deep, waiting for the worst to subside. He still ached from hip to knee, but according to the doctor, no real harm had been done.

His flesh held a different opinion. The doctor had had to scrape out a bullet that had reached all the way to his bone.

Grunting with the effort, Jonah lifted himself from the bed and balanced most of his weight on his good leg. The small room at the front of the doctor's house served as a sleeping area for patients who couldn't yet be moved to their own homes. Doctor Andley's wife had clearly had a hand in decorating this space, as it held far more delicate touches than he'd expected from a recovery room.

He felt more like a guest than a patient, surrounded by the floral-papered walls, finely carved furniture, and thick carpeting. Shouldn't sick rooms be stark, with a table topped with medical instruments?

Voices sounded through the door, and a moment later it

opened, admitting the smiling face of Doc Andley. He took one look at Jonah and the friendly look faded.

"Back in bed with you, young man." He pointed a finger. "That leg's not ready for your weight."

Despite the protest forming on his lips, Jonah sat back on the brightly colored quilt and relieved some of the sharp pain stabbing though his hip. "I need to get to Ma and Lillian. And the girls are still out at the Watson farm. They need to know what—"

Doc Andley held up a hand. "Plenty of young boys with quick feet willing to make a nickel."

"I can send a message, but that won't tell me what I need to know." Like why Ma and Lillian hadn't yet come to see him and what had happened after he'd lost consciousness at the Thatcher home last night. Was Tanner in jail?

Surely the women were finished giving the sheriff their report by now.

Doc Andley ran a hand through salt-and-pepper hair and settled himself into a chair near the hearth. He laced his long surgeon fingers together. "According to the deputy still stationed on my porch, you are not to leave until Sheriff Whittle has come to question you."

Of course the sheriff would need his statement, but why would he need to post a deputy? "I'll head to the sheriff's office right now." He tested his weight again, and a wave of nausea spiked through his belly.

Doc Andley merely waited for Jonah to regain his seat. "There's nothing that can be done by rushing off that can't be accomplished by waiting for the due time."

Jonah had nothing to say to that. He didn't want to sit idly by and wait when he had so many questions, but neither could he walk out of here without fear of landing in a heap on the floor.

The doctor eyed Jonah's leg where his trousers had been cut away. "My primary concern is checking your bandages." He approached and clapped Jonah on the shoulder. "Whatever's going on, I'm sure it'll get worked out soon enough."

Jonah could only hope the man was right. "A fine mess that Tanner made." He winced as the doctor pulled back an edge of the bandage wrapped around his upper thigh. "Locking us in the cellar while he hunted for bootleg hooch." He ground out the words. Frustration at being laid up in bed while the women handled pressing charges against Tanner battled with the lingering nausea in his gut.

Doc Andley looked up from his inspection of the bandages. "Bootleg liquor?"

"Seems Floyd Jackson hid it in the walls, and Tanner came looking for it. Some kind of shipment promised to Atlanta that we discovered while doing renovations for Ma's bakery."

The doctor rocked back on his heels. "They were shipping homemade liquor?" He gained his feet, a frown forming between his brows. "Do you know how long that was going on?"

"Not sure. Seems like Jackson wanted to cut out Tanner, though, best I can tell. But then he died and left everything to Miss Doyle."

The frown deepened. "Did Mr. Tanner know Mr. Jackson was planning to leave everything to Miss Doyle?"

"I don't think so, seeing as how no one even knew he had a daughter." Jonah rubbed at the ache radiating down to his knee. A thought occurred to him, and his gaze slammed into the doctor's. "Last night I overheard Tanner say he didn't have Floyd killed just so the man could swindle him from the grave."

Doc Andley appeared troubled. "I'd wondered why a man previously healthy suddenly had a heart failure. But I've heard quite a bit about this homemade moonshine. Some of it can be nearly toxic. Maybe whatever got him intoxicated that night was from a bad batch."

"Or Tanner poisoned him."

They exchanged a look. After a moment, Doc Andley nodded. "I'll let the deputy know my suspicions." He pointed at Jonah's injury. "Stay off that leg and get some rest. Ignore my orders and I'll mix up a tonic that will make you sleep till tomorrow."

Jonah settled back on the pillows to wait. Soon the truth would be out. Then they could put this entire thing behind them.

A knock sounded on the door, tugging Jonah from sleep. He stirred and sat up against the headboard as Sheriff Whittle entered the room. The man's presence pushed out the last vestiges of sleep and brought Jonah fully awake.

"Sheriff." He looked past the man's shoulder. "Have my mother and Lillian come with you?"

The door clicked shut softly. "They are still being held for questioning until we get this sorted out."

"Held?" Jonah shifted, pulling himself up further. "Why?"

Rather than answering, Sheriff Whittle lowered himself into the chair Doc Andley had earlier vacated and stroked his beard. "What do you know about Miss Lillian Doyle?"

That she was kind, thoughtful, and filled with a determination he'd come to admire. She wrinkled her nose when she concentrated. She hated to admit when she didn't know how to do a thing but wouldn't let inexperience stop her from trying.

She was smart, and when those intelligent eyes turned his way in appreciation, he felt as though he could do anything in the world.

He cleared sudden emotion from his throat. "I know she lived with her mother in Atlanta. Lillian thought her mother to be a widow until she discovered her father's recent passing. She traveled here to claim her inheritance and then decided to stay."

The sheriff nodded along. "Why did she stay?"

"To open a business with my mother." Pride warmed his words. "They're starting a bakery and bookshop."

"And what about her part in Jackson and Tanner's business? What did she do with that?"

The mention of that snake's name had Jonah clenching the blanket spread across his lap. "She sold her share to Tanner, keeping only a small portion of the profits so that she could care for her mother."

"And what do you know of Mrs. Doyle?"

"I only met her once, but I can see why Lillian had no desire to return to Atlanta. That is the sourest woman I have ever encountered."

"So she's been here." He tapped the ends of his fingers together. "Met with Miss Doyle?"

Where was the man going with this? "They talked, yes. Lillian didn't want to marry the man her mother had picked out for her and wanted to start a new life here in Dawsonville. Mrs. Doyle wasn't too pleased and left after their brief visit. I don't believe Lillian has heard from her since."

"And you say Miss Doyle wanted to stay here to open a business with your mother? In her father's house."

"Yes."

"The one where Mr. Jackson hid his moonshine and whiskey."

"Sheriff, I don't know what you are implying, but none of us knew anything about that until we found the bottles hidden in the wall."

"Yet you didn't report it."

"We were going to. But then someone tore up the rest of the house, looking for more." He cocked his head, remembering what Lillian had said about her suspicions that the sheriff had known more than he was letting on. "Which Lillian reported to you."

"Hmm." Sheriff Whittle regarded Jonah for several heartbeats. "Did Mr. Tanner offer to buy the property at any point?"

"Yes." Jonah relaxed his fingers. "My guess would be that he was after the stash, not because he was interested in living in the house."

"And yet Miss Doyle wouldn't sell?"

"No, she and Ma had already entered into a partnership."

"Not even when Mr. Tanner offered her a more than reasonable price?"

Was that suspicion laced through his words? Obviously he already knew that Tanner had offered to buy the house. Ma or Lillian must have told him about the second offer. Defensiveness welled in Jonah's chest. Was the sheriff trying to trap him in a lie? "She didn't want to sell, so the price didn't matter."

Despite himself, doubt wiggled through him. If he separated himself from the situation and looked at it as the sheriff would, he could see where it might seem odd. Why wouldn't someone take more money and open the business elsewhere?

"Were you aware, Mr. Peterson, that Mrs. Doyle and Mr.

Jackson worked together for several years on a bootleg operation ranging from Dawsonville to Atlanta?"

The words hung heavy on the air. "That seems unlikely."

"As unlikely as the daughter of the two of them suddenly moving to our town, turning down a generous offer for her father's property, and instead opening another business in the same location?" He leaned forward, eyes intense. "Does it not strike you as odd that Miss Doyle came here to secure the property holding all the illegal liquor while Mrs. Doyle stayed in Atlanta?"

"But Lillian didn't know anything about those bottles in the wall." He'd seen the look on her face when she showed them to him. Had been there when she found the ledger. Surely that couldn't have been an act. "My mother was with her when they discovered the stores quite by accident."

Thoughts churned in the sheriff's gaze, but he simply nodded. "Tell me what happened last night. From the beginning."

"We spent the day handling the mess Tanner's men had made of the walls. While cleaning, Lillian found a door to a cellar we hadn't noticed before. I went down to investigate. I heard screams and came up to find Tanner and two men. I fought them." Bitterness at his failure welled, and he nearly spat the next words. "They bested me. Knocked me unconscious and put me in the cellar, chained to the ladder. They tied Lillian and Ma with rope."

The sheriff nodded and gestured for him to continue.

"We hatched a plan for escape. I would lead the men to what they were looking for—the liquor that we'd found and I wanted out of the house until I could figure out what we should do with it—and would stall to give the women time to get free. I took Tanner and his men a roundabout way to the crates, hoping I'd given Lillian enough time to escape. Once Tanner was occupied looking at the goods, I made a run for it. Got shot. Next thing I remember was waking up here."

The words seemed to take something out of him, and he leaned back against the pillows.

"So Tanner came looking for the bottles," the sheriff said. "Why now?"

"Said something about getting them to Atlanta or there'd be dire consequences. And it seemed like he thought Jackson had swindled him."

Sheriff Whittle rose. "Thank you. This is helpful information." He turned and headed to the door.

"Wait." Jonah sat up. "What about my mother and Lillian? Will you release them now?"

Sheriff Whittle regarded Jonah for an uncomfortable moment. "Do you not find it strange, Mr. Peterson? This struggle between Miss Doyle and Mr. Tanner?" He opened the door, looking back over his shoulder. "It's almost as though a partnership went bad, and both guilty parties are trying to point the blame at the other." He stepped out, pulling the door shut behind him.

Jonah could only stare at the space the man had vacated, a sense of dread curdling his gut.

Both guilty parties?

CHAPTER THIRTY-FOUR

He didn't care what the doctor said. Jonah hitched the crutch under his arm and hobbled to the door, unable to sit here for another day. He twisted the knob and poked his head outside, feeling a bit foolish. A man shouldn't need to sneak away from another man's house.

From the man's wife, however, that could well be justified.

Loathing every clomp of his crutch through the Andleys' foyer, Jonah slowly made his way to the front door, praying that Mrs. Andley had decided to take the morning in her garden.

"Jonah!"

He cringed. No such luck.

"And just what do you think you are doing, young man?" The matronly form of Mrs. Andley appeared to his left, as though she'd come out of the carved woodwork surrounding the parlor door. She wore an oversized garden hat and a scowl. Seemed he'd not waited quite long enough.

Jonah tried for a pleasant smile. "I'm getting some fresh air."

She tilted her hat in a way that would be almost comical if Jonah wasn't currently trying to escape. "Did my husband give you permission?"

"He gave me this crutch." A truthful statement, and one she might hopefully see as a positive answer.

She lifted one shoulder and waved a gloved hand. "Very well, then. But see that you stay on the porch. I'll not have you opening up that wound under my watch." She wagged a finger at him. "I'm fair with stitching, but I fear it won't be nearly as painless as my dear husband's work."

Jonah couldn't help his grimace. Doc Andley's work had been anything but painless. He nodded anyway and headed for the door. So as not to arouse immediate suspicion, he settled on the rocking chair by the front door and stretched his leg out in front of him.

Worry gnawed worse than the pain. It had now been two days, and he hadn't . . .

The thought trailed off. He rose as a familiar figure bustled down the street, determination in her steps.

Jonah thrust the crutch under his arm once more and gained his feet. "Ma!"

At his call, Ma lifted her head and hastened her steps. Was she still wearing the same dress from two days ago? His stomach clenched. Had Whittle only now released her? Jonah hobbled to the front steps and evaluated the best way to descend.

"I'm here." Ma huffed and placed a hand to her chest. "No sense you coming down." She shooed him like a wayward pup. "Back to the chair with you."

"What's going on?" Jonah angled his crutch and spun around. "Where have you been? Surely Whittle isn't just now releasing you."

Ma grasped his elbow and guided him to the rocking chair he'd vacated, then settled in the one next to it, a small table situated between them holding some kind of flowering plant.

She breathed deep, as though no seat in the world could be more comfortable.

The gesture only increased Jonah's concern. "Ma? Are you all right?"

Her eyes snapped open, and she shook her head as though clearing her mind. "Oh, heavens." She bounced up out of her seat. "Never mind about me." She leaned close, looking him over. "Doc Andley assured me you were perfectly fine, but a mother needs to see these things for herself."

Jonah frowned. "You talked to the doctor, but you didn't come by? What's going on?"

She patted his shoulder like she'd done when he was a child and she was about to deliver a hard truth. Her eyes held the same kind of sadness. "Doc came by the sheriff's office. Giving a statement, he said, and they let me come out to talk to him for a bit to settle this old heart."

Old heart? He'd never heard Ma talk that way. Unease squirmed through him. "Why were you at the sheriff's office that long?"

Ma returned to her seat before answering. "There might be a bit more going on than we thought." She shook her head. "But I don't believe a whit of it."

"Believe what?" The unease coiled tighter.

"They kept me because they thought that me and Lillian were trying to take over Floyd's bootleg operation." She chuckled, but there was little humor in it. "Can you imagine?" She shook her head. "Took a fair amount of questioning before Sheriff Whittle finally realized I didn't know anything about none of it."

"And Lillian?"

Ma's hesitation did nothing to assuage his fears. "I don't know, Jonah. I don't want to believe any of it." Tears welled in her eyes, and she dabbed at them. "I know what God told me, and I was following through. And I know he has a plan and a purpose. But I . . ."

Jonah reached across the table between them and took her hand. "But you're wondering why God's plan seems too hard?"

A tear escaped. "Terrible of me, isn't it?"

He squeezed her fingers. "It's hard not to, Ma, no matter how strong your faith. We can't see what's coming, so when things don't make sense, it's really hard to trust in something that looks like a complete disaster."

Ma smiled. "Look at you. Seems you grew into your faith after all." She cocked a mischievous eyebrow. "It's a gunshot, not the belly of a great fish, and it's only been two days. But I guess the effect is the same."

A chuckle bubbled up out of him. "Ma, you can make a Bible lesson out of anything."

They sat in silence for a moment, and he waited as Ma put her thoughts together.

Finally, she sighed. "Sheriff Whittle says that Mrs. Doyle was in business with Floyd the entire time. If that's true, I still can't believe Lillian knew anything about it."

Maybe. He hated the doubt that nagged at him, but it persisted. "I've thought about this a lot. Maybe she didn't know anything about the bottles in the wall. Or the ledger. But what if she did plan on using the business with you as a new front for the operation?"

"Do you really believe that?"

The truth leaked out of him. "I don't want to."

After another moment, Ma rose and patted him on the shoulder. "I need to get to the bank."

"Why?"

She looked out over the front yard. "The only evidence Sheriff Whittle doesn't have is that ledger." Her back stiffened. "I'm going to give it to him."

Lillian hadn't turned over the ledger? If she was innocent, why not give the sheriff everything? From the look on Ma's face, she knew exactly what he was thinking. Had perhaps thought the same.

He rose and slipped an arm around her shoulders. "I'm coming with you."

"Not on that leg, you're not."

He kept his tone gentle but his words firm. "I am going. I'll not sit here when I'm capable of withstanding a little pain."

Ma opened her mouth to protest but then seemed to think better of it. "I'll ask Mrs. Andley for a buggy."

A short time and a little arguing later, Jonah lifted his crutch into the seat of a small two-wheeled cart. He turned to hand Ma up first, but she skirted the old gelding strapped into the harness and scrambled up on her own. He planted his good foot on the step and pulled his weight up. He plopped down, unable to keep a grunt from escaping his lips.

Ma eyed him. "Don't need you opening up those stitches."

"I know." He gathered the reins and tapped them lightly across the bay's back. The horse bobbed his head as he startled awake, then plodded slowly down the street.

Jonah allowed the gelding the leisurely walk, not in any hurry to jostle them down the road. He avoided as many potholes as he could, and a few moments later, he reined the gelding to a stop in front of the bank.

"I'll be right back." Ma jumped down before Jonah could even garner a response.

He should go in with her, but truth be told his leg already

ached. Best he save his strength for accompanying her back to the sheriff's office.

The sun beat down on his head, reminding him he'd forgotten to grab a hat. His thoughts wandered to the Watson family and his sisters. Were they doing well? Betsy had probably peppered Alma with a million questions by now. Knowing her, she wouldn't mind. But after this long, they were bound to worry.

Mrs. Andley had assured him that word had been sent out to the farm and that all was well, but he'd been surprised—and a little disappointed—that Lewis hadn't come to town or brought the girls. Maybe he'd thought it best to wait until Ma was released from custody. No sense getting the girls worked up over seeing their mother in jail and their brother in a hospital bed.

What a mess.

The thought soured his stomach. Ma never should have been held in the first place. Could Lillian's suspicions about the sheriff be true? Was that why she'd kept the ledger a secret? And if Sheriff Whittle had a part in covering up Tanner's schemes, how would Jonah ever be able to prove it?

A quarter hour and a dozen unanswered questions later, Jonah gathered his crutch. Something must be wrong. Before he could rise, however, Ma hurried out of the bank, a thick book under her arm. She tossed it on the seat beside him and scrambled up.

"I was starting to wonder if I needed to come in after you."

Ma swiped her hand over her brow. "Had to do a little convincing. If Lillian hadn't made it clear we were partners, I don't think Mr. Grimly would have handed it over."

Jonah paused for a buckboard loaded with barrels to pass before he guided the gelding back onto the street. "Why are

313

they still holding Lillian? Is there really any evidence against her?"

"I don't know." Ma clutched the book against her. "We'll pray for the truth, Son. It's all we can do."

Truth, yes. But Jonah would also be asking for justice.

Lillian leaned her head against the wall and counted the stacked blocks for the third time in a vain effort to distract her thoughts. Had her mother really been involved with the bootleg operation? Had she lied about her relationship with Lillian's father?

Of course she had. But in the way that the sheriff had said?

Thirteen. Fourteen. Or was that sixteen? She lost count and started over.

Sheriff Whittle suspected her of criminal activity. She suspected the same of him.

Lord, will the truth not win out?

That snake Tanner had a silver tongue if nothing else. Would he slip free?

The jingle of the lock announced the opening of the door. Lillian rose to face her latest accuser rather than huddle on the cot with her arms wrapped around her knees.

Sherriff Whittle greeted her with a stern nod. "Come with me."

This time he didn't wait for her to walk first so he could closely follow behind her. Perhaps he'd realized she didn't plan to attempt escape. Where would she go, anyway? She wasn't the sort of woman to embrace living a life on the run from the law. Especially when she'd done nothing wrong.

Lillian followed the broad back of the sheriff into the same room where he'd questioned her before. Without invitation, she sank into the chair and laced her fingers on the pocked surface.

She was so tired. Tired of fighting against false accusations. Tired of defending her character.

The sheriff sat across from her, and only then did she notice what he held in his hand. The ledger.

He'd gotten it after all. She shouldn't be surprised. But she did wonder how he'd found it. Of course she'd contemplated telling him about it, but until she could be sure he abstained from corruption, she'd hoped to hold one bit of evidence back for the judge.

"Care to explain this?"

Lillian kept her gaze steady on his. "We found that book in the wall we took down to make a larger space for my bookshop. At first we had no idea what it was. It looks like a bunch of meaningless letters. After we discovered the bottles, we figured it had to be some kind of tracking for the deliveries and types of liquors."

"And why did you keep this hidden?"

Despite her best efforts, Lillian couldn't keep the bite from her tone. "Because I'm still not convinced you didn't already know about the operation and choose to look the other way. I thought I could present it to the judge at my trial."

Surprise flickered through his features. For Sheriff Whittle, that meant a great deal. She must have truly caught him off guard.

"I had once thought to confront Mr. Tanner with the evidence," Lillian continued, "in hopes of getting him to confess that he sent men to vandalize my house—really, who else had any motive to do so? Edith convinced me otherwise. We took that book to the bank right before we came here to report the second intruder incident to you."

The room was quiet for several heartbeats before the sheriff spoke again. "What do you know about your father's death?"

"Very little. He went to jail. He died there." The words came out cold. Wooden. Perhaps the sheriff asked her the same questions over and over in an attempt to catch her changing her story. "And before you ask, I thought my mother a widow. Regardless of that, I find it exceedingly difficult to believe she was involved in any sort of scheming beyond that of pointless society drivel. But if I'm wrong and she flawlessly played a part all these years, then she did so entirely without my knowledge."

He tapped a finger on the desk, watching her carefully. "When we searched your residence, we found not only the letter to you from Mr. Jackson, but also ones from Mrs. Doyle."

Lillian stared at him flatly. If he'd hoped for a reaction to his snooping, she didn't care. She had nothing to hide.

"Wait. What do you mean? You found more than one letter from my mother?" She frowned. "The only letter I have is the one she wrote demanding I come home."

He cleared his throat. "The handwriting doesn't match between those two letters, nor does the writing on the other documentation we have match the letter from Mrs. Doyle that Mr. Carson had." He sat back in his seat. "I have come to the conclusion Mr. Tanner fabricated the documents claiming your mother was involved, as well as her letter to you stipulating the details of continuing the bootlegging operations. I believe he planted those documents in your desk in an attempt to create a false alibi."

The words struggled to find purchase in her parched heart. Did that mean he believed her? Or was this some kind of a game?

"We have suspected such business in our county for some time, Miss Doyle, but we have never been able to catch any of the culprits. So I'm sure you can understand my diligence in wanting to sort out the truth."

"And have you?" Lillian leaned forward, searching his face. "Have you found the real truth?" So help her, if he still thought the truth was some kind of scheme involving her and Mother and leaving out Mr. Tanner, then she'd . . . well, she'd . . .

Lillian closed her eyes and breathed deep. *Then I will leave it in your hands, Lord. I trust you with my future.*

She opened her eyes to find the sheriff watching her intently. "According to the evidence I have gathered from Mr. Tanner's business, both his and your residences, and the accounts of several witnesses, I believe I have finally put together all the pieces of this puzzle." A ghost of a smile touched his lips. "Just as I promised to do."

Lillian laced her fingers in her lap and waited. Whatever conclusion this man had come to, he had clearly set his mind to it.

"Mr. Jackson and Mr. Tanner ran a successful operation transporting moonshine liquor from the hidden distilleries in the northern part of our county—and whiskey from more reputable operations in Tennessee—to a man by the name of Oliver Samuels in Atlanta. We are currently in correspondence with lawmen in Atlanta to share our evidence against the man." He gave a curt nod. "Your ledger will go a long way to building a case against him."

Lillian worked her mouth, but no words formed. She needn't have bothered, as the sheriff continued with hardly a break.

"At some point, Mr. Tanner and Mr. Jackson came to a disagreement. Mr. Jackson then hid the latest and largest shipment from the distilleries, informed Mr. Samuels and several others he would no longer be supplying, and created a new will with his solicitor, leaving everything to his estranged daughter."

Lillian sat forward. "So what he said in the letter was true. He was trying to clean up the business. Do you know what changed his mind?"

The sheriff shook his head. "Not long after, he was picked up by one of my deputies for public drunkenness, something that had never happened before. Doctor Andley suspects that either Mr. Jackson consumed a bad batch of moonshine or he was poisoned."

Lillian gasped. "Poisoned?"

"It's possible. Either scenario could have caused an apoplexy for a man who had otherwise been in good health." He shook his head. "Unfortunately, it is not something we can prove either way."

Energy raced through her, bringing her back up straighter. "Mr. Tanner poisoned my father when he wanted to stop the illegal distributions."

"Perhaps." He spread his palms. "We are still looking into it."

Lillian pulled her lip through her teeth. "I'm guessing Mr. Tanner didn't know about me. He thought my father's unexpected death would mean everything went to him. The fact that my father changed his will so close to his death suggests he suspected he was in danger."

The sheriff watched her for a moment, then inclined his head in subtle agreement. "What we do know is that Mr. Tanner got sloppy after Mr. Jackson dissolved the company's dealings. It seems Mr. Tanner took out a loan to cover the cost of procuring another shipment from the distilleries to send an order to one of his smaller contacts in Atlanta. He then immediately repaid that loan when he completed the delivery. But without finding what Mr. Jackson did with the missing bottles, he was unable to complete a larger shipment he had promised to Mr. Samuels." He tapped a finger on the table, sharp eyes watching her every move.

Lillian waited, a strange sense of peace washing over her.

Finally, Sheriff Whittle gave a decisive nod. "Two of his men turned evidence on him in exchange for a lighter sentence. They admitted to breaking into your house and to the vandalism, as well as providing witness to the nature of the bootlegging operation." His mouth twisted into a slight grimace. "And from the disappearance of one of my deputies, I'm inclined to believe their story that he fed those bootleggers information. That explains why they always seemed a step ahead of me."

Relief poured through her so quickly her shoulders sagged. "So you know I had nothing to do with it."

"Yes."

She'd been right about the corruption in the sheriff's office, but thankfully, the man in charge seemed intent on rooting it out. Lillian searched his face, nearly afraid to ask. "And . . . my mother?"

Sheriff Whittle rose from his chair. "Men in Atlanta will question her, but we believe any evidence against her to be fabricated." He tucked the chair back under the table and opened the door. "You are free to go, Miss Doyle."

Free?

Lillian bolted to her feet and swiped at the tears blurring her vision.

Never had a word sounded so good.

CHAPTER THIRTY-FIVE

J onah's heart twisted at the sight of Lillian emerging from the sheriff's office. She lifted a hand to shield her face from the sunlight, squinting, and her gaze landed on where he sat in the doctor's buggy. Ma emerged right behind Lillian, fussing over her like a mother hen.

"Jonah? Oh!" She lifted her skirt and hurried toward him, concern so evident on her beautiful features that another pang of guilt stabbed through him. He'd so easily doubted her. So easily questioned her integrity because of her father's schemes.

But Lillian Doyle was not her father's daughter.

Ma paused, pretending interest in a flowering bush.

"Jonah!" Lillian scrambled up into the carriage and threw her arms around him. "You're all right." She nuzzled her face against his neck.

He rubbed her back, the nearness of her breaking free something inside him. The guilt surged with such force that words poured unbidden from his lips. "I failed you."

She drew back, concern filling her eyes. "What do you mean?"

Shame pulled him back from her, and she released her grip.

"I couldn't stop Tanner. Couldn't save you and Ma. Instead, I got myself shot."

"That wasn't your—"

"Please, Lillian." He drew a deep breath. "There's more." His gaze drifted over her head to Ma, who gave him a nod of encouragement. He sought Lillian's troubled eyes once more. "When the sheriff said you could be involved . . ." His jaw tightened against the admission, and he had to force it free. "There was a part of me that wondered if he was right. If you planned to use the business with Ma as a way to continue Floyd's operation."

The affection that had blanketed her features darkened to hurt, and Jonah's chest knotted tighter. "I'm sorry, Lillian. You deserve a man who always thinks the very best of you and would never for even a single breath think one drop less."

Lillian studied her hands in her lap for so long Jonah feared he'd lost her. The pain of that realization ripped so deeply through him that he knew he could never live with it. Maybe with time he could rebuild her trust in him. He wouldn't stop fighting. No matter how long it took, he would work until he was worthy of earning her heart.

"None of us is perfect." Lillian's soft words held such tenderness the ache in his chest expanded threefold. "No matter how hard I tried to appear stalwart and in control, those things were an illusion." She turned to face him. "I don't blame you for wondering about the truth, Jonah."

The vulnerability shining in her eyes nearly undid him. He didn't deserve her forgiveness or her trust, but he yearned for them both.

His voice dropped to a rasp. "If you'll let me, I'll spend the rest of my days proving my loyalty."

A small smile played at the corners of her lips. "I might take you up on that." Seriousness replaced her humor a heartbeat later. "You're a good man, Jonah. Respectable and generous. Hardworking and honest. Any woman would be blessed to have a man such as you turn his regard her way."

Unable to resist, he took her hand and drew her to him once more. She settled into his side like she'd always belonged there.

"I must ask your forgiveness for something else too," he said.

Lillian cocked an eyebrow at the mischievousness in his tone. "Oh? What for now?"

He slipped his hand up her neck and gently tipped her head back. "Complete and utter lack of propriety in the middle of a public street."

A laugh bubbled out of her. "I've come to find propriety rather overemphasized."

Jonah lowered his face until his lips hovered just above hers. "That so?"

Rather than answering, she pressed her lips into his. The hurt, worry, and fear of the past days melted under the heat of her kiss.

He drew her closer, letting the depths of his feelings surge through him until he thought the strength of them might sweep him away. He pulled back only slightly, breath mingling with hers. "I love you."

Her tender kiss teased. Lingered. When he thought he might burst from the fire burning within him, she pulled away, eyes sparkling. "That's well and good, Mr. Peterson. A man ought to profess his love when proposing marriage."

Wait, he hadn't . . .

Jonah leaned back and laughed. "Right you are, Miss Doyle."

He caressed her cheek with his thumb. "Would you be willing to marry a humble farmhand?"

"You're far more than that." She looked him over as though in thought. "How do you feel about being a bakery hand?" She scrunched her nose. "That doesn't sound right. A bookshop hand?" Her eyes widened. "No. An electrical engineer. You'll be the pride of the county and we'll be the busiest shop in town when you bring your ma that electric icebox and we have light bulbs."

Jonah laughed again, putting a stop to her flow of words. "Is that a yes?"

"I love you, Jonah Peterson." She scooted closer, nestling into his side once more. "And I'd love nothing more than to be your wife."

As Jonah leaned down to press one last kiss to her lips, Ma cheered.

CHAPTER THIRTY-SIX

S ee? What'd I tell you?"

Betsy's voice broke through the private moment and caused Lillian to reluctantly draw herself out of Jonah's embrace.

"I done told you they like to smush their faces together, Rose." An indignant huff. "I don't know why you never believe me."

Jonah groaned even as Lillian swallowed a laugh. There was simply no accounting for the forthright honesty of children.

"That's because they are getting married." Rose poked her head around the kitchen doorframe. Her cheeks reddened as she caught Lillian's eye.

"What's that got to do with it?"

Rose tugged Betsy from her position in the newly finished dining area and into the fully modern kitchen.

Lillian lifted a basket of warm biscuits from the counter and held it out. "How about you girls take this to your mother?"

Betsy shrugged, easily enough distracted. She took the basket and looked up at Lillian, sweet eyes luminous. "I'm glad you're going to be my big sister now too." She pursed her lips at Rose. "My other one's awful bossy."

Rose's mouth fell open, and Jonah roared with laughter. Betsy bounded for the door without a backward glance at her sister.

Lillian pulled Rose close, wrapping her in a hug. "That means you're doing your job of looking out for her."

Rose looked unconvinced, but she accepted a platter of roasted potatoes and headed for the door. Alone in the kitchen once more, Lillian sought Jonah's gaze only to find him staring at her with a thoughtful expression.

"Three more days until the wedding."

Lillian laughed at the unbridled impatience in his tone. Betsy was right. They'd been spending quite a lot of time "smushing faces." She simply couldn't help herself. Life was too short not to spend a good portion of it kissing the man she loved.

He didn't seem to mind.

Thoughts turned in that direction, Lillian eased close to his side just as a knock sounded at the door. "Who can that be?" she asked. Lewis, Alma, and Edith had already arrived and were with Melanie and the girls out back.

A sheepish look covered Jonah's face. "Don't be mad."

Oh dear. Nothing good ever came from someone starting an explanation that way. Lillian braced herself.

"But with the wedding only a few days away . . ." Jonah let the words trail off as he scooted past and left her standing alone in the kitchen.

Lillian stared after him, the insinuation sinking in. Surely he hadn't. No. He wouldn't.

The door opened and voices sounded, followed by footsteps. One heavy and belonging to Jonah, the other lighter.

A moment later, the visitor appeared in the doorway.

"Mother."

A hundred questions darted through Lillian's mind in rapid succession. Did she intend to try to stop the wedding? Surely she was furious about being questioned by Atlanta policemen. Probably blamed Lillian for all of it. Likely hated her. No telling what had happened to her reputation after that.

Heaven and earth. Why had Jonah asked her here?

Mother lowered her chin, a strange look Lillian had never before seen painted all over her features. Remorse?

"Hello, Daughter." The words had the strangest airy quality to them. She nodded to Jonah. "I'm thankful your young man invited me."

Her young man. Did this mean Mother accepted Lillian and Jonah's intentions?

Emotions tripped through her. Hope for reconciliation. Fury at having been tossed aside. Despite her best intentions to love unconditionally, hurt and anger seeped through her tone. "What are you doing here?"

Mother held her posture perfectly erect, though the usual haughtiness was strangely absent from her tone. "I was invited."

A snort worked its way out of Lillian's nose. "That doesn't explain why you came, when you made it perfectly clear that a daughter who did not follow the very letter of your instructions was a daughter you did not want."

Were those tears glimmering in her mother's eyes?

"Yet you continued to send me a generous allowance and covered my debts." Mother's voice wavered even though her stance did not. "Why would you do that?"

Lillian nearly said, "Out of simple decency and duty to my family," but the words died on her lips. There was more to it. Despite everything, she loved her mother. She cast a glance at Jonah, finding only encouragement there. With time and effort, could she and her mother share the same kind of relationship Jonah enjoyed with Melanie?

But her reasons went deeper than the bonds of family. Lillian eased out a sigh. "God has shown me great mercy. I can hardly be miserly when handing out the same." She gave a little shrug, but the words seemed only to make Mother crumble further.

"I'm sorry." She gripped the edge of Lillian's new kitchen cabinets as though she needed them to keep standing. "All those years I kept you at arm's length, treating you as though you owed me something in recompense for my own mistakes. My own bitterness." She shook her head. "I pushed Floyd away when we might have had a happy life, were it not for my pride."

Lillian's heart squeezed, and she found herself reaching out for her mother. Jonah gave her an encouraging nod and slipped out the back door, leaving them alone.

"I know you must have endured a lot of hurt over the years," Lillian said after a moment, taking Mother's hand. She still had a lot of questions about her grandparents. About the other man her mother had loved. But the past could wait. "Yet in truth, I was quite furious with you for making me believe my father was dead for my entire life. A life where I could have gotten to know him." She heaved out a sigh. Would knowing him have made things different? Would he have made different choices with a family under his care?

"Can you ever forgive me?"

Lillian nodded, tightness in her throat making words difficult. "When I first found out about my father and all the things he was entangled in, I was mad at you and him both. How could God have given me such a father?"

Tears snaked down Mother's cheeks, the unspoken "and mother" clearly registering as well.

"But then I realized, had things not happened as they did, I wouldn't be here now. I wouldn't have found Jonah and loving friends." Lillian took Mother by the shoulders and guided her through the kitchen. "Now I know that God had a plan for me all along." She opened the back door.

The laughter of the Watson and Peterson families greeted them, drifting on the warm summer breeze and dancing in harmony with the fireflies.

Lillian smiled, heart swelling. "I've found a home here, Mother. One where I believe I will be quite happy."

To her surprise, Mother wrapped her in a crushing embrace. It lasted only a heartbeat, then she pulled back, face stoic once more.

Not exactly a loving reunion, but a good start to what would be a long road ahead of them.

They joined the others around the tables, Lillian making introductions and Mother slipping into her usual sociable ways. Lillian had to laugh, though, when Mother was seated next to Edith and the woman immediately began peppering her with all manner of personal questions. No measure of Mother's aloofness would dissuade her either.

Her aunt would be great for Mother.

Lillian took her place next to Jonah and folded her hands in her lap in readiness for Jonah to ask the blessing over their meal.

Before he could, however, Lewis rose and lifted a glass. "Your attention, please."

Quiet settled as all eyes turned to him.

"We've much to celebrate tonight." He tilted his chin to Jonah and Lillian. "Upcoming nuptials." He cast a look to Melanie. "Dreams realized and the upcoming grand opening of Stories and Sweets." He turned loving eyes on his wife. "And the answer to a good woman's prayers."

Alma's eyes shimmered, and Lillian's heartbeat quickened. Did he mean . . . ?

Edith squealed and clapped her hands. "Oh! Is it true? I've been wondering." She launched from her seat, wrapping her arms around her daughter as the two of them released joyful tears.

"What?" Betsy stood on her chair, looking over the adults sharing glances and smiles. "What's happening?"

Rose tried to tug her down, but Betsy shooed her off.

"We've waited to be sure, but Doc Andley says we can expect our first child four months hence." Lewis beamed.

Lillian clapped her hands, joy filling her heart. Everyone lifted their glasses, cheering for the happy parents-to-be.

After the blessing, the food was passed around the table, and the conversations hummed through the evening air.

Peace settled over Lillian's heart. *Thank you, Father, for giving me this family.*

Jonah reached under the table and gave her fingers a squeeze. "I think we should push the grand opening back a week."

Lillian dropped her napkin. Did the man not realize how much work she'd put into planning that opening? They'd made announcements all over town and had worked furiously with the help of several hired builders to be ready in time.

With the money from the sale of the shipping business—a business entirely hers, seeing as how Mr. Tanner would be spending a rather long stint in jail—she'd been able to speed the repairs along. The crates of liquor had all been confiscated by the sheriff's department, and from what Lillian had heard, a rather large bootlegging operation had been rooted out of the county.

She was glad to have all of it behind her. It was finally time to open the shop and get started with the new life ahead of them.

"We are ready for the scheduled time," she said. "And you have classes coming up. The schedule can't allow for—"

He squeezed her hand to stop her. She swallowed the rest of her protest at the excitement in his voice.

"Now that we have more funds than we anticipated since you were able to sell the entire company"—a smile split Jonah's face—"I'm taking you on a honeymoon."

A honeymoon? A thrill shot through her. But they had too much to do. Perhaps in a few months, when . . .

The thought fizzled out. No, she wouldn't waste a moment. Work would always be here, the pressures of life always waiting. If her handsome groom wanted to whisk her away on a romantic adventure, who was she to refuse?

"Are you sure? What about having everything running smoothly before you leave for university?"

Jonah cupped her face. "That dream was always about making something of myself, finding satisfaction somewhere other than this same town." He slowly shook his head. "Now everything I could ever want is right here."

"But—"

"I'm not leaving my new bride." A mischievous smile danced on his lips. "We'll see. Maybe we'll talk about next year."

She returned his smile, letting the matter settle. Truthfully, she was glad to not have him leave so soon. "So, this honeymoon. Did you have somewhere in mind?"

He wiggled his eyebrows dramatically. "You'll have to see."

"A surprise honeymoon?" She gave a mock scoff. "I won't know how to pack."

"I'll do it for you."

Lillian laughed. A man packing for her? Surely he'd forget half the garments required.

As though guessing her thoughts, he chuckled. "You'll have to trust me."

Looking into his eyes, she no longer cared if she'd be wearing winter wool on a sunlit beach or went an entire week in the same skirt. She leaned into his shoulder, bumping him playfully. "Very well. Though I might suggest you let your mother help you."

Jonah tilted his head back and laughed. "Do you think she'd have it any other way?"

"Then I am at your mercy." Lillian entwined her fingers with his and breathed in the fresh Georgia air.

No matter where life took them, one thing she knew for certain. She'd get to do it surrounded by family and with her greatest blessing at her side.

Craving another
enchanting story from
Stephenia H. McGee?

———— ⁓⟨⟩⁓ ————

Turn the page for a sneak peek at
The Secrets of Emberwild

CHAPTER ONE

EMBERWILD HORSE FARM
NESHOBA COUNTY, MISSISSIPPI
MARCH 3, 1905

Freedom rushed through Nora Fenton's veins, erupting with each breath. Invisible shackles didn't bind out here.

Her independence always came at a price.

Nora leaned forward in the saddle. The wind slipped through her hair and snatched it from its pins, letting the honey-brown tresses fly out behind her. Hoofbeats pounded in rhythm with her heart.

The colt's exuberance for the open terrain would soon have to be contained once more and their ride brought to an end. Wild abandon never lasted long, and Arrow's reckless gallop could snatch life away from the both of them without warning. Caution demanded she draw back on the reins.

Not yet.

Freedom tasted far too sweet. It broke through the cloud of oppression and the pall of death that had made the delicate balance of her household all the more unstable these past months. She would pay for the reprieve.

And it would be worth it.

Nora took in one last look at the morning sky painted brilliant pink, then laid her left rein across Arrow's neck, asking him to make the turn toward home. He pinned his ears in displeasure and lowered his head, resisting her attempt at control. He lengthened his stride until they nearly soared above the ground.

Apparently the neck-reining lesson hadn't lasted past the corral. So be it. Gripping the rein in her leather glove, Nora pulled back and applied pressure to the side of the bit. Arrow shook off the command.

Stubborn colt. He would learn. He might be a stallion, but she was alpha of this herd. Nora planted her foot in the left stirrup and snatched the rein down to her hip, holding firm until his stride jerked to a halt. She dropped from the saddle.

"Got the better of you, didn't it?" Nora laughed, ruffling the shock of mane between his red ears already flecked with gray.

Arrow pinned his ears again and tossed his head. Nora squared her shoulders and pushed into his space. He snorted, then flicked his ears forward and lowered his head in submission.

She patted his neck. "See, now. No reason to get ornery. Keep acting like that and you'll spend your sunrises in the stable."

Arrow tilted his head and gave a good shake. As he did, her saddle slipped to the side.

Nora reached for the girth only to find the leather on the right side splitting. It probably wouldn't safely survive another battle of wills with Arrow, and she couldn't risk falling under his hooves if it broke. Roger would likely use this as a mark against her competence. The surly stable master took any excuse he could find.

Sighing, she gathered the reins and turned back toward the stables. They had a long walk ahead of them, and now she wouldn't have time to change. The best she could hope for was to deliver Father's tray before he woke.

Nora strode through the new stalks of bermudagrass, bright green from the spring sun. If the weather held this year, they'd have plenty to sell after they stocked their herd for the winter.

Arrow snorted and pranced. The stallion, two years old last month, was as high-strung as he was beautiful and brimmed with potential. A few more weeks of training and he'd be ready for his first qualifying race—just in time for the fair.

She hoped.

If only she could work with him longer each day. Father's insistence that a woman had no place training horses hadn't waned as his illness worsened, and the stable hands still thought they were doing her a favor by thwarting her efforts. Mother, for her part, seemed to think it her duty to carry on Father's archaic ideals with a fervor. As though doing so would smother Nora's modernized way of thinking and suddenly turn her into the pristine lady they'd both somehow failed to produce.

Nora swatted a thick seed head. She'd show them. Her methods worked faster and better than any of the stable hands', but none of them would admit it.

She smirked. They wouldn't have a choice if she got Arrow ready on her own.

If she could prove to Mother that women were capable of more than just tending home and hearth, then perhaps she could convince Mother to entertain her other ideas for the farm. Father wouldn't get better, and they needed to prepare. Arrow was the key to her independence.

The horse suddenly tossed his head, nearly snatching the reins from her hand as though in direct defiance to her thoughts. As they neared the stables, he let out a shrill call for the other horses, awakening the rest of the barn and earning a chorus of nickers and whinnies in reply.

So much for going unnoticed. Nora glanced up at the sky, its masterpiece of purple and orange light now a swath of blue.

Late. Again.

For the briefest instant she considered leaving Arrow in his stall while she tended Father and then brushing him down later, but she dismissed the notion as swiftly as it came. She wouldn't neglect Arrow just because she'd let herself enjoy his first real ride too long or because they had to walk all the way home.

The massive stone barn of Emberwild fluttered with morning activity. Nora inhaled deeply, breathing in the earthy scents of hay and oats. She felt more at home surrounded by horseflesh than humanity, something her parents never understood. Horses were creatures with pure motives and unveiled intentions.

She led Arrow into his wide stall, pleased it had already been raked clean and the straw replaced in their absence. Her colt thrust his muzzle into the hay bag and snatched out a mouthful with a snort of contentment.

Making quick work with the brush, Nora combed over Arrow's frothy coat and checked his forelocks. After inspecting his hooves for rocks, she tossed him his morning oats and secured the latch to his stall. She replaced her saddle on the stand in the immaculate tack room. She'd have to find a new girth soon.

The heels of her boots clicked down the stone center aisle as the two stable boys, Pete and Andrew, scurried out of her way. She'd long since stopped trying to befriend them. Nora exited through the barn door and quickly surveyed the yard between the house and the stable. Other than the boys tending the horses in the barn, Emberwild roused slowly. Even the hounds didn't seem interested in greeting this humid day.

She passed the exercise track and skirted the pristine, overflowing flower bed on her way into the house. Mother cared about her flowers and the state of the house more than anything—or anyone—else.

The day Father had presented the finished house to Mother, she'd said it looked like a doll's house, with all that gingerbread molding in the eaves and the porch that wrapped around both sides.

For Nora, home became a gilded cage woven with conditional affection and cold conversations.

She entered the still-silent house, praying she didn't leave a trail of dirt behind on the wood floor to condemn her. She rushed through gathering the honeyed milk, the teapot, and the two eggs she'd boiled the night before and assembled them on a silver tray, making sure to leave Mother's sunny yellow domain as spotless as she'd found it.

She lifted the tray and pushed open the door between the kitchen and dining room with her hip, turning toward the wide staircase to the upper floor. All she had to do was slip into Father's room, drop the tray, and then get herself cleaned up before either parent saw her.

She took the steps carefully, avoiding the fourth one, which squeaked. How long had she dallied? She hadn't paused to look at the grandfather clock in the foyer. The chandelier overhead caught morning sunrays, sending diamonds of color over the green papered walls.

She hurried across the thick carpeted hall, coming to a stop next to Father's room, a room he'd once shared with Mother but now called his prison. Maybe that gave him a taste of what life had been like for her all these years. She pushed the bitter thought down and balanced the tray with trembling hands before carefully turning the knob. With any luck, she wouldn't wake him.

The door swung inward on silent hinges, the sunlight barely piercing the shadows. Nora held her breath and listened for her father's ragged breathing. She moved closer to the bed and set the tray on the bedside table, cringing as the rattle of porcelain gave her away. She paused, waiting.

Silence.

There. She'd left his breakfast for him to partake when he woke, just as he liked. She should hurry to her room to don a gown before anyone saw her in men's pants.

But still she lingered.

The silence in the room unnerved her. She needed to get close enough to make certain only sleep claimed him.

Nora inched toward the carved canopy bed draped in summer mosquito netting. With the scant light filtering through the curtains covering the double window opposite, she could make out the shape of his form under the blankets.

She peered closer. Did his body move with breath?

His form suddenly lurched. Nora yelped and stumbled back, her pulse thudding in her ears.

"Nora?" Her father's voice, raspy yet edged in steel, found her in the gloom.

Maybe he hadn't seen her, and she could still slip out. She took another step back.

"I know it's you. I can smell the horse sweat."

Nora set her teeth. "Good morning, Father. I've brought your tray. I didn't mean to wake you."

"But you did."

She turned and headed toward the safe harbor of light beckoning from the hallway.

"Please . . . stay."

Nora froze. Sweat beaded on her brow, and she swiped the moisture away. She turned reluctantly, despising the long-buried need within that still sought his approval.

"Yes?"

"Come closer."

"I've already brought your tray. Do you need me to pour the tea?"

"I . . ." His words dissolved into a racking cough more strangled than yesterday's.

By the time she took hold of the heavy velvet curtain, his fit had subsided. Nora thrust the fabric aside, allowing the daylight to breach the room and fully reveal her disgrace.

"Come. Sit."

Surprised he said nothing about her attire, Nora grabbed a ladder-back chair and positioned it by the bedside. She sat and clasped her hands in her lap, eyes downcast.

She waited, listening to his breathing. Each inhale came with a faint whistle, as though his lungs struggled to fill with air.

"Need to tell you . . . something."

"I know. I shouldn't have been out at the stables this morning—"

"Enough." He barked the single word, cutting off her explanation.

Hiram Douglass Fenton thought women should listen to orders without comment, and children, daughters especially, should be seen more than heard. Nora clenched her teeth to keep her tongue tamed.

Father settled against the multitude of feather pillows behind his back. He'd become a skeleton draped in papery skin. He hardly resembled the thickly muscled man of her youth, and his eyes held none of the laughter that, if she thought hard enough, she could remember from her childhood.

Somewhere deep in her heart, she recalled calloused hands that would hold hers and lips that were quick to form a smile or story in the evening's firelight. Somewhere around her twelfth year, Father had suddenly ceased to be the cheery man she'd loved. As she'd grown into womanhood, she'd seemed to displease him more with each passing year until the man before her was little more than a demanding stranger.

She could feel his eyes upon her but would not lift her head until he spoke again. He kept her in suspense. Another lesson on humility.

"I have something I need to tell you." Father cleared his throat, but his words remained thick. "Something I need to confess before I die."

Her gaze shot up to his face, and she noted the trickle of blood from the side of his lip. Without comment, she handed him a handkerchief. He wiped the blood away, his eyes never leaving her face. Did he expect her to argue? Say he shouldn't talk about death or assure him he would recover?

Such claims were lies they'd both recognize.

He wadded the linen in his gnarled hand. "Everything we have is built on a lie."

Her pulse skittered. "What?"

Father leaned his head back and closed his eyes. "For once, girl, stop talking and listen. I don't have much time, and I need to get this stain off my soul. I've carried it far too long as it is, and if God will have mercy on me, I don't wish to carry it to my grave."

Nora sat back in her chair.

"Fifteen years ago, this place had nothing but four half-starved mares and a floundering stallion that wasn't worth his weight in manure."

While she waited for another fit of coughing to subside, Nora averted her gaze. An uneasy feeling settled in her stomach. She remembered those days. Times when the long winter nights with wind beating at their rickety door left them yearning for thicker blankets and fuller stomachs as they huddled together around the fireplace. Hard times, but happier ones.

"I was desperate to make things better for her, so I didn't question him. That horse was just . . . something."

Nora frowned. What was he talking about?

"But . . . should have known better. Then, all these years, I didn't say anything. Just . . . kept building on the lie."

He clutched at his chest, the coughs racking his thin frame.

"I'm going to get Mother."

"No!" He gasped for air. "I don't like her . . . seeing me . . . this way."

Nora paused, indecision biting at her. He didn't look well. Much worse than yesterday, when she'd honestly thought he wouldn't see another sunrise. Mother needed to know.

"Let her remember me like I was."

His eyes held such pleading and vulnerability that Nora couldn't get herself to move. He clutched his chest again, breaths seeming harder for him to find. His features deepened to a bluish tinge.

"Don't tell her. Don't you d-dare tell her what I told you. Not a . . . burden for her . . . to bear."

Palms sweating, Nora ran them down her hips, only gathering dust in the process. With her hands too dirty to reach for him, she merely watched him instead.

"Promise."

Promise what? What did he want her to do? Promise she would never tell her mother something she didn't even understand? She had no idea what he was talking about.

"Promise!"

Nora nodded, tears clouding her vision. Then he shot forward, his mouth agape, as though he could not catch the breath he desperately needed.

"Mother!" Nora dropped down beside his bed. "Mother!"

Father grabbed her hand, his eyes wild. Not knowing what else to do, she held on, praying that God in his mercy would remember the faith of a younger man and forget the bitterness of the older one. Helpless, Nora watched until her father's body stopped flailing and he slumped back against the pillows. His fingers slacked, then his eyes stared up at nothing.

Biting her fist, Nora fought back the sobs.

Footsteps pounded down the hall, and then Mother's shrill cry splintered the silence.

Historical Note

Thank you to Pat Floyd and the other ladies at the Dawson County Historical Society for answering my questions and for your hard work on the county's historical resources. I took the information I could find on the town and weaved it with a slightly different version to create the fictional version of Dawsonville for this story. I was able to use the names of some of the businesses and the town square, but I also added in other businesses and the residential area to create a town that I hope was similar to the real Dawsonville in the early 1900s yet still suited the needs of the book.

Georgia first passed prohibition laws in 1907, many years prior to the national laws passed in 1917. Interestingly, the trippers from Dawsonville and the surrounding Dawson County became the earliest racers in what we now know as NASCAR. While my story takes place before many of the automobiles started taking to the roads, Dawsonville's ties to racing is an interesting research project.

Another town mentioned in this book is Dahlonega, Georgia, a gold boomtown of the mid-1800s. From what I could find in my research, this was a bigger town than Dawsonville and had a train station that would have connected to Atlanta.

While I dearly love research and all the amazing ideas it gives me for my books, I am not a historian. While I strive to make the settings for my books realistic for the time period, I apologize if there are a few details I may have missed.

The following is a bibliography of some of the resources I used (in addition to all kinds of Google searches!) in learning more about bootlegging and the effect it had on Georgia in the Prohibition era.

Blumenthal, Karen. *Murder, Moonshine, and the Lawless Years of Prohibition*. New York: Roaring Book Press, 2011.

Dawson County Historical and Genealogical Society. *Dawson County, Georgia: A History*. Canton, GA: Yawn's Publishing, 2015.

Dawson County Historical and Genealogical Society. *Dawson County, Georgia, Pictorial: The First Hundred Years (1857–1957)*. Vol. 1. Waynesville, MC: Walsworth Publishing Company, 2007.

O'Daniel, Patrick. *Crusaders, Gangsters, and Whiskey: Prohibition in Memphis*. Jackson, MS: University of Mississippi Press, 2018.

Smith, Ron, and Mary O. Boyle. *Prohibition in Atlanta: Temperance, Tiger Kings & White Lightning*. Charleston, SC: American Palate, 2015.

Acknowledgments

This book makes number nineteen for me. Wow. I can't even believe that as I write it. I'm blessed by each book that the Lord has allowed me to write and for all that he has taught me through each one.

Lillian and Jonah's story is no different. During the writing of this book we had a lot going on, including me losing several weeks to COVID-19 and the aftereffects of a nasty brain fog. But God in his mercy let me get the book finished on time and even helped my imagination along to make the ending even better than I had planned—all while I was panicking I wouldn't make it in time! His plans are always for our good, and he is faithfully with us through every challenge, every victory, and all times in between.

To my very dear friend Patty, my book buddy and quote lady: you might recognize a few of Melanie's quips and maybe even see yourself in her faith and her unwavering resolve. Thank you for making me laugh, for giving me plenty of "patty quotes" during Wednesday night Bible study, and for just being the amazing person God made you. Lots of love, dear lady!

No book is ever complete without thanks to my family: my hubby for his bottomless encouragement, my boys for putting up with my story worlds, and my mom for always being my first reader. Thank you all for being with me through each step of this process. And, though of course she can't read this, my furry shadow for reminding me to take a few breaks every once in a while to play and enjoy the sunshine.

Thank you to Kelsey, Jessica, Brianne, Karen, and all of my other editors, marketing folks, design teams, and superheroes at Revell for making this book possible. Y'all have been a delight to work with.

To my wonderful friends on my Faithful Readers Team, my launch teams, and every reader who thinks, *Hey, maybe I'll give this book written by the gal with a weird name a try.* You have my enduring gratitude. Thank you for allowing me to follow this writing dream and all the adventures it entails.

Stephenia H. McGee is the award-winning author of many stories of faith, hope, and healing set in the Deep South. When she's not reading or sipping sweet tea on the front porch, she's a writer, dreamer, husband spoiler, and busy mom of two rambunctious boys. Learn more at www.stepheniamcgee.com.

The Story of a Girl, Her Horse, and a Stranger Who Is More Than Meets the Eye

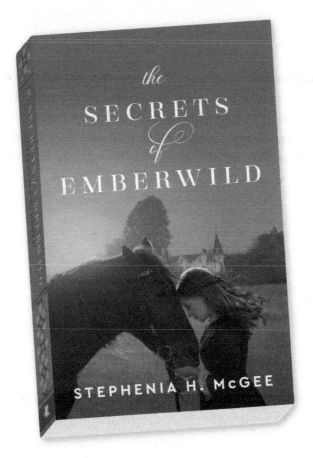

"A spirited woman ahead of her time makes this well-paced novel in an extraordinary setting shine. Rife with suspense and romance—and a horse lover's dream!"

—**LAURA FRANTZ,** Christy Award–winning author of *A Heart Adrift*

Revell
a division of Baker Publishing Group
www.RevellBooks.com

Available wherever books and ebooks are sold.

Meet Stephenia

stepheniamcgee.com

f StepheniaHMcGee

𝕏 StepheniaHMcGee

◯ StepheniaHMcGee